SHADOWS

OF THE

SAND

* * * * * *

BOOK SIX

* * * * * *

D.W. Neuman

ALSO BY D.W. NEUMAN

FICTION

<u>Shadow Series</u>
Shadows of the Mind – Book One
Shadows of the Soul – Book Two
Shadows of the Service – Book Three
Shadows of the Past – Book Four
Shadows of the Heart – Book Five
Shadows of the Sand – Book Six

SHADOWS OF THE SAND
Copyright © 2014 by D.W. Neuman

ISBN (978-0-9907247-0-4)

Words are an injustice,
and will never come close,
to the intense light that emanates
from my beautiful wife.
Connie, you are
my everything.

And to Carol,
thank you, as always,
for falling in love with these characters
and making sure their next adventures
arrive safely in your hands.

The past may dictate who we are,
but we get to determine what we become.

1
Friday April 6, 1973

A middle-aged CIA intelligence officer, with a promising career ahead of him, entered the room.

"You must be Wolf," one of the six men at the table said. "You're the last one to arrive. Please, take your seat and we'll begin."

Wolf sat down in the last open chair. On the round table in front of him was a triangular shaped name card with his codename imprinted on it: WOLF. He glanced around at the other six cards on the table. BEAR. SERPENT. RAVEN. EAGLE. PANTHER. WOLVERINE. The six men, who occupied the other seats, held ranking positions in various U.S. government entities, such as the military, the CIA and the DEA.

"Gentlemen," the man known as Serpent began, "thank you for taking the time to be here today. Now, for security purposes, we will only address each other using our designated codenames. Allow me to make the introductions.

"Serpent is my designation. I work at the highest levels within the Pentagon. I am the creator of this enterprise and I will continue to oversee its operation."

He turned and identified the rest of the board's members.

"Bear; military. Wolf; CIA. Eagle; CIA. Panther; DEA. Wolverine; DEA. And my son, Raven; army.

"You're all here today because you want more out of life. You want to seize control of the present and solidify your future. So do my son and me. With that being said you've been invited here because you've expressed the same ideology; life is for the taking.

"For the past two years, using the Vietnam War as a cover, I created a small pipeline that allowed me to successfully smuggle drugs into the country within the cadavers of our fallen soldiers. The operation has too many possibilities to break down and the chance of the drugs being detected have risen tenfold ever since one of my shipments was discovered. At that point the DEA became involved and I had to immediately shut everything down to avoid detection.

"With your help," Serpent said as he swept his arm around the table, "we will build a variety of secure pipelines that will allow us to increase the quantity of our incoming product. The delivery and distribution of additional product equals more money for everyone here, and that's the name of the game."

There were a number of nods around the table.

"Good." Serpent sat down. "I want to hear your ideas."

* * *

Tuesday May 27, 1975

Major Anthony Palmer, of the United States Air Force, personally observed the final vehicle as it came out of the massive C-130 transport aircraft. The C-130 had arrived from Vietnam earlier that morning and had been filled with military vehicles no longer utilized in the failed Vietnam War America would rather not acknowledge, or talk about.

"Finally, that's the last one," he quietly whispered under his breath.

The thirty-six year old Major had supervised the offloading of more transport planes, than he could remember, but it was this particular aircraft and its contents that had kept him on edge. Anthony had been approached a few years prior to join a unique group of military personnel. His recruiter, a friend he had grown up with, had told him he'd be paid handsomely for his assistance and that no one would be hurt. Anthony was assured that all he had to do was make sure the contents of certain flights were placed in specific storage facilities and then look the other way. At that time Anthony's wife was pregnant, on the verge of giving birth, and he knew his family desperately was in need of extra money. He mulled over the offer and eventually decided the risk was worth the reward, especially since he was in charge of the military airbase and all of its operations. He knew he could mitigate any surprises that might pop up.

What Anthony didn't count on was that his conscience would catch up to him after four successful endeavors. He decided he no longer wanted to be a part of anything illegal and tried to back out. However, he was informed that if he stopped following orders he'd come home to find both his wife and two year old son's necks slit wide open. Shocked, and with nobody to turn to, he never brought up his trepidations again. Instead, he kept his head down and continued to follow the instructions he was given.

Major Palmer watched as the last vehicle was taken to the designated storage area. The Lieutenant, he'd put in charge of the offloading, walked up to him with a clipboard and saluted.

"Any problems Lieutenant?" he asked as he reciprocated the salute.

"No sir," he replied and handed over the clipboard for review.

Major Palmer ran down the inventory list, signed it and handed it back. "Very well. Carry on."

"Yes sir." The Lieutenant snapped off a quick salute before he jogged back towards the storage facility to finish up the task assigned to him.

The Major watched his subordinate leave before he turned around and walked two buildings over to an empty phone booth. He fished in his pocket for a dime, inserted it, and used the rotary dial. His call was picked up after two rings.

"Everything's set on this end."

"Any problems?"

Anthony looked around to see if anyone was watching him. "None. This was the last flight scheduled out of Vietnam. Can I take that as an indication that you will no longer have any additional work for me or my base?"

"You do seem a little tired Major. Perhaps a short respite is in order before I require your assistance in the future."

Anthony's face flushed with anger. "I don't want to do this anymore. My wife and son are counting on me. My entire career is in jeopardy Goddammit."

"Relax and take a deep breath Major."

Anthony looked around once more and gripped the phone tighter.

"No Bob, you need to back off."

The man's voice didn't waver. "No names over the phone."

"You pulled me into this and used our lifetime of friendship to do it. You manipulated me and this situation. I can't do this anymore. I don't care what you say."

4

"You'd better care. Your wife and son, like you said, are counting on you. The people I work with, and you for that matter, will not take kindly to their operation becoming exposed. More specifically, if they realize you're not onboard anymore I won't be able to protect you or your family." Bob paused for a few seconds. "Tell me you understand exactly what I'm saying?"

Major Palmer mulled it over. "Yes," he finally managed to say.

"Good. Now, while I have you on the phone I will tell you this much. I'm going to go to bat for you since we grew up together."

"I don't understand. What the hell does that mean?" Anthony irritably asked.

"It means you need to sound a little more grateful. I'll convince them to put off using your airbase until the end of the year. That should give you five or six months to come to your senses. But in the same breath I also have to warn you, don't say no to me ever again. You're in this whether you like it or not. And now, before I forget, your money has been placed in the same location as before. Enjoy your few months off Anthony."

The line went dead. Anthony silently cursed himself for betraying his oath as he hung up the receiver. *What the hell am I going to do?* He left the phone booth and slowly walked back to his office. Regardless of how he felt he still had an airbase to manage.

And, even though it made him sick, he still retrieved his money later that evening on the way home from work.

5

2
Wednesday May 28, 1975

Beepbeepbeepbeep.

It's too early. Sam Paige rolled over in his bed and slapped the top of his alarm clock. The incessant sound immediately stopped. *Finally.* As he rolled back over to get comfortable the door to his room swung open.

"You and I both know you're going to be late for school if you don't get up right this instant."

"Come on mom. How many times have I told you not to just barge in my room without knocking?" Sam tried to cover his head with a pillow.

Janet Paige didn't miss a beat as she approached her son, sat down on the bed next to him and ruffled his hair. "More than I can remember young man. But that doesn't stop me. Before I know it my little boy will have left my nest and spread his wings."

"Barf. You're going to make me puke if you keep talking like that," came his muffled response.

"Oh, so you can hear me? Good. Now get your butt up mister. You don't graduate high school until next Friday; so until then no son of mine is going to slack off on my watch."

Sam uncovered his head. "Do you know if dad is going to be at my graduation?"

He didn't see as his mother's face faltered for a second. "I don't know. Maybe you should call and remind him about it," she said with a touch of disdain.

Sam turned over and sat up. "Are you ever going to tell me what happened between you two? I mean, you got

7

divorced when I was in second grade and I still have no idea why."

She bristled somewhat. "You know I don't like talking about your father and I wish you'd stop putting me on the spot about him. I'm with your step-father now and that's all that matters."

"Sure, to you, but what about what I want?"

His mother ignored him and turned to walk out of his room. "Time to get up and get ready for school Sammy. Tonight, as a family, we're going to sit down and talk about your future."

Great, just great. And my name is Sam, mom.

Sam rolled his eyes, shrugged off the bed covers and got up. He found his way into his adjoining bathroom and turned on the shower. He brushed his teeth and stared at his reflection while the water warmed up.

My future. What do I know about my future?

He spat into the sink, rinsed his toothbrush and stepped into the hot water.

I don't know what I want to do. None of the colleges I applied for accepted me so I'm sure tonight's conversation will be about going to Junior College. But I don't even know if that's something I even want to do. I just don't know.

Sam finished his shower, dried off and got dressed. He checked his backpack to make sure he had his necessary school books, not that it really mattered. He was graduating with the rest of his class, and he knew everyone was merely passing time before next Friday's big day. Even the teachers had relaxed on their classroom agendas and couldn't wait for summer to commence.

8

Sam walked into the kitchen and found his mother and step-father sitting at the table. He picked up a piece of toast covered in jam and took a bite.

"Morning son," said his step-father Jacob.

"Morning Jacob," Sam replied without looking at him.

"So what's on deck for school today? Anything interesting?"

"Same shit, different day."

"Language!" his mother exclaimed.

"I don't know what's gotten into you lately son but…"

"I am not your son!" Sam exclaimed. He tossed the remaining toast on the counter and stormed out.

"Don't you walk away from me," Jacob commanded. "Get back in here!"

They heard the front door slam and a few seconds later the sound of Sam's car started up.

Jacob turned to his wife. "What the hell was that all about? What's gotten into him?"

"I don't know, but he asked about his father again," was her reply.

"Again? I thought we made it clear it was not a topic for discussion?"

"He has a right to know. He's going to hear about it at some point."

"Maybe," Jacob replied, "but not from us."

"I also told him we'd be having a talk about his future tonight."

Jacob nodded. "That has to be it. No wonder he was in such a disrespectful mood. He knows his friend Tom is heading off to USC. Not having any future prospects has got to be eating away at him."

"Well," Janet replied at she picked up the half eaten toast and threw it away, "I guess we'll figure that all out tonight, now won't we?"

3
Wednesday May 28, 1975

Beepbeepbeepbeep.

Bill Nicholson turned off his alarm and reluctantly sat up in bed.

"Just one more week until I don't have to do this shit anymore," he said out loud.

"Until you don't have to do what anymore?"

Bill jumped and looked over at his mother standing in his doorway. "Seriously? I have a door for a reason. It's my room and I deserve some privacy."

"Not in my house you don't Billy Boy."

"Cut it out ma. You know I hate that stupid nickname. And for all you know I could have been masturbating."

Louise Nicholson raised one eyebrow. "Well looking at the poor condition of your room your ejaculate would just be one more thing I'd have to put gloves on to clean up in here. Maybe I'll find that risqué Sears's catalog that suspiciously went missing last week."

"Gross ma."

"So is your room young man."

Bill grimaced. "I just love it when you call me young man."

"Good," she replied not taking the bait. "Now get up and get ready for whatever they're calling this week before graduation." She turned and walked back down the hall.

Bill shook his head, stood up and began to get ready for school.

Twenty minutes later he appeared in the kitchen and found his mother sitting at the table.

"Hungry?" she asked.

"A little. I'll just get a bowl of cereal."

"I figured as much," she replied.

Bill opened the pantry and removed the Cheerios box. After adding milk and procuring a spoon from the utensil drawer he sat down at the table. She stared at him.

"What?" he tried to ask with a mouthful of cereal.

"What are your plans?"

Bill chewed and then swallowed. "Plans?"

"Don't play coy with me young man. Are you planning on getting a job, going to community college or to do both? Your father and I would prefer both."

"My father doesn't live with us now does he? However, if you're referring to Reggie, the man you married after the divorce, then I'd understand the question."

"I swear. Raising you hasn't been easy. You really have no idea what it's like day in and day out with a child in tow."

Bill shot back. "Is that what I am to you, a child?"

"You certainly act like one. We had high hopes for you but you seem to be more than content on just throwing it away. You don't seem to grasp the real world. You just want to hang out with your friends and not plan for a damn thing."

"I'll figure it out, okay? Get off my back will ya."

"I am your mother and it's my responsibility to see that I send you off, into this world, to become successful. Don't ever tell me to get off your back because I love you too damn much to stop trying."

Bill put his hands up. "Fine. Fine. I love you too. Can we just drop it for now?"

12

Louise readjusted in her chair. "Fine with me. So what's the plan for graduation?"

"What'ya mean?"

"I don't know. How many seats are we allotted?"

"I haven't the foggiest. I think families just show up and sit down."

"I see. Well, I talked to your father and…"

Bill stopped eating. "You talked with him? When?"

"Recently and…"

"What'd he say? Did he ask about me?"

"If you'd stop interrupting I could tell you."

"Sorry."

"That's better. Now, as I was trying to tell you, he won't be able to make it to your graduation."

Bill's heart sank. "Oh."

"He said he was going to be on a business trip but to look for a card in the mail."

"Great, a card."

She got up to comfort her son but Bill quickly scooted his chair back and stood up. "I'm going to be late for school."

"Honey, are you okay? You know he wanted to be there."

"I'll see you later ma," he responded on his way out the door.

4
Wednesday May 28, 1975

Beepbeepbeepbeep.

Tom Clark opened his eyes and glared at the alarm clock that had been annoying him for years. He tapped the button and it stopped beeping. *And just think, I'll get to hear the same irritating sound at college too.* He rolled his eyes as he sat up in bed. *I can hardly wait.*

Tom looked around his room, the same room he'd called his own ever since his grandparent's took him in after his father died eight years before. They'd raised him in the wake of that tragedy with a firm but gentle hand. In time they determined Tommy was going to be alright even though they had purposely kept the real truth from him. And his friends, Sammy and Billy, had been there for him over the years, not to mention a million birthday parties and sleepovers.

Tom made his way to his bathroom and got ready for school, although at this point it was really considered hanging out until graduation day. Afterwards he made his way to the kitchen where his grandparents were.

"Morning," he said.

"Good morning sweetie," Claire replied.

"Hey champ. How's it hanging?"

"Ed, of all things." Claire scolded.

Tom and Ed shared a smile as Tom took a seat.

"And don't think I didn't see you egging him on," she said with a grin.

"You don't miss a thing do you grandma?"

"At our age it's all we can do to keep up with you I'm afraid. Now, what would you like for breakfast?"

Ed spoke up. "He's going to have to start cooking for himself. Before we know it he'll be down at college and we'll be having our meals prepared for us."

Tom caught on right away. "Another trip I take it?"

Claire smiled. "Indeed."

"But there's more to it than that," his grandfather added.

"Oh?"

"As soon as you graduate, and head off to college, your grandmother and I are moving to Rossmoor."

Tom knew exactly where that was. "It's that retirement community in Walnut Creek? Wow, that's a huge change."

"Well," said Claire, "with you gone at college there's no need for such a large house here in Orinda Woods. We've decided to downsize and then spend more time exploring this world we live in."

"That's fantastic. I guess that means I should pack everything I own and take it with me to USC?"

"No no no, of course not," his grandmother replied. "You'll always have a place to stay with us sweetheart."

"That's right," added Ed. "We're not kicking you out. Just think of it as changing venues."

Tom smiled. "It's okay. I totally get it. It's your time now. College seems daunting and a bit scary to me but that's what's happening. You certainly didn't ask to raise me..."

"It's not about that at all," interrupted Ed.

"It's okay grandpa. You two have been wonderful. I had to adapt just as much as you did. It is what it is. But now with me heading down to southern California I understand your need to stretch your legs, and it's about time too. The truth is that both of you have been cramping my style."

Ed and Claire looked at each other, grinned and then turned back to their grandson.

"Funny. We'll have a talk after graduation next week my boy," said Ed. "Until then why don't you grab an apple and head out to school."

"Love you Tom," said Claire.

"Love you guys too," Tom replied as he headed to the door. He turned back for a second and added, "And this place better be packed before I get home or no supper for either of you."

"Get out of here before I put you over my knee," Ed warned.

"Ha! Good luck with that grandpa." And with that Tom closed the door behind him.

Claire finally sat down at the table next to her husband. "He's a good kid."

"The best actually. I think we did something right by him."

"Did we?" she inquired.

"Please, let's not bring that up again."

"But he needs to know the truth."

"Why for God's sake?" Ed pleaded. "What good would that do him? All he knows is that his father died. He doesn't need to know the awful truth. What do you think that would do to him right now? I'll tell you exactly what it'd do. It'd crush him. And after that we can forget college and, more to the point, he'd never trust us again, that's for damn sure."

"But..."

17

"No buts. We hid this from him for a good reason. But next week, at least, I can finally explain part of the truth to him."

"The money Michael left him."

Ed nodded. "He's no dummy. He knows something's been going on for a long time. Our getaways, the new house, the upcoming vacations, etcetera."

"I suppose. I just hope it doesn't bring back any painful memories for him. I know he must live with that every day."

"As do we my dear. As do we."

<u>5</u>
Wednesday May 28, 1975

Tom found an available parking spot, parked his '67 Chevy and got out. He pulled his backpack over his shoulder and headed towards the front entrance of Miramonte High School. A slew of students walked to and fro, along with a number of small social groups that were gathered wherever they had found room. Tom had ten minutes before his first class began, so to kill time he began to browse the postings on the school's Information Board.

"Hey dickhole."

Tom turned towards the familiar voice as Bill appeared by his side. "And good morning to you too asshole."

Bill smiled. "What're you up to?"

Tom shrugged. "Nothing I guess. I was just wasting time looking at the board before class started."

"Class. Now that's a joke. The school might as well send us seniors on vacation for the next week and come back to graduate."

Tom noticed Bill's not so subtle tone. "You okay?"

It was Bill's turn to shrug. "I dunno. Parent shit. I got in to it with my mother this morning."

"Oh yeah? What about?"

"She's harping on me about my damn future again."

"Who's harping on you?" Sam inquired as he walked over.

"Hey Sam," greeted Tom.

Sam gave Tom a nod and then turned back to Bill.

19

"My mom," continued Bill. "She's been on my case about 'my future'," he said using his fingers as air quotations. "It drives me crazy."

"Apparently you and I are in the same damn boat," said Sam. "My mom wants to have *the talk* about my future tonight as well."

Bill shook his head. "Are they getting this shit out of the same playbook or something? Christ. At least our buddy Tom doesn't have his folks on his back. He's off to college and shit."

Tom cringed a bit but quickly recovered.

Sam elbowed Bill in the ribs. "Dude. Uncool."

Bill turned to Sam. "What the hell was that for?"

"Seriously? Do I have to spell it out for you?"

"What? All I said was he doesn't have his folks to…" Bill trailed off as he realized how far he'd stuck his foot down his throat. He turned back to Tom. "Oh shit man. You know I didn't mean anything by that. I was just running my mouth like usual and…"

Tom put his hand up. "Forget it. It's okay." A couple of seconds passed without any words so he changed the subject. "So both of your parents are riding you pretty hard about your future, right?"

Sam and Bill nodded in unison.

Tom pointed at a poster on the Information Board behind him. "The school must have just put this up this morning."

"What is it?" asked Sam.

"It's an army recruitment poster," Tom stated. "It has a date for taking something called the ASVAB tomorrow here at school."

Bill moved in closer and looked at the poster. "It says here that the ASVAB stands for Armed Services Vocational Aptitude Battery."

"What's that mean?" Sam asked.

Bill continued. "Apparently they score tests in the following four areas. Arithmetic reasoning, word knowledge, paragraph comprehension and mathematics knowledge. All of those count towards your AFQT or Armed Forces Qualifying Test score. If you do well that score determines if you're qualified to enlist in the U.S. military or not."

Sam looked over Bill's shoulder and looked over the poster. "Interesting."

"Maybe we should check it out," said Bill.

"Maybe we should," Sam agreed. "That might piss off our folks."

Tom stepped back. "Come on you guys. I was just joking around."

Sam and Bill turned to face Tom again. "What are you worried about? You think we're going to head off and join the military or something?" Sam joked.

"I...I don't know," replied Tom.

Bill chuckled. "Yeah, right. Could you imagine the two of us in the military? That'd be a laugh. Following rules and regulations. Saying shit like 'yes sir' and 'no sir'. You wish."

Sam put a hand on Tom's shoulder. "Relax brother. Your future's looking bright and we're proud of you for that. We give you a ton of shit about your writing but secretly we're just jealous of your talent."

"Jealous?" Bill said as he pretended to be insulted. "I think not good sir. I do hath not a jealous bone in thine body."

Tom and Sam smiled as Bill acted.

"Enough you fuckers," said Tom. "You can both kiss my ass."

Bill laughed. "Heh heh. I'm just fucking with you. The truth is, Sam and I know you're destined for greatness. He and I, on the other hand, don't have our shit together and we're scrambling for answers."

"But the military?" inquired Tom.

"The test doesn't mean a thing," Sam answered. "Hell, I think Bill and I will take it for shits and giggles."

"Not to mention getting out of class for a while," Bill added.

"Good point. That too." Sam smiled. "We have nothing better to do."

Tom relented. "Hmm. Maybe I should take it with you guys."

"Oh hell no," said Bill. "There's no need to derail what you're already good at."

"I'll have to agree with my esteemed colleague, Dr. Nicholson," said Sam with a puffed up chest and held an imaginary pipe up to his mouth.

"Why thank you, Dr. Paige," Bill joked back.

"Think nothing of it, Doctor."

"Do you think our patient is tiring of us yet, Doctor?"

"Indubitably, my good Doctor."

Tom couldn't wipe the smile off his face. "Would you two please shut the fuck up already. We're going to be late for class."

Sam and Bill couldn't stop as they all walked into school.

"After you, Doctor."

"Why thank you, Doctor."

"My pleasure, Doctor."

"Doctor."

"Doctor."

"Oh shut up!"

6

Friday June 6, 1975 1:30pm

"Hey Tom! Tom!"

Tom looked across the quad and saw Bill coming towards him. When he reached Tom he asked, "Hey, have you seen Sam yet?"

"He said to meet us right here. He knows we only have thirty minutes until the ceremony starts," said Tom.

Sam snuck up behind them both and tapped them on the shoulders. They all were wearing graduation caps and gowns. Bill and Tom turned around. "Way to know your surroundings, Bill. They're going to murder you at Basic," Sam said.

"What the hell are you guys talking about?" ask Tom.

Bill looked at Sam and said, "Do you wanna tell him or should I?"

"I don't know, he might faint," said Sam and they both laughed at Tom.

"Fuck you both very much. What's going on?" asked Tom.

Sam put his arm around Tom's shoulder and said, "Well my friend, it's like this. While you're headed off to college to become smarter, we're heading off to the Army to protect the country."

"Aww man Sam, you fucked up the delivery," complained Bill.

"No I didn't. Shut up." Bill and Sam started mock fighting while Tom smiled.

"Quit it you guys, you might hurt each other's pussies."

Sam and Bill stopped and looked at Tom. Bill piped up and said, "At least I know what one is." Sam and Bill started laughing but Tom didn't find it nearly as hilarious.

"Ha ha," Tom mocked.

"Hey, I'm just kidding buddy," said Bill slapping his buddy on the back. "We're all friends here. You're just not a lady's man. Give it some time. No sweat brother."

"You're wrong Bill," said Sam.

"I am?"

"Tom has had two steady girlfriends for a while now." Sam held up both his hands and made fists, then pumped them up and down in the air. They were practically rolling on the ground now.

"God how I hate you both," said Tom, but he smiled nevertheless. The only people that could cut you that deep were the people you trusted.

"But seriously, I didn't think you guys were going to go through with it."

"Why not?" the two asked in unison.

"Well, I guess because the Vietnam War ended two years ago," Tom said.

"Tom," started Bill, "It's not all about going to war in some other country."

"No?"

"No. It's more than that, and this is going to sound cheesy, but we want to help people. There are a lot of bad guys out there, and Tom, we want a crack at them."

Sam jumped in. "Remember back when we were Freshman and we had that altercation on the field?"

"Altercation. Nice big word for you Sam," Tom poked.

"Fuck you too. My point is, we didn't get fucked with from that day forward." Sam looked at Bill and then back at Tom. "We're just going to take the ass kicking from local to global." Sam and Bill smiled.

"You guys are hilarious but I wish you both well. Don't quote me on this but, if this shit is real, I'll fucking miss you both," Tom said.

"You'll be fine Kemosabe," said Bill.

"High School is about to be behind us and the world is our oyster," Sam added. "Speaking of, how's the USC process? We know you got in but when are you taking off to find a place to live?"

"I don't know. I need to talk to my grandparent's about that. The paperwork from school says the sooner the better or I could get stuck pretty far from campus."

"So, can I ask a favor?"

"Sure Bill," Tom replied.

"Can I pwease have a bedtime story now?" Sam and Bill died laughing again.

Tom grabbed Bill's graduation cap and tossed it away. Bill ran after it still laughing.

"Listen Tom, you're the smart one out of our trio," Sam stated.

"What? Shut up," Tom replied. Bill returned with his cap.

"No seriously, listen. Go out in the world and kick its ass. Leave the other shit behind you. We're going to be friends forever and you know we'll always have your back. Just make us proud at USC, okay?"

"What he said," Bill added and then got really serious. "I may give you a ton of shit brother but it's only because I love you. That day, at the sandbox, you guys could have turned me

27

away, but you didn't. We've been through more shit than I want to remember, and if it wasn't for you two I don't know if I would have survived."

Tom was speechless. They all looked at each other, and without speaking took the moment to hug each other.

* * *

Tom found his grandparents while they were walking to the field's bleachers.

"Hey grandma. Grandpa."

"Hi Tom."

"Hi sweetie," said his grandmother.

"So where are we sitting for this shindig?"

"Over here grandpa." Tom led them to a specific section and seated them. "I'll be over there with my class," Tom said pointing to the chairs below the raised podium.

Tom joined his class and waited for the ceremony to begin.

* * *

"Congratulations to the class of 1975! May all your dreams come true!" said the Principal over the speaker system. A myriad of hats flew in to the air. Everyone was screaming and hugging each other. High school was now behind them and college was on the horizon.

"Congrats," said Sam.

"Yeah, congrats you guys," Bill said.

"Congrats," Tom heard himself saying.

"We'll catch up with you later tonight Tom," said Sam. "Drop by the house around 7pm."

28

"You got it." Tom wasn't feeling like himself. He knew that he'd be heading off alone on his own adventure soon. He didn't know when he'd see his best friends, who were joining the Army. *So many changes.*

A strong hand landed on Tom's right shoulder. Tom turned and saw his grandparent's standing there.

"Congratulations honey," said Claire.

His grandfather said, "Tom, let's go to Loard's for some ice cream."

* * *

Claire drove back to the house while Tom drove his grandfather to downtown Orinda. He found a spot right outside Loard's Ice Cream and they both headed inside.

"Good afternoon and welcome to Loard's," a young woman said.

"Thank you."

"What can I get the two of you?"

"Tom, what would you like?" his grandfather asked.

Tom smiled. "Like you don't know." He turned to the young woman behind the counter. "I'll have a double scoop of Rocky Road on a sugar cone please."

"Coming right up. And for you, sir?"

"That sounds good, but just make it a single for me."

"You got it."

Soon afterward the two of them were sitting at one of the tables and began to work on their cones.

"Your ceremony was nice."

"It was okay I guess."

Ed raised an eyebrow. "Is there something on your mind Tom?"

Tom sighed. "Yeah. I just found out that Sam and Bill are joining the Army."

"Voluntarily?"

Tom nodded. "I know. It seems bizarre."

"And you're worried about their decision?"

Tom looked his grandfather in the eye. "That's partially it. The other part is that I'm starting to feel isolated."

"What do you mean?"

"Well, there are a lot of changes that are right around the corner for me. There's college, a new city to get used to, new people to meet and my two best friends that I won't see for a long time. I'm having a hard time processing everything."

Ed nodded. "And add to that list that your grandmother and I are moving to a new house. That's a lot to take on in such a short amount of time."

"It feels that way, kind of."

"Only kind of?"

Tom shifted in his seat. "Yeah. I'm excited and nervous about all these changes at the same time."

"Good. That's a great way to look at your future. Speaking of, you must be curious why I asked you here?"

"I figured it was to celebrate graduating high school."

Ed shook his head. "No Tom. It's time to share something that your father left for you."

A puzzled look appeared on Tom's face. "What do you mean? I don't understand."

"To tell you the truth, your grandmother and I didn't understand either."

"What does that mean?"

Ed extracted an envelope from his coat, paused for a few seconds in contemplation and then handed it over to his grandson. Tom gently took it.

"What's in it?"

"You'll have to open it to find out."

Tom could sense that this was a very unusual experience and his grandfather appeared somewhat nervous as he'd handed him the envelope. *What the hell is going on?* Tom looked down at the envelope and then carefully slit it open along the top. He slowly removed the official document within and read it. *Wait. What?* Tom reread it just to make sure and then looked at his grandfather. The document shook slightly in his hands.

"Is...is this for real?"

Ed nodded. "It is. That statement you're holding is current as of a week ago."

"But...but I don't understand. This isn't a joke?"

A new customer walked in to Loard's and up to the counter. Ed leaned forward and lowered his voice. "Your father gave your grandmother and I money as well. He wanted you to be taken care of, to be provided for, so you could live your life and pursue your talents."

"But this statement says the trust he setup for me has twenty-two point seven million dollars in it. Million." Tom pressed his hand against his forehead before speaking again. "This is insane. What did my father do for a living? How did he get so much money? What the hell is going on?"

Ed didn't respond immediately.

"What?" probed Tom. "What is it? What aren't you telling me?"

"Tom, when your father was alive…well, let me back up. That Christmas morning, before he passed, your father gave me some envelopes. Inside were the trusts he'd created for us. You can imagine my surprise was similar to yours. I asked him the exact same question Tom, about what he did for a living. And do you know what he told me?"

"What?"

"Nothing. He didn't tell me what he did or where he got the money."

"Why not?"

Ed shook his head. "To this day I still don't know. However, what I do know is that the money he gifted your grandmother and I has changed our lives for the better. Your father intended the same for you Tom."

"But why now? Why not eight years ago?"

"You know the answer to that. You were too young but now you're mature. You're an adult and you're headed off to college. You have your entire life ahead of you."

"But what am I supposed to do with all this money?"

Ed put his hand back on his grandson's shoulder. "That's for you to figure out. I do have a couple of suggestions while you're going down that particular road, if you'd like to hear them."

"I'm all ears."

"Keep this information to yourself, like your grandmother and I have from the people we know. Its human nature to want what you don't have and if nobody knows you have money then no one will be able to take it away from you. Do you understand what I'm saying?"

Tom slowly nodded. "I think so. What about Sam and Bill? Can I tell them?"

His grandfather looked him square in the eyes. "You can do whatever you feel is right Tom. This is your money now and you can do whatever you'd like with it, or tell anyone about it. Just be careful. People with money are typically treated and looked at differently, even by close friends. I'm sorry to say, but money changes the status quo."

"I get it. Wow, I...I don't know what to say. This is more than I can take in right now. I'm positively overwhelmed."

Ed smiled. "Good. You weren't supposed to be instantly okay with this." He paused for a few seconds. "Listen. You have a good head on your shoulders Tom. Your father would be proud. Now, let's go home so we can talk about USC and try to alleviate some of your nervousness about heading off to college."

7
Thursday July 24, 1975

A month and a half later Tom pulled in to the Orinda Community Center and parked. He got out and walked towards the park. It wasn't long before he spotted Sam and Bill watching two women play tennis on the courts in the distance.

"How's the view?" he said as he snuck up behind them.

They both jumped and turned around.

"We knew you were there," said Bill.

"Yeah. Totally," added Sam.

"Sure you did," said Tom. "You two jumping jacks want to grab a seat?"

The trio walked off the grass behind the large sandpit and found an available table located in the shade.

"So what's everyone been up to since graduation?" Tom asked.

"Has it really been that long since we saw you brother?" Bill asked. "What's been keeping you so busy that you haven't had time for your buds?"

"Yeah. Listen. Sorry about that. I've been helping my grandparents move from the house to their new place in Rossmoor. We also took a drive down to USC and found me a place to live off campus."

"That's great," said Sam. "Are you excited?"

Tom nodded. "It's growing on me. It's a big change. But speaking of big changes, you have to tell me how badly your parents freaked out."

Bill rolled his eyes. "Over the top freak out."

35

Sam agreed. "Oh yes. It couldn't have been worse. My mother even resorted to getting my father on the phone to try and talk some sense in to me."

"Oh shit. How'd that work out?"

"About as well as you can imagine."

Bill piped in. "It took some time but once our folks heard that we were enlisting together that seemed to calm them down somewhat. They're still pissed at us but the paperwork has been signed. Everything's moving forward."

"Holy shit! So you're really doing it? Goddamn. So how's it all work?"

"We're getting shipped out at the end of September to Fort Benning, Georgia," said Sam.

"You'll never guess our MOS," Bill said excitedly.

"What's an MOS?" Tom asked.

"Military Occupational Specialty."

"Okay, what specialty?"

"Guess."

"Umm, artillery?"

"Bzzt, wrong. Try again."

Tom thought for a few seconds. "How about sniper?"

"Good guess but that's not it either."

"Okay, I give up. What the hell are you two knuckleheads going to be doing in the Army?"

"We're going to be Rangers," Sam said proudly.

"What he said," added Bill.

"Shut up. No you're not."

"Yeah, we are," Bill said with a huge smile on his face.

"Get the fuck out of here. How'd you manage to pull that off?"

"Our recruiter had some job openings and our ASVAB scores, surprisingly mind you, fit the requirements. He asked if we wanted the jobs."

"Just like that?"

"Almost," said Bill.

"What do you mean by 'almost'?"

"Well," said Sam, "there was a catch."

"Here we go."

Sam continued. "Typical enlistment time is a four year commitment. To get the Ranger MOS we had to commit to eight years."

Tom was stunned. "What...what does that mean? Does it mean I won't see you guys for eight years or something? That's not right."

"Easy Tom, take it easy," said Bill as he tried to console his friend. "Our recruiter assured us that we'd get leaves of absence. So to answer your question, we'll be able to get together plenty. Besides, you'll be at college for the next four years anyway."

"What Bill is trying to say is that it's going to be a tough transition for all of us. We're used to seeing and talking to each other every day at school. We haven't seen you for over a month now so and that hasn't been right."

Tom looked back and forth between his two best friends and then lowered his head. "You're right. I haven't been myself. I'm not good with change and it's been so much all at once. I'm sorry I've been avoiding you guys. I just know I'm going to miss the hell out of you both."

"It's okay man," said Sam. "We still have a month before we leave. When are you heading down to college?"

"In a week and a half. Time enough to get settled and ready for classes."

"Now that's something I won't miss," said Bill. "Class."

"Well shit," said Sam. "That doesn't give us a lot of time together. But you know what; let's make the best of it before you do head out."

"Agreed," said Tom as he smiled.

"Hell yeah," Bill added. "So with your grandparents moving and you heading off to college, is there anything else going on?"

Decision time. Tom hesitated. "Well, there is one thing."

"What is it?" Sam probed.

"My father…"

Bill and Sam shared a glance.

"Your father what brother?"

They'll look at me differently. They'll treat me differently. They might even stop being my friends for all I know. "My father left me a graduation card. He must have had it prepped for years. It was weird to get is all."

Sam and Bill understood. "You okay?"

Tom nodded. "Yeah. You guys want to go hit up a movie at the theater or something? I mean, I only have a week and a half left and you two have been avoiding me for the past month so…" Tom stood up and began to run away.

"Get him!" Sam cried out as he sprang from the table after his friend.

"Get that lying bastard," Bill yelled as he chased after Sam.

Little did any of them know that it'd be years before the three of them would sit down together again.

8
Friday, September 19, 1975

Tom closed his notebook and returned it to his backpack as his final class of the day came to an end. *My first week of college and I've already got two papers due next week. Fantastic.* He stood up, slung his bag over his shoulder and followed everyone else out of the lecture hall.

Tom had driven down Interstate 5 the entire way south and at the last minute cut down the 110 towards USC earlier that month. His first major decision had been to rent a modest single family home a few miles away from the college. The owners were thrilled to have met his family the month before and even more thrilled when they heard he wanted to rent the house for four consecutive years as the only occupant. A deal was quickly settled and Tom had the keys to his place before his final trip down before school. He pulled off the 110 and drove straight to his new house, unloaded what few possessions he's brought with him and began to settle in. His grandparents had held on to the majority of his possessions, including his favorite little brown chair he'd had since he was a small boy.

He had a week before school started and Tom's plan was to get the lay of the land beforehand so he'd be more comfortable. And his plan worked. He located the local market and gas station right away. Soon afterward Tom began driving the neighborhood, challenging himself by jumping on and off the various freeways to navigate his way back home. Before the first day of college began his confidence level had risen tenfold.

The USC campus had been another hurdle to conquer altogether. But after two days he already knew how long it would take him to walk from one location to another. Tom enjoyed the routine and he was used to tackling schoolwork without his grandparent's asking if he'd finished it. He felt free, but he knew that was the wrong word for it; it was more like energized. It was a new and exciting time for him.

But various thoughts invaded Tom's mind. *I'm rich now. Do I need to stay in college?* But he knew the answers to those tempting questions long before he even asked them. However, there wasn't anyone to talk to about it since his grandparents had already left on their world trip, and he knew on Monday that Sam and Bill would be relatively out of contact once they headed out to boot camp. He was effectively alone and he knew it.

Tom's biggest obstacle, amongst the numerous other changes in his life, he still needed to overcome and that was making new friends. It was either that or spend the next four years alone in a sea of students.

9
Monday September 22, 1975

Sam and Bill bid goodbye to their respective parents
Sunday evening at San Francisco International Airport. The
parents watched their boys walk through the boarding gate and
down the ramp only to disappear into the belly of the plane.
Both of their mothers were crying and guessed that their sons
had enlisted to somehow hurt them. Images, of the Vietnam
War from television, still stuck in the parent's memories and
they prayed Sam and Bill would not have to endure any of
those hardships.

Sam and Bill looked back one more time before they
entered the large plane that was headed to the east coast
overnight. They were directed to their seats, sat down and
buckled their seatbelts as they began to settle in.

"Sam?"

"Yeah Bill?"

"I don't want to sound like a pussy or anything, but do you
think we're doing the right thing?"

"You nervous?"

Bill nodded.

"Honestly, so am I. We've signed away eight years of our
lives. And getting on this plane, well, it's just starting to sink
in how long that really is."

"Me too. I mean, did you see our mother's? They were
both crying and shit."

"Yeah," said Sam, "I saw. But it's too late to back out
now. When we get there all it's going to be is running around,
doing push-ups and pull-ups. It's going to be a cakewalk.

Aside from that we're doing this together. So relax and get some sleep. The reality, that we're used to is about to take a right turn."

* * *

Their plane landed at Hartsfield-Jackson Atlanta International early the next morning and Sam and Bill were jostled awake as the wheels hit the tarmac. The plane taxied to the terminal and everyone disembarked. As the two entered the terminal they immediately noticed a few uniformed military men with clipboards. Behind them, against the wall, were a number of other young men nervously standing around.

"Are your names Sam Paige and Bill Nicholson?"

Sam and Bill stopped, turned to their right and came face to face with one of the clipboard wielding men.

The man was clearly impatient. "Are you deaf? Are your names Sam Paige and Bill Nicholson?"

They nodded their heads.

The man looked over their heads and yelled, "Got'em. I've got the last two." He turned back to the duo. "Grab your shit and get your asses over with the rest of the new recruits. No talking. No questions. Just do it. Understand?"

They nodded again.

"Then why are you still here taking up my space? Move it!"

Sam and Bill hefted their bags over their shoulders and made their way to the existing group. Bill leaned towards Sam and whispered, "We're not in Kansas anymore, Toto."

Before Sam could say anything a large hand came out of nowhere and landed on Bill's shoulder. He was spun around and ended up two inches from the man's face.

"You're here for less than two goddamn minutes and already it's apparent you can't follow directions. What's your MOS you sorry piece of shit?"

"Ra…ranger," Bill stammered.

"Ra..ra..ra..ranger? Are you fucking sure because you certainly don't sound sure?"

"I'm…"

"Shut the fuck up and get back in line. One more fucking word out of you and I'll personally tear you a new asshole. Now, if you can manage it ra..ra..ra..ranger, follow the other shitbirds outside to the bus."

* * *

The bus held twenty-five recruits and upon boarding Bill sat down next to Sam who had saved a place for him. They drove south out of Atlanta down the I-85 and then merged onto the I-185 towards Fort Benning. During the entire two and a half hour drive no one said a word to each other, under the watchful eyes of their chaperones, and could only watch the scenery as they headed into uncharted waters.

Somehow the group of young men got collectively quieter, as if that was even possible, as one of the Sergeants announced they were a few minutes out from their destination. Anxious eyes darted to and fro outside as the bus entered Fort Benning, cleared security, and continued on towards its destination.

"Fuck, this just got real," whispered Bill.

"No shit."

43

The bus route drove them right pass the two extremely large jump towers that dominated the base's skyline. Parachutes fell from the towers with men attached beneath them. Five minutes later the bus pulled to a stop outside a large complex.

"This location is what we call Reception. You will call this place your home for the next week or so until you are assigned out. Right now you will keep your mouths closed unless you are asked a direct question. Grab your belongings, exit the bus and get in line for processing. Don't give us a reason to fuck with you."

All twenty five of them silently did what they were told and soon enough they were lined up against the side of the building. Another sergeant, with a clipboard, walked down the group and reaffirmed that all recruits were present and accounted for.

"Alright. Listen up. You're going to follow the person in front of you inside where you will sit down and continue to keep your mouth shut."

The sergeant looked over and gave a nod. One of the other sergeants told the first young man in line to head on in. The rest followed as instructed. There were benches inside and before long the first few rows were filled up with wide-eyed boys who only thought they were men.

"Before you're officially admitted into this processing facility, you will have your bags 'thoroughly' searched for any contraband. Contraband includes, but is not limited, to the following items. Alcohol. Cigarettes. Pornography. Drugs. Weapons of any sort. Do I need to go on?"

A few of the twenty five boys shifted nervously.

"If we discover any of the above on you, or in your belongings, you will be disciplined. However, I will give each of you a one-time opportunity to 'dump' any contraband in this bin, before the other sergeants and I inspect you and your belongings, without any consequences. You have five minutes before inspection commences."

He motioned to the other three sergeants and all four of them left the room. The contraband bin remained at the front of the room. Initially nobody moved for a few minutes. But as the clock on the wall ticked down a couple of the recruits unzipped their luggage, removed some items, and then made their way up front to dump whatever it was in the bin before returning to their seats. The last minute ran out and the four sergeants immediately re-entered the room.

"I hope you all decided to make your lives easier. You were given one chance. There won't be a second chance." He paused and looked around the room before he continued. "Immediately following this procedure you will be issued lunch. After that we will continue with your processing. The inspection will begin immediately. Once you have been cleared you will sit on the left benches and NOT return to your seats. If you fail to follow this simple direction, and go back to where you are sitting now, you will repeat the inspection process. I hope I've made that perfectly clear. Now, when I call your last name you will grab your belongings and come forward. Archer. Baker. Diego. Franklin."

Those four recruits got up and took their bags up to the front. The four sergeants meticulously searched the belongings of a different boy and then proceeded to pat each one down, going through their pockets and looking for contraband anywhere it could be hidden.

45

Within a matter of minutes the names Nicholson and Paige were called. Sam and Bill made their way up front and handed their assigned sergeant their luggage.

"Stand on the white line," Sam was told as the sergeant unzipped his luggage and began to roughly go through it.

"Put your feet on the white line and don't move," another sergeant instructed Bill.

After the two sergeants found nothing but clothing and their shaving kits they zipped the luggage back up, put it aside and turned to Sam and Bill.

"Face the wall. Hands over your head and spread your legs." They both complied.

"Do you have any contraband hidden on your person?" Sam's inspector asked him.

"No sir."

"Wrong. The correct answer is 'no Sergeant'. I am a NCO which stands for non-commissioned officer. I actually work for a living. Do you understand me?"

"Yes Sergeant," Sam replied.

"Better." The sergeant proceeded with the body search.

Bill's inspector addressed him. "And what about you cupcake? Do you have any contraband on your person?"

"Yes Sergeant."

Sam quickly turned his head and looked at his friend. The sergeant addressing Bill continued.

"And why didn't you dispose of it when we gave you the chance?"

"It won't come off Sergeant."

"What contraband are you holding on your person Nicholson that won't come off?"

"My cock Sergeant." Bill tried in vain to hold his smile back.

The sergeant, however, did not find it humorous whatsoever. "GET ON THE GROUND RIGHT NOW NICHOLSON!"

Bill's smile immediately faded and he froze. The sergeant's iron hands grabbed hold of Bill, yanked him off his feet and in less than a second Bill found himself face down on the cold floor.

"GIVE ME TWENTY RIGHT THE FUCK NOW!"

"Twenty what?" Bill replied somewhat stunned to have been manhandled so easily.

"YOU MUST BE AN IDIOT TO HAVE JOINED THE ARMY NICHOLSON! TWENTY GODDAMN PUSHUPS RIGHT NOW!"

Bill pushed his body up by his arms and then down again as he began the pushups.

"Count them out so I can hear them."

"One," said Bill.

The sergeant turned around and addressed the recruits. "You were told not to fuck with us."

"Two."

"I hope this little demonstration properly illustrates the situation you are all in now."

"Three."

"Each and every one of you is now the property of the United States Army.

"Four."

"The only rights you have are the ones we give you."

"Five."

"The only freedoms you have are the ones we allow you."

"Six."

"The only property you will be allowed to call your own will be the items we give you."

"Seven."

"Let me be very clear. Your mothers are not here to coddle you."

"Eight."

"Your fathers are not here to protect you."

"Nine."

"After this week of Reception is over you will begin your eight weeks of Basic Training."

"Ten."

"Trust me ladies, what funny man Nicholson is pumping out on my floor right now is nothing compared to what each of you will experience."

"Eleven."

"Welcome to the Army." He stopped and turned back to Bill. "Nicholson. Recover. On your feet."

Bill stopped and picked himself up off the floor. He had a slight sheen of sweat across his brow.

"Do you seriously think you have what it takes to be a soldier?"

"Yes Sergeant," Bill replied.

"I'm sorry, I can't hear you."

"YES SERGEANT!"

"I highly doubt it," he responded dismissively. "Complete funny boy's inspection and then get him out of my sight."

* * *

After lunch their luggage was tagged with their names and stored. They were taken for buzz haircuts and then issued a set of military greens, boots and covers. In the barracks they were assigned a place to sleep and told to organize their areas until the call for dinner came. That first night everyone was quickly taught how to properly make a bed so a quarter would bounce off of it.

The next morning, albeit not as early as everyone imagined they'd be woken up, the medical process began. Anyone with corrective lenses was pulled aside for eye exams. The rest stood in multiple lines, with their profile folders to hand off to the next medical personnel when requested. What seemed like a never-ending array of needles, containing who knows what, were injected in to both the left and right upper arm region. The entire operation felt like a cattle call. Hand your folder over. Sit down. Injection. A notation in your paperwork. Folder handed back. Next.

However, the level of panic and fear over joining the Army subsided for the two of them relatively quickly. Reception turned out to be very relaxed and as long as you didn't do anything stupid there wasn't any yelling by any of the sergeants. Even the food was surprisingly good. Hamburgers, fried chicken, donuts and even ice cream. The hard nose rumors about the Army seemed to be just that, rumors as all the recruits were in a good mood and well fed.

Sam and Bill met a variety of recruits, in various stages of Reception, and quickly ascertained the routine of the place. It didn't take long for word about what Bill had pulled to spread. Some of the recruits cheered him on while others openly told him he was a disgrace to the uniform. And with such a melting pot of people from all over the United States it was

49

very apparent that there were many different opinions. The biggest issue that they observed was the constant racial tension. More than once the sergeants had to split white and black recruits apart and discipline them in front of everyone. The lesson was clear and concise. They didn't care what color you were or where you came from. You would follow the rules and guidelines set forth or face the consequences, period.

* * *

During the sixth day of Reception Sam and Bill, along forty-six other recruits, were issued new orders. The following morning they were to muster at zero-seven-hundred. Excitement rippled through the two of them. Their basic training was about to get under way.

* * *

Three cattle trucks idled, spewing diesel fumes in to the air, as the forty-eight recruits gathered in the quad. The recruits stood around, chatting to each other, as a clipboard was brought out.

"LISTEN UP!"

Everyone quickly fell silent.

"When I call your name you will take your duffel and enter the cattle car. There are no seats. Do not sit down. You will hold your duffel in front of you and squeeze in. It will be uncomfortable but your comfort is not our concern."

The sergeant began to read off names and young men began to pile in to the back of the trucks aptly named cattle cars. The first truck filled up quickly. As the second truck was nearly full Bill and Sam's names were called. They took their duffel bags, climbed in to the second truck and were forcefully wedged into a sea of flesh. The outer door was closed and they found themselves locked in with everyone else. The truck was so tightly packed there wasn't room for anyone's duffel bags to fall to the floor, even if they let them go.

The third truck finally filled up with the remaining recruits and the trucks lurched from a dead stop. Sam and Bill had their breath knocked out of them as they were crushed from the momentum of the other recruits towards the rear of the truck. Dust flew up from the tires, choking everyone, and added to the intense claustrophobic situation. Ten minutes later the cattle car hell ended as the three vehicles pulled to a stop in front of a new set of barracks. As the dust began to settle they saw new sergeants split off and approach the back of the trucks. The metal bars unlatched and their real hell began.

"GET THE FUCK OUT OF MY TRUCK!"

Without any warning the sergeant grabbed Sam's arm and yanked him out of the truck. Sam and his duffel hit the ground. Before he could recover Bill landed on top of him. Someone else's duffle hit the dirt right next to Sam's head and he knew he didn't want to have anyone or anything else crush him. He and Bill rolled a few feet and sprang to their feet.

"GET YOUR ASSES OVER HERE YOU LIMP DICK MOTHERFUCKERS!"

Sam and Bill grabbed their bags and moved towards the large men yelling at everyone.

"YOU'RE MOVING TOO SLOW!"

"YOU STUPID IDIOT! DROP AND GIVE ME TEN
YOU SONOFABITCH!"

"YOU'RE A GODDAMN JOKE! YOUR MOTHER
SHOULD HAVE SWALLOWED YOU WHEN SHE HAD
THE CHANCE! AND SINCE SHE DIDN'T, NOW IT'S
OUR JOB TO RAISE YOU!"

The four sergeants seemed larger and more intense than
those they'd had at Reception. Sam, Bill and the rest of the
recruits were all wide-eyed as they scrambled to follow the
directions screamed at them. The yelling never stopped. The
sergeants got in everyone's face, forcefully pushing bodies and
bags towards the center area as recruits piled off the trucks. It
was chaos, the kind of controlled chaos the sergeants wanted
so they could instantly obtain control.

"MOVE YOUR ASSES!"

"FORM UP! DO IT NOW!"

"DROP YOUR DUFFEL AND SIT DOWN ON IT. I
DON'T GIVE A SHIT IF IT'S NOT YOUR DUFFEL. SIT
RIGHT THE FUCK DOWN NOW!"

Forty-six confused, abused and bewildered recruits either
immediately dropped their duffels and sat down or scrambled
to locate the nearest one. The seconds seemed to tick off
agonizingly slow. The air was filled with dust, making it
difficult to breath. Sweat poured down everyone's faces. A
few recruits didn't react fast enough to the command as they
tried in vain to find an available bag.

"WHAT THE FUCK IS WRONG WITH YOU? CAN'T
YOU FOLLOW A SIMPLE ORDER YOU WORTHLESS
PIECE OF SHIT?"

The sergeant grabbed the recruit and literally tossed him at
an open bag.

"AND WHAT ABOUT YOU SHITHEAD?" screamed another sergeant at one of the two remaining recruits. "WHAT THE FUCK DO YOU THINK YOU'RE DOING?"

"Looking for a bag," came the meek reply.

The sergeant pointed at one of the remaining two bags that didn't have a sweating recruit sitting on top of it.

"Thank you sir."

"STOP RIGHT THERE!" The sergeant moved quickly to the recruit's side. "WHY WOULD YOU INSULT ME AFTER I SHOWED YOU SUCH KINDNESS!?"

"I…I…"

"SHUT YOUR PIEHOLE! GET ON THE GROUND AND GIVE ME TWENTY!"

The recruit dropped and started pumping out the pushups as the sergeant addressed everyone.

"WE ARE NOT OFFICERS. DO NOT MAKE THE MISTAKE OF CALLING US SIR! YOU DO NOT SALUTE US! THE TWO PROPER RESPONSES TO ANY OF US IS YES DRILL SERGEANT OR NO DRILL SERGEANT. IS EVERYONE CLEAR!?"

"Yes drill sergeant," the recruits responded weakly.

"I SAID, IS THAT FUCKING CLEAR!?"

"YES DRILL SERGEANT!"

The sergeant looked down at the recruit doing pushups. "Recover and find a bag." He looked up and addressed the group.

"Listen up because I'm only going to say this once. My name is Drill Sergeant Sheffield. My second's name is Drill Sergeant Hicks. The other two are my assistant Drill Sergeants, DS Smith and DS Rutger. You are now under my command and will be known as Platoon Alpha, which is part of Company A, for the next sixty days during basic training. Your parents are not here to hold your hand anymore. My drill sergeants are not here to hold your hand. We are here to train you to become soldiers. Now, with that said, there are a number of different MOS's represented sitting in front of me."

He flipped through the clipboard pages for a few seconds.

"Where are my artillery recruits?"

A few hands shot up.

"Good. What about my tank crew?"

Another group of hands.

"My riflemen?"

The majority of the boy's hands went up.

"Oh my. Gentlemen, it would appear we have some celebrities in our midst. Where are Nicholson and Paige?"

Sam and Bill reluctantly raised their hands.

"These two want to be Rangers. The rest of you better watch out for them because Nicholson and Paige are here to become elite soldiers."

Sam and Bill lowered their hands as beams of hatred and jealousy shot out from recruits all around them. The sergeant handed the clipboard off to one of his assistant DS's.

"Regardless of whatever MOS you're pursuing, our job is to train you; to mold you all in to a cohesive team to work together towards a common goal. There will be hardship and you will hate us for what we make you do. But trust me when I tell you this. We don't care what you think. We don't care what you feel. You will do what we tell you to do. You will do what's expected of you. And you will do it willingly and with purpose or there will be consequences. Some of you will test us and I invite you to do so. Drill Sergeant Hicks," DS

Sheffield commanded as he turned and walked away, "get these recruits a bunk to call home."

* * *

The first week of Basic consisted of a 03:30 bed rousing, 04:00 headcount followed immediately by PT, or Physical Training until 06:00. After a quick breakfast they would muster and then head off to classroom lessons such as first-aid, military customs, drills, Army Core Values and various other soldiering skills. Seven minutes was allocated for lunch with a strict no-talking policy sometimes followed by a run or PT afterwards which left many lunches all over the ground. The afternoon was filled with more of the same including two mile road marches. After dinner their time was spent studying for spot examinations by the sergeants, cleaning their clothes and/or Company area, polishing their boots or keeping their area organized. The Drill Sergeants would come around and spot check the barrack on a whim. If they found any infraction they would pull everyone outside and smoke them. To get smoked meant extremely rigorous and non-stop exercise. It was meant to tire you to the very core, very quickly. If the platoon was able to hit their bunks by 23:00 there was still Firewatch. Firewatch consisted of a one hour detail, for two soldiers in full uniform, to patrol the barrack. At the end of their hour they would wake the next two scheduled, remove and properly store their own uniforms, and fall asleep only to be woken at 03:30 when the routine would start all over again.

Needless to say, Sam and Bill, just like everyone else, were very tired and extremely sore.

Week two and three expanded on what they'd been taught already. More marching and drilling; proper saluting and interaction with superior NCOs and Officers; four hour road marches in full battle gear; rappelling; the Obstacle Course, both with and without gear. There was also the never-ending cycle of classroom instruction and PT. Night and day, day and night. It all felt the same. Their minds played tricks on them. And even when they were allowed to sleep they never dreamed. Their bodies were destroyed. Blisters, sores, scrapes and rashes appeared all over their feet and where their equipment constantly rubbed their bodies. They were being torn down bit by bit.

* * *

"Shut the fuck up and line up maggots."

Forty-six recruits quickly formed up and shut their mouths.

DS Hicks turned around and watched as DS Sheffield and a few other sergeants entered the building behind him. He turned back around and addressed the platoon.

"I hope you all enjoyed what you just had for lunch because right now you're all going through the Gas House. It will be filled with CS gas, otherwise known as Tear gas."

The majority of the recruit's faces turned nervous.

"Five at a time will line up outside this door," DS Hicks said as he pointed to the same one the other DS's had used. "You will then don and secure your gas mask. After that all five will enter the Gas House and line up. You will follow all instructions given to you. Have fun."

Sam and Bill, like the other recruits, had heard stories about this place and none of them were happy stories. They happened to be in the first five and lined up right outside the door.

The command was given. "Masks on."

Sam, Bill and the other three recruits extracted their gas masks from their hip bags and pulled them over their heads. After that they pulled the various head straps to tightly secure it. Once secure each recruit covered the filter and blew out and in hard to verify the integrity of the seal around their face. If there were any gaps each recruit would instantly know it because they'd be sucking raw and not filtered gas.

Each recruit gave a thumbs up and DS Hicks sent them on their way through the door. Inside Sam and Bill walked into a hazy room and instantly they smelled the CS gas, even though it was filtered. A multitude of nerve endings flared as any exposed cuts on their bodies began to tingle and hurt. On a number of tables were coffee cans that emanated white CS gas.

"Line up," a masked DS ordered. "Now, as I approach each of you I will give you a signal. At that point you will remove your mask, take a deep breath and answer three questions I will pose to you. The only way you will exit this gas house is by successfully answering my questions. I recommend that you do so as quickly as possible."

He approached the first candidate, gave the signal and the recruit lifted his mask and took a deep breath. Immediately he began to cough uncontrollably as tears ran down his face.

Sam shifted in his boots. *Well this doesn't look like fun.*

Bill looked on as well. *Fucking great.*

Eventually the first three recruits managed to answer the questions and exit through the back of the gas house. The DS stepped up to Sam and gave him the signal.

Here we go. Sam lifted his mask, took a deep breath and his lungs were instantly assaulted. A wave of panic set in as his body revolted. He coughed and spat out a gob of phlegm. Tears flowed down his face as his eyes, nose and mouth were stricken with the foul gas.

"Name, rank and serial number."

Cough. "Sam...Sam Paige. Private." Cough. Sam barely rattled off his social security number as another round of coughing overtook him.

"You're done. Head out the exit."

As Sam left the back of the gas house the fresh air slapped him in the face and his eyes uncontrollably slammed shut. Tears and mucus ran freely from his eyes and mouth.

"Breath soldier."

Sam moved his hand to touch his face and had it slapped away.

"Don't touch your face, that'll make it worse. Breath while I pour water over your face."

Sam listened and did what he was told. The cold water felt as if a life preserver had been thrown to him and he welcomed every drop as it washed the CS gas from his pores. It didn't take long for Sam to catch his breath as fresh air replaced the gas in his system.

Bill emerged from the gas house and Sam, through squinted eyes, saw his friend in the same condition he'd been in. Sam smiled. *Well, that was one hell of an experience.*

* * *

Towards the end of the third week they had another classroom lesson. Sergeant Hicks walked up to the front and

58

held up an M16 rifle. All eyes, even the sleepy ones, became focused on the weapon.

"This is your primary weapon. It is known as the M16. It is a magazine fed, gas-operated, air-cooled, semiautomatic or fully-automatic, hand-held, shoulder-fired weapon. The M16 uses five point five six millimeter cartridge and has a muzzle velocity of three thousand feet per second. On full automatic this weapon will shoot approximately eight hundred rounds per minute. Its effective range is five hundred and fifty meters for a single point target.

"All of you will now be issued an M16. You will be held responsible and accountable for your weapon. When your weapon is placed on the floor in front of you do not touch it. I repeat, do not touch it."

The other drill sergeants proceeded to dole out forty-six M16s for the next few minutes. The anticipation started to rise.

DS Hicks continued. "The first lesson will be to familiarize you with the exterior of the weapon and how it operates. After that we'll go through disassembly and proper maintenance. Following that we'll run through some loading and unloading simulations which will include the use of SPORTS. It's going to be a busy day and you have a lot to learn."

Bill put his hand up.

"What is it Nicholson?"

"When do we get to shoot them?"

The DS sighed. "It never fails. Every rotation we get the same question. And every rotation we give the same answer. Stand up Nicholson."

Bill rose to his feet.

"Now drop and give me thirty. We'll wait while you finish."

Quite a few of the other recruit's grinned as Bill grunted out thirty pushups.

"Retake your seat."

Bill sat back down.

"Now, before we begin you need to partner up with some…"

Bill put his hand back up.

DS Hicks stopped cold. "Nicholson. You're playing with fire. What is it?"

"Was the answer the thirty pushups or was it something else drill sergeant?"

A collective gasp could practically be heard throughout the room. Even Sam couldn't believe his friend was this stupid to test the DSs.

"On your feet Nicholson," ordered DS Hicks.

Bill stood up once again and all eyes darted between him and the DS.

"Nicholson. Are you familiar with the M16?"

"No Drill Sergeant."

"And yet you'd like to shoot it before learning how to operate it?"

"No Drill Sergeant. I only asked when we get to shoot them."

"Are you attempting to mind fuck me recruit?"

"No Drill Sergeant. I'm just very interested in shooting the weapon. Besides, Drill Sergeant, you're not my type."

Sam waited for Bill to get annihilated. *Holy shit, here it comes. He's done for.*

The seconds ticked by as Bill's words hung in the air. Everyone waited for Bill to get his ass handed to him in one way or another. DS Hicks finally spoke up.

"Here's the deal Nicholson. You'll be the first recruit to shoot if, and only if, you pass the weapon's handling exam with flying colors. In a few days everyone will be tested on how the M16 operates including jams, disassembly and reassembly. If you pass that without any mistakes then you'll shoot first. However, if you miss one iota, or fuck up one tiny thing, then you'll run fifty concurrent laps around the field. Do we have a deal?"

Bill only smiled. "Deal Drill Sergeant."

DS Hicks smiled. He liked the kid. "Sit the fuck down Nicholson."

Bill sat down and Sam whispered, "Are you fucking insane?"

Bill shook his head. "If you can't beat'em, join'em. I got this."

* * *

DS Hicks loomed over Bill as he completed the reassembly of the M16.

"Hand it over," he commanded and Bill gave the rifle to him.

The Sergeant pulled back the charging handle, let it go and then squeezed the trigger. Click. He handed it back to Bill along with a magazine.

"Demonstrate SPORTS and explain the steps to me."

Bill inserted the magazine into the rifle and then pointed the weapon downrange. Everyone was still gathered around and craned forward to seeing if Bill would finally make a mistake.

"SPORTS stands for Slap, Pull, Observe, Release, Tap and Squeeze. When a malfunction occurs, SPORTS is the first thing you try to attempt to clear the weapon and get back in the fight. To start with you Slap the magazine to make sure it's seated. Pull the charging handle back to the rear and Observe if a live round or expended cartridge ejects. Release the charging handle and then Tap the forward assist to make sure the bolt is closed. Squeeze the trigger."

Bill demonstrated each step as he talked his way through the procedure. He then ejected the magazine, pulled the charging handle back to expel the live round currently in the chamber, placed the weapon on safe and placed it on the table.

DS Hicks spoke up. "You made one mistake Nicholson." A number of the recruits standing around smiled.

Bill's smile faltered but he kept quiet.

"Do you know what your mistake was?"

Bill shook his head.

DS Hicks leaned in so only Bill could hear him. "It was making that deal with me. Now you get to shoot first and everyone else dislikes your overconfidence just a little bit more."

A smile appeared on Bill's face. "You're saying I passed Drill Sergeant?"

The DS pulled back and spoke up. "That's exactly what I'm saying. Listen up. Nicholson will be shooting first. Pair up with your battle buddy, line up to get your assigned ammo and take a firing lane. You will not load your weapon until instructed to do so."

Sam patted Bill on the back. "Nice job. Fifty laps would have been brutal."

"No shit."

Ten minutes later the platoon was in position.

DS Hicks spoke over the loud speaker and began to issue commands. "Insert a five round magazine in to your weapon. Charge your weapon. On my mark Nicholson, and Nicholson only, will commence fire. You have five rounds Nicholson, the range is yours. Commence fire."

Bill lay prone and lined up his iron sights on the target one hundred yards away. He breathed out and squeezed. BLAM! He resituated his sights and squeezed. BLAM! After three more shots he ejected his magazine.

DS Sheffield and DS Hicks looked through their binoculars.

"And the kid can shoot."

"That he can," DS Hicks replied as he brought the microphone up. "All bays. I repeat. All bays. Five rounds only. Commence fire."

* * *

A week later, after multiple trips to the range, Sam and Bill's ability put them in the platoon's top five shooters. Along with that skill they constantly excelled at running, navigating the obstacle course, marching, grenade throwing, land navigation, classroom testing and other physical challenges they were presented with.

The one thing either one hadn't been assigned yet was the temporary Platoon Leader or squad leader positions that were constantly rotated. The Drill Sergeants changed up who ran each of the twelve man squads, as well as the entire platoon to see how each recruit would manage under various circumstances. During the platoon's downtime the four DSs talked about just that.

"It's about time Paige and Nicholson were assigned squad or platoon role," said DS Smith.

"I agree," added DS Rutger. "They haven't been tapped for a leadership role yet."

DS Sheffield shook his head. "I want to wait on those two."

"Why?"

"Because the longer we wait the more anxious they'll get. They're heading from Basic down the Ranger path and I want to wait to see how they handle real adversity. When the time comes, at the end of Basic, we'll put Paige in charge of the platoon and Nicholson in charge of his squad. The rest of the platoon, and any animosity that those two have accumulated, will come to a head. That'll be a perfect time to see how they handle soldiers who don't want to follow them."

"I like it," said DS Hicks. "And truth be told, I like Paige and Nicholson. They've got heart, balls and brains."

"Nicholson seems to have a bigger death wish, seeing how he continually enjoys testing our resolve."

DS Hicks chuckled. "Yeah, he does do that. But he and Paige aren't slackers. They listen, adapt and get the job done."

"Indeed," agreed DS Sheffield. "The final week is coming up and that means live fire exercises, the three day overnight in the field followed by the final road march. We'll see how they do when the time comes."

10
Monday November 24, 1975

Ring Ring.

Major Anthony Palmer walked over to his home phone
and picked up.

"Hello?"

"Major. I hope you enjoyed your respite. You know who
this is I take it?"

A pained look instantly appeared on Anthony's face. "I'm
afraid I do."

"Good. I hope you can save me the trouble of having to
explain what will happen if you don't comply with my next
request?"

Anthony rubbed his head with his free hand. He knew he
was trapped in a no-win situation and he hated it.

"Are you still there Major? Would you like me to repeat
the question?"

"No. I heard you the first time." *You asshole.*

"Make sure that you did. Now, this is how you're going to
proceed."

* * *

Two days later Major Palmer anxiously waited as the
plane, bound from South America, began its final decent to his
airbase late at night. He'd completed the preparations he'd
been asked to setup and there was nothing else for him to do
but look the other way yet again.

What the hell am I doing? I hate myself for agreeing to this agreement years ago. If this delivery goes south my family and I are completely screwed.

"Lieutenant. I'm going to head down and meet that plane," he said to the officer guiding the plane in from the control tower they were in.

"Sir? I don't understand. That's unusual and will be dangerous."

"I'm not asking for your opinion Lieutenant. Inform the ground crew that I'm on my way." He turned and headed down the tower stairs.

The skeptical lieutenant turned back to his console and spoke into the radio. "Ground crew. Ground crew. The Major is on his way to meet the plane. Look lively."

By the time the Major made it out to the hanger the large plane had landed and taxied to a stop. The ground crew supervisor walked over to him.

"Sir, can I help you with something?"

"No. I just haven't seen one of these things offloaded in a while. As you were."

The ground personnel appeared relieved. "Oh. Excellent. Please be careful sir." He jogged away and started to issue orders to his crew.

Major Palmer watched as the contents of the plane were taken out and placed in systematic rows within the hanger. As the last crate was dropped off he began to slowly walk through the aisles.

"Is there anything I can do for you sir?"

The Major turned and came face to face with the supervisor. "No. Thank you. Dismissed."

"Very well. Have a good night."

The Major nodded in return as the man walked away. He resumed meandering and ten minutes later he stopped. *What the hell am I looking for? I'm sure it's drugs. It has to be drugs. Nothing else makes sense.*

Suddenly a dog barked and a number of flashlights bore down on him.

What the hell?

"Stay where you are! Hands up! Do not move!"

Are they talking to me?

"I said hands up!"

Before he knew it a number of Military Police had surrounded, searched and detained him.

"What the hell is this?" he asked. "Do you know who I am? I'm Major Palmer and I run this airbase. Get your damn hands off me."

Someone the Major had never seen before in his life walked up to him and spoke.

"You might not be commanding anything if my hunch is right, Major."

"Who are you? What's going on?" Anthony shot back.

"My name is hardly important. What is important is that I'm from the USACIDC. That's the Criminal Investigation Command. I've been investigating you for some time Major. It appears that you've been living outside your means."

The Major tried to look surprised but came up short.

"Your home phone was tapped. And truth be told, I almost lost interest in you until the other night. And from that conversation, well, here we are."

"I don't know what you're talking about."

The agent smiled. "I expected as much." He raised his hand and two men began to lead their dogs through the off-boarded equipment. He turned back to the Major. "I guess we'll just have to wait and see what they find. Maybe you're right, maybe this is just a huge misunderstanding."

Five minutes later one of the dogs began barking uncontrollably. It didn't take long for a couple of other CID agents to discover a huge cache of cocaine stashed within the equipment.

"Is there anything you'd like to tell me?"

"This is as much a shock to me as it is to you," the Major replied.

"I bet. And yet, here you were, looking for something all on your own in the middle of the night. Strange coincidence, don't you think?"

"I'm not saying another word."

The agent nodded. "That's probably the smartest thing you've said all night. Take him away." The agent spoke up. "I want pictures, plenty of pictures. Then bag and tag it all. And make sure nobody visits the Major before I do."

* * *

Major Palmer was searched and then placed in a base holding cell. As he sat there fuming at his stupidity he knew the case against him was strong. *Maybe I can make a deal? If they have the phone conversation then it shows I wasn't a compliant participant. I can tell them what I know in exchange for immunity. I don't have any other choice. My family needs me.*

The cell door opened and a MP stood in its opening.

"Sir, a representative from JAG is here on your behalf."

68

Well shit, that was fast. Major Palmer stood up and was escorted to a private room where he was handcuffed to the table. A woman, in professional attire, walked in and placed her briefcase down on the table.

"Working a little late, aren't you?"

"No rest for the wicked," she shot back. "And apparently I'm looking right at the wicked, isn't that right Major? Hand in the cookie jar, so to speak." She paused and then said, "My name is Anna Garland." She extended her right hand towards his shackled hands.

His eyes narrowed as he accepted her handshake. *Sweaty hand.* "Fine. I don't want to play any games. I want immunity for my family and myself in exchange for what I know."

"We'll get to that tomorrow. Right now I just dropped by to let you know I'm going to be your lawyer, unless of course you wanted to hire someone else. In the morning make sure not to talk to anyone unless I'm present. Any deals you want to make I will verify are genuine before I allow you to speak. Do you understand?"

"Yes, of course." A wave of relief washed over him. "Thank you Ms. Garland."

"That's what I'm here for."

She knocked on the door and the MP let her out. A minute later the Major was escorted back to his cell.

Maybe I'll get out of this? My career is over and my wife will be furious, but at least we'll all be safe.

He stifled a cough as his mind wandered.

If she was just assigned to me then how would she have known what I was doing in the hanger?

He coughed again and he covered it with his hand.

She arrived so quickly, but JAG is closed this time of night.
This time a violent fit of coughing startled him. His throat felt wet and he spat out what he thought was phlegm into the toilet. Bright blood floated in the bowl and stared back at him. What the hell? The next round of coughing began and it didn't stop. Blood sprayed out of his mouth and all over the opposite wall. Two minutes later Major Palmer lay dead in his cell.

* * *

Anna Garland, or whoever she claimed she was, exited the building and walked to her car. She opened the door with her left hand, got in and closed it behind her. Very carefully she used a pair of tweezers and removed the thin membrane that was lightly adhered to the palm of her right hand. She bagged the membrane that has been coated with the contact poison, and then removed her wig. She then started the car and pulled away.

11
Tuesday December 2, 1975

The library door closed behind Tom and he made his way over to his favorite table he liked to use for studying. It was located in the far corners of the large room and allowed him to observe the interactions of his fellow students. He'd come to enjoy watching people from a distance and he'd begun only a few conversations with fellow students. But ultimately they'd felt forced and far from the ease he'd felt talking with Sam and Bill.

I wonder how they're doing in Basic?

Tom placed his backpack down on the table, pulled out a few books and took a seat. He opened one of the textbooks but instead of reading the contents his mind began to wander.

Is this what my life's going to be like for the next four years? Is it all studying, tests and isolation? I feel alone and it's been difficult without my buds around to talk to. Part of me is jealous that they're together and that I'm all alone.

Tom sighed.

I don't know. I suppose life is what you make it. Maybe being alone isn't that bad. Besides, in a couple of weeks it'll be Christmas break and I can drive back up to see my grandparents. I could also...

Tom's train of thought instantly derailed as a stunning redhead, a few years older than him, entered the library and walked his way. *Wow.* He couldn't stop staring at her. As she drew closer she caught him looking at her and whatever look he had on his face caused her to smile right before she sat down at a table twenty feet away.

Did...did she smile at me? Nah, couldn't have been. But I swear she did. What am I supposed to do? Do I go talk with her? What would I say? I don't know but I'd probably blow it anyway. Forget it. He gave up. *Concentrate Tom. Back to work.*

Tom averted his gaze and looked back down at his open text book. What he failed to notice was that the redhead looked over her shoulder not ten seconds later to check on his interest level. When she saw that he wasn't paying her any attention she went back to her own schoolwork.

His loss.

12
Tuesday December 2, 1975

"MOVE OUT!"

The platoon headed out on their initial march. An hour and a half later, after they arrived, they quickly setup a base camp. Security patrols were scheduled and it wasn't until later that evening when the Drill Sergeants tasked them with a final night mission.

Two months' into Basic Training recruits were all working as a cohesive unit, for the most part. Early on the DSs made a point of always punishing the entire platoon when one recruit failed. That form of mental manipulation worked wonders and pressured the recruits who consistently failed to excel, or face the wrath of the rest of the platoon. However, the repeat offenders who didn't care if they affected the rest of the platoon or not, had to have their will bent in a different fashion. When those particular individuals failed the DSs gave them donuts while the rest of the platoon was punished instead. That led to a number of beatings, by the other recruits, during early morning Firewatch. It wasn't long before those smug individuals decided to get their shit together.

Tonight the platoon's mission was to infiltrate, engage, and then successfully exfiltrate an enemy base using the intelligence provided to them. That specific intel turned out to be a few grainy overhead pictures and a hand drawn map of where that base should be located. The current Platoon leader gathered his four squad leaders and had just begun to create an assault strategy when DS Sheffield spoke up.

73

"Brown," he said as he addressed the platoon leader, "you've just been injured. You've been relieved of command."

"What the…"

The DS turned around and yelled, "Paige! Nicholson! Get your asses over here!"

Sam and Bill stopped talking, disengaged from the group and jogged over to where the Drill Sergeant was.

"Paige, Brown here has suffered an injury and needs to be relieved. You're the new Platoon leader. Nicholson, you're now in charge of Squad Alpha. The mission commences in t-minus two hours. Don't fuck this up."

"Yes Drill Sergeant."

Brown's mouth still hung open as the DS walked away.

"The squad's all yours Nicholson," said Alpha's previous leader and headed back to the platoon.

"Sorry," Sam offered to Brown who had remained behind.

"Fuck you," Brown heatedly shot back. "Who the hell do you think you are?"

"It wasn't my call. You know that."

"It's not right. This was my shot. I'm going to do whatever I can to sabotage you."

"You should walk away right now," Bill countered, "before you really need a medic. And if you do anything to fuck this mission up I'm sure the rest of the platoon would love to know it was you."

"Like it or not," Sam said, "this is my command now Brown. I need you supporting me one hundred percent. If that's something you're not capable of then let me know right now."

74

Brown's eyes darted back and forth between the two before he finally relented. He handed off the intel and sulked away. They watched him leave before the five of them turned and huddled up. Sam looked through the photos and the hand-drawn map, passed them to Bill and then spoke up.

"The rest of you have seen these I take it?"

Squad leaders Bravo, Charlie and Delta all nodded. They liked what they just heard and how Paige and Nicholson had handled Brown. They were eager for a successful mission now more than ever.

"Good. Thoughts?"

Bravo, Charlie and Delta looked at each other.

Charlie spoke up. "You want our opinion?"

Sam nodded. "You're not here to blindly follow what I have to say. I need to know what each of you would do so I can come to an informed decision."

"He's kind of funny that way," Bill added. "I'll start if that helps." Bill laid the photos and map out on the ground so they could all see them. "The compound, for lack of better words, is located at the top of a small hill. It appears that all four sides are open which gives them a three-hundred-sixty degree angle of fire down the hill."

"That doesn't bode well for us," said Charlie.

"I agree," Delta added.

"But it's nighttime," Bravo offered. "Maybe they won't see us?"

"Or maybe they should," Sam said with a sly grin.

* * *

"Delta in position."

75

"Bravo in position."

"Charlie in position."

Three minutes later. "Alpha is now in position."

"Roger that," Sam replied over the radio. "Make sure you're not seen and that your squads are spread out evenly. We're only going to get one chance at this."

For the past hour all four squads had successfully navigated through the forest and had crept up to the tree line. Two hundred feet away was the enemy compound, slightly raised above them on top of the hill. For two hundred feet in every direction there was absolutely no cover to hide behind. A frontal assault on the compound would be suicide as any attacker knew they'd be cut down by gunfire in a matter of seconds.

"Delta. What's the opposition look like?"

"Delta here. The light is terrible. I can make out a few sentries."

"Charlie reporting. I agree with Delta. The light is terrible. Total number of enemy force is unknown."

"Roger that," Sam replied. "Stick with the plan. Don't open fire until I give the order. And when you do make sure you hit what you're aiming at."

"But…"

"I know," Sam countered. "All I'm saying is once you have their attention make sure to keep it."

Everyone's weapon in the platoon was loaded with blanks. Using live rounds was out of the question since their final mission pitted them against live opponents.

"That we can do. Waiting on your signal."

Sam had ordered Bravo, Charlie and Delta to spread out along the southern tree line while he, along with Alpha, had gotten into position along the northern tree line.

"Is everyone ready and know what they're doing?" Bill asked his squad.

A collective nod was returned from within the darkness of the woods.

* * *

A flurry of automatic weapon's fire erupted from the southern woods. Instantly the alarm sounded within the compound.

"Report!" DS Hicks demanded.

"Based on the amount of firepower it looks like the entire platoon is down there shooting at us."

"Idiots. What they hell were they thinking. Give me four flares right now."

Ten seconds later four flares launched from within the compound. Each one drifted down along the four compass points.

The shooting continued from the southern trees.

"Anything!?"

"Nothing to report on the north side."

"Ditto on the east. No movement."

"West is clear. Hillside has no movement."

"Fine," replied DS Hicks. "Time to show them a trick or two."

* * *

Four flares launched into the sky above the compound.

"Shield your eyes," said Sam. "Don't look at them. Preserve your night vision."

A single flare wafted down the northern hill completely illuminating the entire hillside. Any attackers would be been spotted immediately. The flare finally hit the ground and burned out. When it did Sam burst out of the foliage and sprinted up the hill towards the compound. Squad Alpha was right on his heels.

* * *

"Give me four more flares."

The weapon's fire continued without pause from the southern edge of the forest.

* * *

Sam saw the flares rise into the air when he was fifty feet from the compound wall. He pushed himself even harder. He reached the wall just as the parachute popped and the flare began its slow decent. Bill, and his squad, arrived a second later and immediately hugged the wall just as Sam had done.

* * *

"What's out there?" demanded DS Hicks.

"Not a damn thing. The only contacts are from the south."

"Well, we might get to wrap this up earlier than I thought. I can't wait to smoke the entire platoon for fucking up this mission this badly. I thought Paige would be a much better leader than this. I want mortars focused in on the southern tree line. Hit them with smoke rounds. That'll let them know they would have been blown up."

Of the sixteen man crew that was in the compound, four of them left the DS to go adjust the mortars. Eight were on the southern wall returning fire. The other three each watched the other compass directions which left DS Hicks talking all to himself.

"I guess I win my bet with DS Sheffield. He thought Paige had leadership potential. He was wrong."

DS Hicks turned around and froze. Nine recruits had somehow materialized within his compound walls. Sam and Bill had their weapons trained on him. The other seven members of Alpha instantly aimed their weapons at the backs of the other fifteen enemy defenders.

"How in the…"

"Cease fire," Bill said into the radio. A few seconds later the tree line gunfire stopped.

"Tell your men to surrender or I will kill them where they stand," Sam ordered.

"I…"

The rest of the defenders finally turned their heads and realized the precarious position they were in.

"Do it now!" Sam ordered.

Suddenly all of the compound lights came on all at once. The loudspeakers boomed.

"ATTENTION! ATTENTION! THE SIMULATION IS OVER. I REPEAT, THE SIMULATION IS OVER. PLATOON ALPHA, RALLY ON THE COMPOUND ON THE DOUBLE!"

The remaining recruits emerged from the southern trees and ran up the hill. DS Sheffield came out of a small shack and walked over to Sam.

"Stand down."

Sam, Bill and the rest of Alpha lowered their weapons. Thirty seconds later the rest of the platoon joined them. When they had all quieted down DS Sheffield finally addressed them.

"Gentlemen. It is with great pride that I get to congratulate you on passing your final exam!"

Cheers and high fives rippled throughout the group.

"It's been a grueling two months but each and every one of you deserves to graduate tomorrow. In ten minutes trucks will arrive to take you back to basecamp. There you will eat and drink like kings. In the morning we march back in time to graduate!"

DS Sheffield showed a little admiration in his eyes.

"Great job Paige."

"Thank you Drill Sergeant. But I didn't do it alone. It was a collective effort."

"Is that so? DS Hicks, what do you think?"

DS Hicks scrutinized Sam and Bill before he said anything. "I think I just got my ass handed to me." He smiled and then said, "Fucking great job. It looks like I owe DS Sheffield a drink."

DS Sheffield slapped DS Hicks on the back. "Damn straight you do. Now Paige, do me a favor and get everyone ready to head back to basecamp. You haven't graduated yet."

"Yes sir," Sam said with a wink.

"Now you had to go and say something stupid like that, didn't you Paige," he replied with a grin. "Drop and give me twenty before you get your platoon ready for transport."

"Yes Drill Sergeant." Sam hit the ground and started pushing them out.

Bill squatted down next to him. "Stop taking my lines brother."

* * *

The road march back to the barracks might have been the easiest one any of the forty-six recruits could remember. Their hearts and sprits were at an all-time high. When they arrived back at the barracks they showered and then finally got ready in their dress uniforms.

Graduation was routine. The bleachers were filled with parents and relatives. After the ceremony finally finished DS Sheffield made his way over to Sam and Bill. He handed them each a box.

"Congratulations. You've both been promoted to PFC. That's Private First Class."

"Thank you Drill Sergeant."

"Yes," added Bill. "Thank you Drill Sergeant."

"Don't thank me. Going from an E-1 to an E-3 is a big deal, but you both earned it. I still can't get over what you did to DS Hicks on that hill." The DS chuckled. "He won't be getting over that for a long time."

Bill and Sam smiled.

"Anyway, I understand that neither of your folks showed up. Is that right?"

"Yes Drill Sergeant," they replied in unison.

"That's an unfortunate side effect of this career I'm afraid." He pulled two envelopes from his uniform and handed them over. "You've been issued new orders. You're to report to Airborne Training sooner than you thought."

"How soon?" Sam asked.

"This evening. You start tomorrow."

Bill joked. "No rest for the wicked, eh?"

"Certainly not. You're both superb soldiers. Good luck on your path to becoming Rangers. It's been a privilege gentlemen."

DS Sheffield extended his hand and shook both of their hands to their utter surprise. He turned and walked away.

"Well shit," said Bill. "Is tomorrow free for you Sam?"

"I'll have to check my schedule."

"Yeah. Of course, looks like our folks didn't check theirs too closely."

"You know they don't approve of what we're doing. All we really have is each other."

"That's deep brother, really deep."

"Fuck you too," said Sam.

* * *

That evening Sam and Bill were dropped off at their new barracks and were the last to arrive. Their class consisted of officers and other enlisted personnel from both the Army and other military services. Their three week course was broken up in to three separate phases: Ground, Tower and Jump weeks. Regardless of the training phase, every morning the class endured PT followed by a three to four mile formation run.

Ground week prepared Sam and Bill on how to jump out of a plane and land safely. Time after time they worked on their PLF, Parachute Landing Fall, until they were sore from constantly hitting the ground. The trick was to keep your legs and feet together. As you land they would transfer their energy of the fall from the lower to the upper body. Various heights along with various landing areas of sand and pebbles were used to instill the proper PLF. At the end of Ground week a thirty four foot tower was introduced to their training. Jumping off the high tower simulated the feeling of an actual jump due to the sensation of falling. Sam and Bill loved every minute of it.

Tower week focused on tower jumps. The thirty four foot tower was used, but added to the mix was the swing landing trainer, the suspended harness training as well as the monster two hundred and fifty foot tower. Throughout Tower week Sam and Bill were taught the different phases of exiting an aircraft; parachute malfunctions and how to identify and deal with them; not to mention recovering from drag.

Jump week took everything they had been taught and put it to test. The plane would fly twelve-hundred feet above the ground traveling at one hundred thirty miles per hour. Sam and Bill jumped a number of times, from wearing no gear to wearing a full load.

The experience was taxing, to say the least, but it was not as grueling as Basic had been. Training lasted approximately eight hours a day. Evenings and weekends they were free to do whatever they wanted provided they show up early and rested the following morning. Sleep had never felt so good in their entire lives.

After three long, but fun weeks of Airborne training, Sam and Bill graduated once again with no one there to share it

with. But they had their Airborne wings and their new orders
to attend Ranger school in a week, at the beginning of the year.

Christmas was the day after graduation and both of their
parents had expected them to fly home during their week break
before attending Ranger school. On the phone Sam and Bill
each informed their parents that they weren't coming home for
the holidays. That news did not go over well but the last thing
Sam and Bill wanted was a week of hearing how disappointed
their parents were in them. Instead, they stayed on base and
decided to spend the week exploring the area surrounding Fort
Benning.

13
Friday January 2, 1976

"SO YOU ALL THINK YOU HAVE WHAT IT TAKES
TO BE A RANGER DO YOU!?"

Seventy-seven soldiers stood at attention while Ranger
Instructor Hansen began his welcoming speech. The classes
age group ranged from eighteen to twenty-five and
encompassed the ranks of PFC through Lieutenants. However,
none of that mattered to the numerous RIs that had seventy-
seven Ranger wannabes at their mercy.

"WELL I'M HERE TO TELL YOU THAT YOU DON'T
HAVE WHAT IT TAKES. I'M GOING TO PERSONALLY
MAKE SURE EACH AND EVERY ONE OF YOU FAIL,
AND I HOPE LIKE HELL THAT PISSES YOU OFF."

RI Hansen took it down a notch.

"I'm here to inform you that becoming a Ranger is no easy
task. The training you're about to endure is considered to be
the hardest the United States Army has to offer. And it only
gets worse. Trust me when I tell you that I don't give a shit if
you believe that or not. The only thing that should matter to
you is whether you can dig deep down inside yourself and
discover the will, the courage and the strength to continue on
regardless of how exhausted, sore, injured or hungry you may
be.

"For the next four weeks, or until you get dropped by
either one of the RIs, or you voluntarily pussy out, each of you
will have to make that hard choice. And your choice is
whether you have what it takes to earn that coveted Ranger
Tab. Believe me when I say that this Ranger Indoctrination

Program will weed out the non-believers. Only those that survive will be invited to Ranger training, and certainly not before. Oh, and if I didn't mention it before, I especially enjoy these winter months for training because the class dropout rate will be much higher than normal. Welcome to RIP. RI Bass, get these sorry looking sonsofbitches out of my sight."

RI Bass took over. "IT'S TIME FOR A FIVE MILE FORMATION RUN TO GET EVERYONE WARMED UP. ON ME. MOVE OUT!"

Sam and Bill shared a glance as they began the run. Both of their expressions had the 'what the hell have we gotten ourselves into' look. Their week off for Christmas hadn't been as fun as they'd expected and even though they didn't talk about it they both missed spending the holiday with their families. And without a vehicle at their disposal they only made two endeavors off the base using public transportation. The rest of the time they'd practiced running, exercising and resting to prepare themselves for all the rumors they'd heard about the Ranger Indoctrination Program. What they didn't realize, just as the other seventy-five hadn't, was just how grueling the training was going to be.

* * *

Within the first week alone twenty-one soldiers had either been dropped or quit which left fifty-six. Twenty hours a day Sam and Bill were constantly trained, pushed and prodded to their breaking point. They were sleep deprived, hungry and exhausted. Push-ups, sit-ups, pull-ups, running, road marches, classroom training, water survival, day and night land navigation, map reading and what seemed like the kitchen sink

86

were thrown at all of them. Each RI constantly badgered everyone, degrading and sowing seeds of doubt to see what they were made of.

By the end of the third week another fourteen were gone. The remaining forty-two knew more about themselves then they'd ever thought possible. Through all the hardship, the blisters, the bruises, injuries, rashes, sleep deprivation, hunger, thirst, rain, cold, bugs and the constant harassment from the RIs, they had all survived it. They had each pushed through their own doubt and knee jerk reaction to quit. They had overcome all odds and were determined now, more than ever, to finish their RIP training.

* * *

It was the beginning of February when the forty-two survivors of RIP were assigned to the 75th Ranger Regiment. There was only a one day period of downtime before their actual Ranger training began at Camp Darby, a separate area within Fort Benning.

Sam and Bill were exhausted but elated at both of their progress, not to mention stubbornness. There had been numerous occasions where Sam and Bill had wanted to quit but the other had pushed them on. Without each other to lean on they knew they might not have succeeded where so many others had failed.

The following morning, after arriving at Camp Darby, they got a glimpse of what was expected of them. A new set of Ranger Instructors met the remaining forty-two and a whole new level of hell began. They stood at attention as the lead RI addressed them.

"You will refer to me as RI Johnson. I and the other RIs are not here to hold your hand or be your friend. We are here to instruct you, to punish you in ways you can't even imagine. Becoming a Ranger is not easy, and each of you will find that out. For some of you this sixty-one day course will end with accepting a Ranger Tab. For the others, they will fall to the wayside and fail to negotiate this program. RIP culled a number of the weak. Trust me when I say I'm here to finish what they started.

"For the next twenty days your home will be here. We like to call it the Crawling Phase. The first week you'll be rigorously tested in RAP, or Ranger Assessment Phase. It will be grueling and will include such evolutions as a six-hour, full ninety pound pack road march; water survival; land navigation and the fitness test. That test includes a five mile run in forty minutes or less, a minimum of forty-nine push-ups, fifty-nine sit-ups and six pull-ups. If you happen to pass the first week, the remaining part of the Crawling Phase will consist of ambush and combat training, recon patrols, airborne operations and obstacle course navigation.

"The second part of training will move us to Camp Merrill, located in the Georgia Mountains for another twenty days. We call that the Walking Phase. That training is based around leadership and survival in extremely harsh conditions which includes hunger, sleep deprivation and emotional stress. It will be fucking cold up there gentlemen.

"And for those of you who happen to survive Phase Two, the third portion of training will take us to the swamps of Florida, based out of Camp Rudder. Survival and leadership skills will be tested extensively during this Running Phase.

Small boat operations, ship-to-shore and stream-crossing training will all come in to play.

"You all proved yourselves during RIP, but now it's time to dig deep and really see what you're made of. Remember, fifty to sixty percent of this class will not make it. Welcome to Ranger School."

* * *

Sam and Bill finished the three mile terrain run, at the head of the pack, and came face to face with a large obstacle course. A seventy-five foot shallow and muddy area, topped off by knee-high barbed wire, was the first thing they began to tackle. An RI began to yell at them.

"THE OBSTACLE ISN'T GOING TO COME TO YOU! ATTACK IT! GET ON YOUR GODDAMN BELLIES AND HIT IT!"

Without any hesitation Sam and Bill dove into the thick, oozing, smelling mud and maneuvered their way towards the far end with the razor sharp barb wire just a few inches above them. They finished dragging their now mud encased bodies out of the obstacle and began the climb up the cargo net that towered in front of them. Another RI, with a firehouse, constantly showered them with freezing cold water as they climbed up, over and down the other side. They were both dripping wet, tired, sore, hungry, pissed off and determined as they began the next obstacle.

"Having fun yet brother?"

"Not as much fun as you Sam. The RI with the hose missed a shitload of mud that just doesn't want to dislodge itself from my asshole."

89

Sam jumped to catch a stationary rope that dangled over a deep watery pit and nearly missed it because of Bill's comment. He swung over the pit and Bill followed closely behind.

"You fucker. Don't make me laugh like that. I almost took a header into that pit back there."

White teeth appeared on Bill's mud covered face from out of nowhere as he smiled.

"SINCE YOU TWO THINK THIS TRAINING IS A JOKE, DROP AND GIVE ME TWENTY!"

Sam and Bill's smiles faded instantly as they obeyed the command given to them. They pounded out the twenty push-ups in no time and then continued through the rest of the obstacle course.

* * *

"You will have no more than three hours to complete this march. This twelve mile march will be conducted in full gear. Your gear will be weighed before you leave and once again after you arrive to eliminate cheaters. This is the final step of RAP week and is a pass or fail event. If you fail you will be dropped from this course. You have five minutes to gather your gear, your weapon and muster back here."

Sam and Bill brought their rucksacks outside and lined up to get them weighed. The past week had been hellish. There never seemed to be any downtime for sleep, rest or even meals, which had been reduced from three a day to two. The raw amount of physical exertion their bodies outputted easily exceeded their daily calorie intake. During RIP they had each lost six pounds. During the last week alone they'd dropped another two pounds already with no relief in sight.

Their eighty-five pound packs were weighed in and recorded. They were told to put them on and wait until the rest of the weigh-ins were finished. Twenty minutes later, and already with sore shoulders, the twelve mile march began. Sam and Bill's goal was to stay together and keep a brisk five mile an hour pace, which is really just a very fast walk. Some of the others decided to take off running instead while others took on a slower pace. Within twenty minutes Sam and Bill were all alone on the open road.

"How're you doing?" Sam asked between breaths.

"Don't worry about me. I'm good with this pace so far. You?"

"Just peachy."

They both smiled and kept going, backs hunched over with their rifles in their hands. It was going to be one hell of a tiring day.

* * *

"Everyone take a moment and look around," said RI Johnson. "Nine of your peers are no longer with us."

Sam and Bill, along with the remaining thirty-one classmates, were solemn. They knew a number of their peers hadn't completed the forced march in time and had been cut from the program.

"You should congratulate yourselves on passing RAP, but don't let that get to your head because your training is far from over. That Ranger Tab won't be yours until you've earned it.

"You've been allotted a few extra hours of sleep and a hot meal this evening. Tend to your wounds and get some sleep. You'll all need it. Tomorrow morning, bright and early, we start this shit all over again."

* * *

Two weeks later, after tackling endless obstacle courses, constant five mile runs, airborne operations, and a variety of other training, all thirty-three candidates moved on to the Walking Phase and relocated to the Georgia Mountains at Camp Merrill. It was the end of February and the weather was unsavory at best, dropping very low at night. Winter training was going to be harsh and they all knew it.

* * *

"Nicholson. Stop fucking around. You're up."
Bill stepped up and secured the belay to his harness. Wearing full combat gear he leaned backwards off the sheer mountain cliff and abruptly disappeared. At the base of the cliff a number of his classmates watched as Bill negotiated his repel down the mountainside in a controlled but brisk pace until he landed next to them. He unhooked himself from his gear and took up a security position amongst his peers as the next soldier hooked in and began his rapid descent.
Bill quickly shot a glance over to Sam and received a nod in return before he went back to scanning for any incoming threats. Even though they were both constantly tired and hungry they were actually having a blast. They both had come so far together and were determined to become Rangers. What

other choice did they have? They knew it was either succeed in the military or come crawling home to their parents as failures. When the nights were so cold, as the wind whipped over them tugging at their will to continue, Sam and Bill knew more and more that this was the life they wanted to be a part of. The comradery alone was overwhelming. To know that you'd to anything for the guy next to you and he would do the same is a feeling that was indescribable. They felt that in spades and that, in turn, made it feel like they were part of a family.

* * *

Twenty days on that God forsaken mountain were behind the thirty-two remaining students. Unfortunately one man suffered frostbite and had to be pulled from the class and sent to the hospital. The rest of the class, having successfully negotiated combat patrols, climbing, moving cross country over mountains and a variety of other training were now in a bus heading towards the nearest airfield. The Running Phase was coming up and most of them had passed out as soon as they sat down in the bus. The group was tired, beat up and quiet, reserving all energy for what lay ahead of them in the swamplands of Florida.

The bus eventually arrived at the airfield and pulled up next to the large plane, which they boarded after they dismounted the bus and put on their jump gear. The plane took off and carried thirty-two tired, but willing soldiers, towards their new home in Florida. Sometime later the red light came on. They all stood up and double checked both their own gear as well as the soldier's gear in front of them.

The red light switched to green. Immediately they began to exit on both the left and the right side of the plane as open chutes began to fill up the previously empty sky.

* * *

Bill melted into the foliage. The rest of his squad slowly crossed the stream, one-by-one, while he provided cover for them. Bill slowly scanned the area and looked for any of the teams sent to locate and capture them. Mosquitos, gnats and other insects constantly picked at his open skin, especially around his neck, but he ignored them lest he give away his position. It was quiet in the jungle, or rather, the jungle sounds continued unabated as Bill's team moved deeper towards their goal.

Bill's eight man squad had been given twenty-four hours to navigate ten miles through dense jungle. They were tasked to locate, recon and call in an airstrike on an enemy encampment without being detected. Once the recon was complete the team was to exfiltrate via small boats. The caveat was that the other three team's jobs were to prevent them from succeeding.

Bill's was the last team to attempt this mission. The three previous attempts, made by the other teams, had concluded with one successful mission and two failures, when those teams had been caught. Sam had been in charge of the one team that had completed their mission without any complications. Now it was up to Bill, since he'd been tapped to be the squad leader this time around.

The last of his men finished the stream crossing and crouched out of view in the bushes. They had been on the

94

move since noon and the weather conditions had been punishing. It had rained heavily a few hours before and all of his men were soaked to the bone and extremely tired. Each of them tried to focus on the task at hand but after weeks of punishment they were all at their breaking limit. Bill extracted himself from his hiding spot and moved up to whisper to his assistant squad leader.

"It's seventeen hundred hours, which means we've been pushing through this shit for the past five hours without a break."

"Tell me about it," his second replied.

"We're stopping here until midnight. We need to dry out, rest, tend to our wounds and eat before we tackle the objective. Full noise restrictions. I'll take first watch. Pass the word."

"Roger that."

Bill gripped his weapon tighter as he watched his men begin their process of quietly moving off the trail fifty feet before removing their gear. He kept his eyes and ears open for anything out of the ordinary. His decision to stop was risky, but, traveling through a jungle is tough enough, but attempting it during the night was foolhardy. The opposite side of that coin was that, if successfully executed, his plan would allow his team to bypass the other exhausted teams without incident as they were asleep. It was a gamble and he knew it, but those were the risks of leadership.

A few hours later another team had come close to their location but had passed by without seeing them. Around midnight Bill's squad moved out cautiously, under the light of a partial moon, towards their final destination. The air hung thick with humidity but due to the earlier rain the ground was moist and pliable. These conditions enabled the eight man squad to move faster and quieter than they had anticipated.

It was an hour before dawn when they determined they were only half a click away, or five hundred meters from the encampment. Bill had his team stash everything but their weapons, and the radio, under a pile of fallen palm tree leaves. He then took point and carefully led his men onwards knowing full well that since they hadn't been caught there was a good chance one or two opposing teams could be planning an ambush for them.

An hour later, just as the glowing light of a new day barely broke the horizon's edge, Bill's squad finally spotted their target in the distance. Bill used hand signals and his team slowly lowered themselves onto the ground, out of sight and blended in with the surrounding jungle. Bill raised the binoculars to his eyes and scanned. The encampment consisted of two guard towers, a few buildings surrounded by a rudimentary wood fence line that was approximately eight feet high. A number of enemy personnel stood still throughout the complex and in the guard towers. Bill looked closer and quickly determined they were all dummies dressed up for the training mission.

He lowered his binoculars and began to point at his team members. Three would come with him while the other four would move around the opposite side of the encampment. Along the way each of the four-man sub team would take pictures using the two cameras provided until they'd regroup on the opposite side. With a few nods, and growing anticipation, Bill's group moved off to the right while the other four men moved off to the left.

* * *

"I believe we finally have something," Sam barely breathed out from behind one of the dummies. He'd setup watch in one of the guard towers with another one of his men. Two others were in the other tower while the remaining four had hidden themselves just inside the fence line. He and his team had been up all night waiting for Bill to arrive while the other two teams had gone out to flush Bill's team out. Sam was tired and agitated from the constant insect harassment that continued to feast on him throughout the night.

There. Movement. Sam's eyes shifted and he slowly moved his head to verify his peripheral vision hadn't played tricks on him. *Definitely movement.* Sam hit the button and an alarm filled the entire encampment.

* * *

Sirens came alive all over the camp.

Shit!

Bill had expected something like this, but not this soon. His group of four were still hunkered down in the jungle so it must have been the other part of his team that had been seen. *No matter.* The plan he'd set in place with his men would have to work or else they'd all get caught.

"Radio the strike in," he ordered. "The rest of us will provide cover."

Moments later the man next to him sent off a rapid transmission that provided the coordinates for the artillery target. Bill took a number of quick pictures and then they made their way towards the rendezvous at a brisk pace before

97

anyone from the camp could come out to capture them. Thirty seconds later the remainder of Bill's team met up with him and together they sprinted towards the nearby river as a multitude of shouts were heard in their wake.

* * *

The game is afoot. Sam stood up and yelled to his team.
"They're heading south! They're heading south! Head them off at the boats!"
The four men on the ground moved out towards the beach to get ahead of the invading team. Sam pulled his radio out and informed the other two teams of the situation. Unfortunately, none of them were within adequate striking distance. Sam tore down the tower ladder, regrouped with the other tower team, and headed off south into the jungle after Bill's team.

* * *

We're so close but this mission is far from over. We have to escape! Bill's squad raced south through the jungle at breakneck speed. The large river that drained in to the sea was only a hundred feet away. All eight men, as planned, plunged into the swift flowing river together.

* * *

The three men with Sam weren't able to keep their prey in view as the jungle enveloped Bill's team. The trail left behind

98

in their wake was enough to track and they followed it quickly until it abruptly ended at the river's edge.

Fuck!

Sam raised the radio and spoke. "Group one, tell me you have them. Over."

"Negative team leader. We've seen zero movement."

"Check the ocean where the river dumps into the sea."

"Oh shit."

The radio in Sam's hand went dead.

*   *   *

Eight men rose out of the salty water with their weapons trained on the backs of the four men in front of them.

"Check the ocean where the river dumps into the sea," they heard Sam's voice over the radio.

A RI stood off to the side, strictly as an observer to the exercise, and watched everything unfold.

"Consider yourselves dead," Bill said calmly.

The four opposing team members whirled around and froze as they came face to face with eight rifle barrels.

"Oh shit."

The RI spoke up. "Four confirmed casualties!" He had the four men lay down on the ground.

Bill's team wasted no time as they commandeered an amphibious raft and headed down the coastline towards their exfiltration point. Bill looked back just in time to see Sam appear out of the jungle and watch the boat disappear around the bend.

"Well played brother," Sam said under his breath.

* * *

"Yes sir. I'll let you know when I'm ready."

"Make sure to keep this conversation to yourself," Raven replied. "We do not tolerate loose lips."

"I understand. You can count on me."

"Good."

Captain William Slater hung up the encrypted phone and smiled. He had an extensive amount of planning to do in the next two weeks but his mind had already begun to work on the necessary solutions to the problems at hand. He'd always had bigger aspirations for his life than he knew the Army could ever provide him. The man he'd just talked too had promised him a shitload of money and a position within the organization. It hadn't taken much to convince him to come on board.

On the other end Raven began to smile as well. He dialed another number and spoke when it was picked up.

"Yes?" Serpent responded.

"Raven here."

"Are we encrypted?"

"Of course. I called to say that our new pipeline will be up and running within a month. I just got off the phone with Captain William Slater. He works behind the scenes in distribution."

Serpent jotted the new name down. "And you vetted him?"

"Absolutely," Raven replied.

"Just as much as you assured me that Major Anthony Palmer, your childhood friend, could be relied on. And we both know how that turned out, don't we son?"

Raven fumed. "That was my mistake and I've handled it. All I know, dad, is that we need to be more careful as we branch out. But since you have me compartmentalizing our operation it does help me minimize any future losses that we might encounter."

"Be sure that it does," Serpent hissed. "This operation is quickly growing bigger than I anticipated and we need to be able to cover our tracks."

"Trust me. I'm covering all the angles."

14
Saturday April 3, 1975

"Bravo. Let me know when you're in position," Sam said over the radio.

"Roger. Wilco."

"Charlie. ETA?"

"We need 10 mikes."

"Understood," Sam replied.

Alpha, the squad Sam led, and Delta, Bill's squad, were dug into the hillside that overlooked their island objective. A light sprinkle bore down on everyone's heads and added to their level of discomfort. The daylight had receded in the last two hours and evening was upon them. Sam knew that if he could just coordinate the mission successfully then all thirty-two members of the class would graduate. He didn't stop to contemplate a failed mission because Rangers weren't allowed to think that way.

The previous week's training and testing had been brutal in all aspects; physically, mentally and emotionally. The past nine days had consisted of field exercises and scenarios. Numerous stressful and challenging exercises had been placed in their paths and at every turn the instructors reminded them that they were being evaluated. Raids, ambushes, assaults and anything else the RIs could throw at them they did. The entire class was exhausted and many of the students were constantly at their breaking point. The RIs told them that only one mission remained and those men pulled themselves back from the brink of quitting. Collectively the class elected Sam as their platoon leader for the final mission, especially since he'd led the only successful squad, during the last training mission, to recon and escape without being spotted.

Yeah, no pressure. Sam took the time to survey the two squads and the status of the men that were with him. For the past two months he, and everyone else in the class, had endured an unfathomable version of personal hell. Everyone looked ragged, destroyed and they were all mere shadows of whom they once were. They'd all lost a significant amount of weight during training and it was clearly evident. Uniforms hung loosely on their bodies as if the men had been issued clothing larger than necessary to wear. Sam managed to smile. *Yes, I've been through hell but I'm still here and so is Bill. And that's all that matters.* The island compound was their final obstacle to overcome. It was the pinnacle of their training and each and every one of them could taste how close they were to the end.

The mission briefing the RIs gave them had been explicit and to the point. Engage an unknown number of enemy forces at the island compound utilizing a multi-faceted and coordinated assault. As platoon leader it was on Sam's shoulders to make sure the attack went off without a hitch. He had risen to the occasion because he had the entire platoon backing him up. They all wanted and needed to succeed and had unanimously placed Sam in the leadership role rather than have him assigned to it by an RI. It was an honor and he wasn't about to let his platoon down by failing this late in their training.

The radio came to life. "Bravo in position."

"Roger that," Sam replied. "Hold for go code."

"Holding."

The light rain that had accompanied them all day began to come down harder. *Excellent.* Overall the additional rain was good news to Sam. It provided noise cover, reduced visibility and irritated the RIs who populated the compound Sam was preparing to attack. All he was waiting on now was Charlie squad.

Sam peeked over the brim of the ridge and verified the OPFOR, or Opposing Force, were still in their same positions. The increasing weather conditions hindered his visibility somewhat but Sam saw that nothing significant had changed. If anything there were a few less sentries guarding the compound than before. *Good. They don't like the rain either.* He lowered his head back down.

The radio crackled to life again. "Charlie ready."

"Roger that. Stand by."

Fifteen men, including Bill, looked over at Sam. It was time. Everyone was ready and eager. Sam motioned to prepare with his right hand and brought the radio up in his left.

"All squads. Commence Operation Decoy at twenty-one hundred fifteen hours."

* * *

Damn rain. RI Johnson looked out over the compound walls towards the water. He couldn't see or hear much because the sound of the rain hitting the surrounding jungle drowned out any ambient noise. *My guess is that they should primarily be attacking from the water. A quick beach landing and their attacking force would be at our gates. Of course, Paige has a tendency to do things differently.*

As if on cue the feint sound of onboard motors could be heard out on the water. RI Johnson depressed the alarm button and everything happened at once.

Floodlights instantly illuminated the water and honed in on the source of the motors.

The loudspeakers spewed out the tornado warning all over the compound.

A multitude of lights sprang to life on the external walls, changing night to day in a matter of seconds.

Every single RI prepped themselves for the impending attack.

* * *

Sam gave the command and Alpha and Delta squads belly crawled, in the mud and water, down a narrow stream towards the compound as quickly as they could. Any noise they made paled in comparison to the ambient rain. The plan was simple. Reach the compound walls undetected and then use decoys to draw the attention of the OPFOR to a different section of the compound. Sam knew the plan was similar to how he attacked the hill a few months prior, but this plan changed the game completely.

* * *

"Prepare to defend and give me a shitload of flares!" RI Johnson ordered. "Watch all sides! They're coming!" He moved away from the command console

106

The sky filled with flares and added to the existing illumination. The jungle and the open ground lit up. He didn't see any movement whatsoever.

The floodlights finally honed in on two inflatable boats that were headed towards the shore.

The alarm bell, floodlights and external lights expectantly turned off.

What the hell? RI Johnson whirled around to look at the console and came face to face with Sam whose body was covered from head to toe in mud. Behind Sam was a number of his squad.

"We're already here. You lose."

They had taken control of the compound's command center without firing a shot. RI Johnson wasn't used to losing but his feeling of pride easily outweighed his ego. He smiled.

In the distance the two boats hit the beach. Sixteen men poured out of them and immediately took up defensible positions.

"Congratulations you fucking ghost. I look forward to hearing about this over a pint of beer." RI Johnson approached the console and flipped on the speaker. "Now here this. Now here this. Stand down. I've been captured. The command post has been taken and this operation is hereby terminated. You have all passed. Congratulations!"

* * *

"So you managed to sneak two full squads up to the perimeter and then breach the wall. Then, while your decoy boats were inbound you gained access to the command post without firing a shot. Impressive." RI Johnson had been true to his word and treated everyone to beers at the Gator Lounge back at Florida's Camp James E. Rudder.

"Truth be told, it was the rain and all the men working together that allowed this operation to be so successful," Sam replied.

"Humble to the end. Regardless, the other RIs and I are impressed. We've also noticed that you and Nicholson make a great team."

"He's my best friend. We've known each other since elementary school."

"Well it shows. You two really pushed both yourselves and other members of this class to the distance." RI Johnson stood up, raised his glass and addressed the rest of the class. "Men. You have been through an experience that no one else can ever understand. Beside you are your brothers; fellow soldiers in arms. You all are now members of an elite group and no one will ever be able to take that away from you. To my new Rangers!"

Cheers went up throughout the room followed by copious guzzling. Even though each and every one of them was in a fantastic mood, they were also starving, beat up, sore and severely sleep deprived.

"For the next six days your orders are as follows. Rest, eat, seek medical care and clean your equipment. You all look like hell and I don't want your relatives to see you like this on Saturday when you graduate. Put some pounds back on gentlemen, you've earned them."

RI Johnson sat back down and turned to Sam. "What are your plans for your future?"

"My future RI? I don't know. I guess Bill and I get assigned to a Ranger Battalion and we go from there."

"Maybe. Maybe not. I'll see what I can do."

Sam was puzzled. "What does that mean?"

"Don't worry about it. Just enjoy your beer and get some rest."

"It's my first one."

"What is?" RI Johnson asked.

Sam held up his beer. "This is my first beer I've ever had."

"No shit."

"And it's going straight to my sleep deprived head."

RI Johnson chuckled. "Have fun and then get some rest this week. You've all earned it."

He wandered away and started to talk with some of the other men. Bill took that moment to come over and join Sam.

"What was that all about?"

"Apparently he likes our interaction. He says we work well together."

"Shit. I could have told him that and saved ourselves the last two months of hell if he had just asked."

Sam laughed, raised his glass and Bill did the same.

15

Saturday April 10, 1976

RI Johnson stood with both hands on the podium and looked out over the numerous family members that had attended the graduation.

"Each and every one of these thirty-two soldiers has earned the right to wear the Ranger Tab from now until the end of time. They have all demonstrated true courage, commitment and dedication."

He turned around and looked out over the men who continued to stand at attention behind him.

"Rangers! What is your creed!?"

In unison they began to recite the Ranger Creed.

"Recognizing that I volunteered as a Ranger, fully knowing the hazards of my chosen profession, I will always endeavor to uphold the prestige, honor, and high esprit de corps of the Rangers.

"Acknowledging the fact that a Ranger is a more elite soldier who arrives at the cutting edge of battle by land, sea, or air, I accept the fact that as a Ranger my country expects me to move further, faster, and fight harder than any other soldier.

"Never shall I fail my comrades I will always keep myself mentally alert, physically strong, and morally straight and I will shoulder more than my share of the task whatever it may be, one hundred percent and then some.

"Gallantly will I show the world that I am a specially selected and well trained soldier. My courtesy to superior officers, neatness of dress, and care of equipment shall set the example for others to follow.

"Energetically will I meet the enemies of my country. I shall defeat them on the field of battle for I am better trained and will fight with all my might. Surrender is not a Ranger word. I will never leave a fallen comrade to fall into the hands of the enemy and under no circumstances will I ever embarrass my country.

"Readily will I display the intestinal fortitude required to fight on to the Ranger objective and complete the mission, though I be the lone survivor."

The thirty-two men finished the roaring creed. RI Johnson smiled. He couldn't have felt more pride for the soldiers he'd led through training; through the hell he'd created for them. But he'd seen them stumble, pick themselves backup and overcome incredible odds to be where they were today.

"Family and friends. Please indulge me as I call each Ranger up to the stage to receive their Tab. Directly following this presentation you'll have the opportunity to visit."

* * *

"Well look at you two sorry looking sonsofbitches," Tom said as he approached Sam, Bill and their collective parents. "You both look pretty beat up."

The two looked very happy to see Tom and they exchanged hugs.

"It's really good to see you brother," said Sam. "It feels like it's been forever."

"It really has. Aren't you supposed to be in college or something?" Bill asked.

112

"Something like that," Tom replied, "but I wasn't going to miss this for the world. You guys are Rangers now. Holy shit that's awesome."

"Language," Bill's mother Louise cautioned.

"Relax mom, we're not kids anymore."

"My apologies Mrs. Nicholson," Tom offered.

"She hasn't gone by Nicholson for years now," said Reggie, Bill's stepfather.

Sam and Bill both rolled their eyes.

"I...I meant no offense," Tom stuttered.

"Of course, it was good to hear the words Mrs. Nicholson again," said Stuart, Bill's real father. "I haven't heard that used in years."

"Oh screw you Stuart," Reggie shot back. "She left you. Get over it already."

Louise interjected. "Why don't we all take a breath and relax. We aren't here to cause a scene or embarrass ourselves now are we?"

Reggie and Stuart backed down.

"So sweetie," Louise continued, "we are so proud of you but you look so skinny. Didn't they feed you while you were out camping in the woods?"

"Camping in the woods? Is that what you think this was, like a Boy Scout camp or something?"

"Well," she replied, "whatever you boys were doing out here in Georgia is beyond my understanding apparently. All I do know is that you left me to join the Army on a whim."

"On a whim? Are you fucking serious right now?"

"Watch your language young man."

Tom, Sam, and Sam's parents were uncomfortable.

113

"Guess what ma. You don't get to tell me what to do anymore."

"Now the Army will do that for you," Reggie shot out.

"Go to hell Reggie," said Stuart. "You might have stolen my wife but you don't have the right to talk shit to my son."

Reggie began to step up to Stuart and both men had their fists balled up. Bill quickly intercepted Reggie and before anyone knew how it happened his stepfather was face first in the dirt.

"Oh my God!" exclaimed his mother. "Bill, what did you do? Let him up this instant."

Bill got off his stepfather and stepped away. Other people in the crowd noticed the scuffle and continued to watch from a distance. Reggie stood up, regained his composure and dusted himself off. His face was deep red.

Bill's mother continued. "How dare you attack your father."

"He's not my father," Bill shot back. "He's just some guy I had to live with after you got rid of dad."

"Why I never…"

"Typical. Just typical."

The group collectively looked over at Jacob, Sam's stepfather who had just spoken.

"What the hell does that mean Jacob?" Reggie angrily asked.

"Now honey…"

"Don't honey me Louise. I want to know exactly what he meant."

"Typical dysfunctional family bullshit is what I meant," Jacob answered. "I mean, stop and take a look at our two families. We're split at the core. Our boys wanted to get away from us and they succeeded."

"Now I have to weigh in," said Ray, Sam's father. "For Stuart and me it's cut and dry. Sam and Bill are our boys, not yours. You stepfathers are married to their mothers but you'll never be their fathers."

"Well said," Stuart added.

"Go to hell Ray," Jacob replied. "You make me sick."

"Oh, yeah? How's that?"

"You're never there for Sam but I am."

Ray didn't like that.

Jacob continued. "Why don't you tell your 'son' what really happened between you and his mother? Go on, I dare you."

That peaked Sam's interest.

"You sonofabitch," Ray shot back. "How dare you."

"So what happens now?" Janet, Sam's mother suddenly asked, as she changed the subject.

There was an awkward silence before Sam finally spoke up.

"What do you mean?"

"When do you get to come home and get away from all this?"

Sam, Bill and Tom all shared a glance before Sam spoke up again.

"What are you asking?"

"I thought I was pretty clear," Sam's mother replied. "When are you coming home?"

Sam shook his head in disbelief. "What do you think?"

"I don't know. That's why I'm asking. I made up your room and everything."

"Wow. Okay. I don't even know where to begin. How delusional are you mother?"

"You don't talk to your mother like that," snapped Jacob and Ray together.

"Great," said Sam. "This is just what I need right now; two fathers. And to top it all off you, dad…, Ray to be more specific, now you take the time to come around? Where the fuck have you been all these years? Why don't I know what happened between you two?"

"Lang…"

Bill cut his mother off with a look.

Sam continued. "Where were you when I was growing up?"

"Around Sam. I was around."

"Yes, that's my point. You were around but never close enough when I needed you."

"That's not fair Sam," Janet said.

"You don't get to talk about fair mother. The only ones that have ever been there for me are my friends, Bill and Tom."

"But we're your parents."

"That's rich. You all," Sam waved collectively, "all have a shitload to work out between yourselves. You're all fucked in the head."

The group grew quiet and shuffled their feet. Bill's mother finally spoke up.

"So, when are you two coming home?"

"They're not coming home."

They all swiveled their heads and looked at Tom.

"They have an eight year contract. Joining the Army might seem like a whim to all of you but to me, their friend, this is a career that I know they'll make the most of. You should be proud of them rather than second guessing their decision."

"At least you went to college," Ray quipped. "It's safe to say I'm not proud of my son. I think he made a huge mistake."

Sam's mouth hung open as his father finished his sentence.

"I'd have to agree," Stuart added.

"Gee, thanks a lot Dad," said Bill.

"Come on Bill. Do you really think we'd be proud of you? A soldier? Being sent to other parts of the world to be shot at and kill people? No way. At least Tom will have an education. What the hell are you two ever going to have? I'll tell you what. Nothing. You'll be able to pull a trigger and that's it. No marketable skills. Nothing."

"Well shit. Why don't you tell me how you really feel?"

Bill turned to Sam and then to Tom. "Why don't we get out of here? Sam and I can tell you all about the past year."

Sam and Bill took a long look at their parents, turned and walked away with Tom.

"Where are you going?"

"Get back here right now!"

"This discussion isn't over young man."

* * *

The bar was used to its clientele consisting mainly of soldiers, so none of the bartenders ever asked for identification. Tom had driven his two friends out of Fort Benning and to the bar and Sam ordered the first round of beers and brought them over to the table.

Tom raised his glass to make a toast. "Congratulations are in order."

Sam and Bill smiled and drank. There was a small silence before Tom spoke up again.

"So, uh, seeing your parents all ganging up on you was, well, interesting."

They smiled at first and soon afterwards started to laugh. It didn't take long before all three of them were in stitches.

"You fucker," said Bill. "I don't know how you do it but you can always cheer us up."

Sam held up his glass. "To Tom."

"To Tom," as Bill joined in.

Tom raised his glass and said, "To my friends. That's all the family you two will ever need."

"To friends," Sam and Bill repeated as they finished their beers.

Bill picked up the next round and came back to the table.

"So," said Tom, "like I was saying, you guys look like hell."

Bill nodded. "You should have seen us a week ago."

"Yeah, we were worse off then. We've put a couple of pounds back on and gotten a shitload of sleep since."

"But the description of hell is accurate."

"What happened?" Tom asked.

Sam leaned back in the booth. "It's something we could try and tell you about but any words would actually be a disservice. Let's just say that it was the most intense experience Bill and I ever had in our entire lives."

"So what's next?" Tom inquired. "I hear you have a couple of solid offers to head back home." He smiled.

Sam and Bill both spit out their beer they'd been drinking. "You asshole!"

They wiped up and collected themselves but it didn't take long for them to fall back into their old rhythm, and that rhythm felt very comfortable.

Tom got the third round and brought the drinks back to the table.

"Thanks for coming out for graduation brother," Bill said. "It means a lot."

"No shit," Sam added. "Thanks. It's really good to see you. How's college life?"

"Truthfully?"

"Is there any other kind?" Sam asked.

"Intellectually it's rewarding. Socially it's lonely as hell."

"You're telling me," Bill started, "that you still haven't bagged a babe?"

"Come on. Keep your voice down. And no, embarrassing enough as it is to admit, I have a hard time talking to women."

"That's nothing to be embarrassed about," Sam said. "The good news is that you must be surrounded by smart women. At some point they're going to notice you and sparks will fly. Trust me. It's all about the timing."

"Speaking of timing," Bill added, "have you noticed the two beauties sitting at the end of the counter?"

Tom tried to turn his head but Sam stopped him.

"You can't just look. It's too obvious. And yes, to your question my friend, I saw them some time ago."

"Shall we then?"

"As much as I'd like to I'm not going to bail on our friend Tom just like that."

"It's okay," Tom said. "Maybe I can pick up some pointers to take back to California."

Sam smiled. "That's the spirit."

Before he knew it Sam and Bill had left the booth and walked over to the two women, who were clearly older than they were and started up a conversation.

How do they do that so easily? Tom took another sip of beer and continued to watch. A few minutes later all four of them walked over to where Tom sat.

"Tom, this is Katie and Sarah. Ladies, this is our best friend Tom."

"Very nice to meet you both," Tom replied.

"And so polite too," Katie said as she giggled. "You sure you don't want to invite him along?"

"Oh Katie," Sarah snickered, "you're just drunk, but he is cute."

Tom blushed while Sam and Bill couldn't believe what they'd just heard.

Tom recovered. "Actually, I have a flight out in a few hours that I can't miss, but thank you anyway. You're both in good hands. Sam and Bill will take good care of you."

Sarah laughed. "Well that's what they keep promising but we're still here."

"I know," Katie added. "Let's go."

"Give us one minute ladies," said Sam as he and Bill sat back down and got serious. "Seriously, thanks for making the trip. You have no idea how much it means to us."

"What Sam said brother."

Tom nodded. "No problem. It was fun. Any idea when I'll see you guys again?"

Sam and Bill looked at each other and shrugged. "We haven't received our next round of orders. For the time being we're based out of Fort Benning, but that could change. I honestly have no idea."

Tom stood up and hugged both of his friends. "Be safe and look after each other. Until we meet again."

"Come on, let's go drink some more," Katie badgered.

"See ya brother," said Bill as Katie took his hand and dragged him towards the front door.

Sarah licked Sam's ear and whispered something that Tom couldn't make out.

"Got to go my friend. Apparently I've just been given a new mission to complete."

"Take it easy Sam," Tom said to his friends.

And with that Sam and Bill disappeared out the front door. Tom sat back down and took his time to finish his beer.

16
Tuesday June 1, 1976

It was the final week of school and Tom only had two finals left to take. He wasn't worried about them, as he hadn't about his other classes; because he was confident that he knew the material cold. It'd been nearly two months since he'd seen his friends and that weighed heavy on his shoulders.

I know I'm moving on with my life, going to college and whatnot. And I should be happy that they're moving on. I mean, I am happy for them. Tom sighed. *I guess I'm just bummed that they're charging ahead in life together and I'm charging ahead all alone. And with summer around the corner what the hell am I supposed to do with myself?*

Tom closed the textbook he had been studying, put it aside and got up from his desk. He headed to the kitchen, picked up the phone and dialed. After a couple of rings the other end picked up.

"Hello?"

"Hey Grandma. How are you?"

"Tom? Is that you?"

"Yes, it's me. Do you have another grandson I don't know about?"

"Cute. How're your finals?"

"Straight to the point as always, right Grandma?"

"Your studies are important and you can't blame me for caring. So, how're you doing?"

"I feel like I'm acing my finals. I won't know for sure until next week but there's no need for concern, I'll be a Sophomore next year."

"Well you know me dear, I wasn't worried, I just like to ask."

Tom smiled. "How's Grandpa?"

"Well, here's around here someplace. Our new house in Rossmoor has changed quite a bit since you've been gone. We've been decorating it little by little."

"That's good Grandma."

Tom heard his Grandfather's voice in the background. "Have you told him yet?"

"No. I was just about to get to that."

"Is everything alright?" Tom asked.

"Everything's fine," Claire assured him. "Ed's just impatient is all. Anyway, before we get into that, any idea of what you're going to do during the summer break?"

"I don't know. I've been busy with studies so I haven't come up with anything solid." Tom thought about it. "I suppose I could come and visit you two."

"Well, Ed and I would love to have you except for one minor detail."

"Oh, what's that?"

"We're actually going to be out of the country."

Tom hadn't expected that. "Oh."

"We're taking an extended trip to Europe. That's what your Grandfather wanted me to tell you. I'm sorry."

He recovered. "No. No, it's okay. You two deserve to get out and see the world."

"You're not disappointed?"

"No Grandma. If anything I'm jealous. That trip sounds wonderful and exotic."

"Oh, I'm sure it will be. Ed and I can't wait to leave in a week. We've been packing and repacking nonstop." She

124

caught herself. "But given that, any ideas for your summer now?"

"I don't know. I'm sure I'll figure it out."

"Hold on a second, Ed wants to talk with you."

Tom heard the sound of the phone being passed.

"Hello, Tom?"

"Hi Grandpa. How're you doing?"

"Couldn't be better. How's school treating you?"

"I just have a couple of finals left. After that my freshman year is behind me."

"Listen Tom. I wanted to tell you something and had to make sure you heard it before your Grandmother and I head to Europe."

"What's on your mind Grandpa?"

"Tom." His voice took a serious tone. "You've experienced more heartfelt loss in your life than anyone should have to bear. Through all of it, and from all of it, you have become a survivor. What I wanted to tell you is simple in comparison. Your Grandmother and I are very proud of you. You've grown into a young man and you should be proud of the path you're on. There was a chance, at Loard's, that you could have easily thrown everything to the wind and done anything you wanted. Instead, you stuck to your guns and headed off to college. We're very proud of you."

"I...I don't know what to say. Thanks Grandpa."

His tone lightened up considerably. "Don't mention it. Now, while Claire is out of the room, let me ask you a question."

"Okay. Shoot."

"How're you doing with the ladies? Are you getting any trim?"

"Grandpa!"

"I'm just asking, man to man, is all. It's important to get that poison out of the system from time to time."

"Poison?"

"You know what I mean, or maybe you don't. In either case maybe you should spend the summer at the beach chasing the skirts around. Oh crap, here comes your Grandmother."

Tom heard the phone changing hands once again.

"Tom?"

"Yes Grandma?"

"Ed has a guilty look on his face. Anything I should know about?"

"Nope. Not a thing."

"Well then. We'll be gone in a week so if we don't talk before then please have yourself a great summer."

"You too Grandma. Take a lot of pictures for me."

"Will do. Bye Tom. Love you."

"Love you too."

Tom hung up the phone and stood there for a few minutes as he tried to collect his thoughts. *Well, visiting them is out. What else can I do?* Images of the beach and scantily clad women raced through his head. *Maybe I could go to the beach, but by myself? I dunno if I can do that.* He thought some more. *What about visiting the house I grew up in? Oh hell no, why would I think of that? I don't want to relive those nightmares.* Tom shuddered. *Shit, I'm not coming up with anything good right now. Maybe I'll just head down to the burger shack to think about it.*

* * *

126

With a chocolate shake sitting aside a large burger and fries, Tom started a list of the things he could do to keep himself busy over the summer.

The beach
Women
Bike riding
Write letters to Sam/Bill
Go to the movies
Hide in my house
Studying for next year
Short stories

Tom paused at his last entry. *Short stories? I am at college for creative writing. Maybe I should actually start writing and see what I can come up with? I mean, the beach and the women will always be there when I need a break.*

Tom listed his name out a few times in a new column.

Tom Clark
Tom Clark
Tom Clark

I don't know. It doesn't reach out and do anything for me. If and when I become a writer I need a penname that jumps off the cover of a book and slaps people in the face. I need something that doesn't sound quite as harsh as Tom Clark.

Tom thought for a few minutes before he wrote out a new name on the page.

Thomas Clark

Tom smiled as the reality of becoming a writer began to take hold. *I really like the name Thomas. It flows from my lips. And it fits with my name's evolution. I was Tommy and then Tom. But from this moment on I will now be known as Thomas.*

17
Wednesday June 2, 1976

It'd been nearly two months since Sam and Bill had become Rangers and continued to be stationed at Fort Benning under the 75th. Their weekdays consisted of rigorous training from morning till the late afternoon, with their evenings and weekends unscheduled. The routine was easy for them and they enjoyed learning more about the other Rangers in their unit. Competitions arose daily between men, typically with the loser providing beers later that evening.

Sam and Bill were in their element and felt on top of the world. What they'd overcome and accomplished together to become Rangers made for one hell of a story, but a story they would always keep to themselves. No one would understand the full extent of what they'd put their bodies and minds through. Looking back it seemed unfathomable that they had endured it. They often told each other that if it wasn't for the other they probably would have thrown in the towel.

Their respective parents had sent them a few letters asking how they were doing, but ultimately those letters would end with condemnation on their choice to join the Army. They never wrote back, foregoing their family relationships until they might have a chance to converse on their terms at an undetermined time in the future. For now Sam and Bill just wanted to concentrate on just being the best Rangers they could be and prove they continued to deserve to wear their uniforms.

* * *

It was Friday night when they found themselves at the local watering hole, relaxing and talking shit with a group from their unit. Two distinguished men, in uniform, sat at a booth in the corner and discretely observed Sam and Bill. The elder of the two leaned back in his seat and spoke to his subordinate.

"Keep tabs on them. They come highly recommended but I want a profile created for each of them and on my desk by the end of the month."

"Yes sir."

18
Tuesday September 21, 1976

Sophomore year here we go. Wow. Where did the summer go?

Thomas parked his bike, that he'd purchased over the summer, and secured it with a lock. He'd spent most of the three and a half months sequestered in his rental house brainstorming ideas and writing short stories. The time had flown by as his excitement for his craft grew. Scores of legal pads and the *wapwapwap* from his typewriter filled the house. One idea led to another which always seemed to lead to another. His constantly massaged his cramped right hand, and more than often, bore through the pain in an effort to capture every random thought.

There were a few occasions where he drove west to Venice, parked his car and strolled up and down the beach. Thomas had experienced a variety of people at school already, but he wasn't prepared for the onslaught of artists, performers and entertainers that worked Venice Beach. He would sit and watch the performers wow the crowds all day as he indulged himself on penny sweets and anything else that caught his eye. And his eyes caught many enticing forms at the beach, in two-piece bathing suits, playing volleyball, walking or laying on the beach. His perpetual shyness stopped him from ever making a move and part of him wished his friends were here to show him the ins and outs on how to talk to women.

At the beach, and even around town, Thomas saw many people that were clearly in need of help and he willingly gave them money. He felt badly that he had millions, but he had decided long ago not to be a flamboyant spender. He only spent money on what he needed rather than what he wanted. Besides, Thomas knew he had two pressing issues when it came to his wealth. The first was that he wouldn't tell anyone about his money for fear of being targeted. The second, and the issue that haunted him the most, was that he didn't know how his father came into possession of such a vast amount of money. That bothered Thomas to no end and kept him awake at night more often than he could remember.

A month into summer Thomas had left his house when he decided he needed a break. Yes, he knew he was lonely, but he was used to it to some extent by now. He was tired of driving wherever he needed to go, aside from trips to the beach, and purchased a Schwinn Speedster one day. He hadn't ridden a bike for some time, but once he started peddling around town he instantly felt the freedom again. He was hooked and anytime he went out of the house he rode his bike, even down to the store for groceries.

By the end of July even his nineteenth birthday had snuck up on him. He knew it was coming, just like anyone does, but without friends and family around to remind him he had practically forgotten about it. The day before his birthday, Thomas received a postcard in the mail. It was from his Grandparents. On the front was a picture of the Colosscum in Rome. On the back, in every available space, they had told him about their adventures and where they'd been. They had also written that they were proud of him and to have a happy birthday. Thomas smiled and used a pushpin to secure the postcard above his desk. Every time he looked at the Colosseum he just smiled and then went back to whatever he'd been doing.

Thomas also looked forward to other forms of reality. When he wasn't writing his own adventures, or out bike riding, he read books. A lot of books. And going to the movies alone bothered him at first, but over time he didn't mind and enjoyed such titles as The Omen and Logan's Run that had premiered over the summer.

By the end of the summer, and with the next year of school right around the corner, Thomas had chiseled out a very safe lifestyle for himself. He worried about Sam and Bill, and had even sent them a few letters, but as it turned out they weren't too good at reciprocating. He was excited about college starting up again and couldn't wait for the first day to start.

Thomas left his bike secured behind him and headed off to class. He quickly opened the door to the lecture hall and promptly ran into someone on the way out. The person's books tumbled and hit the floor.

"I'm sorry," he said. Thomas bent down to start collecting the fallen items.

"It was my fault," was the female reply as she bent down as well. "I'm in the wrong hall and in a hurry."

The enticing scent of her hair was the first thing he noticed. His nose breathed it in as if it couldn't get enough. *Is that Jasmine?*

"Excuse me?"

Thomas faltered as he handed over the few books he'd picked up and finally gazed in to her face. Her brunette shoulder length hair surrounded a face of beauty. Two soft blue eyes stared back at him.

"I'm sorry?" he stammered.

She smiled at him. "Yes, it's Jasmine."

"Jasmine?"

"You asked if it was Jasmine."

"I did?" *Holy shit, did I say that out loud?*

She cocked her head at him but kept her genuine smile. "Are you okay? I certainly didn't mean to bump in to you that hard."

She's talking to me. What do I do? They stood up slowly together and he finally opened his mouth. "You definitely have my head spinning. If you'd like you can try knocking me off my feet?"

She giggled. "You're sweet. My name's Samantha. Samantha McDermott."

"Tom....Thomas. Thomas Clark."

"Very nice to meet you Thomas Clark. Listen, I'm seriously going to be late, and with this being the first day and all that might be frowned upon."

"Absolutely," he replied as he stepped aside.

"You probably get this all the time but would you like to have lunch with me today? Maybe we can continue our conversation?"

Thomas smiled. *Sure, I get this all the time. Holy fucking shit. Just be cool. Be cool.* "I'd really like that Samantha."

"Great. See you in the quad at twelve fifteen'ish?"

"I'll see you then."

And with that the sweet smell of Jasmine, and Samantha, disappeared out the door. He eventually collected himself, found a seat and sat down. Regardless of how much he tried to concentrate on the lecture, Thomas couldn't get the image of Samantha out of his head.

* * *

Friday October 8, 1976

Thomas got out of his car, walked around to the passenger side and opened the door for Samantha.

She smiled and said, "Thank you. You're always such a gentleman."

After she sat down he carefully closed the door and got back in behind the wheel. She leaned over and began the date by kissing him. Fireworks went off in his head.

"Wow," he breathed.

She giggled as Thomas started the car, pulled out of the dorm parking lot and began to make his way downtown.

"So Thomas, what do you have in store for us this evening?"

Ever since they'd inadvertently bumped in to each other, they had instantly hit it off. Samantha had been born and raised in Southern California. Her parents owned a number of dry cleaners but insisted, as she'd grown older, that their only daughter get more out of life. She had decided to pursue a major in Biology and so far the classes she was taking at USC interested her.

When she asked about his upbringing he deflected and told her that it was like any other kid's childhood; two parents, friends and school. He focused on Sam and Bill and their adventures together rather than indulging in his dramatic childhood. Thomas said he was majoring in creative writing and ever since she had been badgering him to let her read some of his stories.

For the past few weeks they'd gone out on three dates, and at the end of the last one she made the move and initiated the goodnight kiss. It was the first time Thomas had kissed a woman and his entire world had melted away as her soft lips gently, and then with more force, engaged his own. He was in heaven as he walked back to his car that evening.

"Well, I thought we'd start by getting something to eat and then maybe check out a movie. What'ya think?"

"I could eat, but maybe we could do something other than watch a movie."

"Okay. Do you have something you'd like to do in mind?"

"Let's play it by ear. I'll let you know what ideas I have when we're finished eating."

* * *

During dinner they chatted, switching from topic to topic with ease. Thomas always had a hard time talking to women, but he found it easy to talk with Samantha. He enjoyed her company and she clearly enjoyed his. Thomas paid the bill and they slowly walked back to his car, hand in hand, amongst a cool breeze. They closed the car doors and sat.

"Thank you for dinner Thomas. It was delicious."

"It was my pleasure. The theater is right around the corner if you..."

"I don't want to see a movie," she said softly taking his hand in hers.

"Oh. Did you have something else in mind?"

She nodded. "I thought about taking you to the point, the pullout above the Hollywood sign, but now I think I want to go somewhere more private."

What is she saying? "Private?" he squeaked out.

She nodded again and brought his hand up to cup her face. She felt him tremble ever so slightly. "Take me back to your house."

They didn't talk as Thomas drove back home. His brain was in overdrive and with so many thoughts careening and bouncing around the inside of his skull he was lucky enough to get them home in one piece. After pulling into the driveway they walked up to his front door where he promptly fumbled his keys. As he bent over to retrieve them she cupped his ass. Electric shocks shot through him and he dropped them again. She found his reaction hilarious and giggled as he finally managed to get the door open.

"So, did you want to watch some tv or maybe play a game or something?"

"Or something," she purred as she approached him.

What's happening? What is she doing? But Thomas' instincts knew exactly what she was doing. That didn't stop his uncontrollable nervousness to kick in to high gear.

Samantha pulled Thomas close to her body and kissed him like he'd never been kissed before. His entire body shuddered as she took both hands, placed them behind his head and pulled him into her. His brain exploded with a myriad of new and amazing sensations. His breath shortened and his pupils dilated. He returned the energy she was giving to him and she let out a small whimper.

"Oh my Thomas. Aren't you a quick study."

He managed a shy smile as she took his hand and began to lead him towards his bedroom.

"Where…where are we going?"

"Oh, you know exactly where we're going."

And he did. "But…I'm…"

She turned and gently placed a finger on his lips. "I know you're a virgin but it's going to be alright. In fact, it's going to be better than alright. Trust me."

Can I do this? Oh my God. Oh my God. Oh my God. Is this actually happening? What do I do? I don't know what to do.

She led him to the bed and pushed him down. He ended up sitting on the edge looking at her.

"Why don't you take off your shoes?"

Without taking his eyes off her he deftly kicked off both shoes.

"Do you trust me?" she asked.

He nodded.

"Good. That's good." She turned around so her back faced him. "Would you mind holding on to one end of my bow?"

Thomas, as if in a drug induced haze, watched his hand grab hold of the bow on her dress. She walked forward and the bow unraveled. He let his end go. His eyes widened as she pulled her dress up and over her head. He glanced back over her shoulder and loved the look she saw on his face. It was a combination of shock, shyness, awe and wanting. Samantha let her dress drop to the floor as she turned back around.

Oh my God. Thomas' heart began to race even faster. He'd never seen a woman in her bra and panties before. She sauntered over to him with a sly smile on her face. The look on his face was priceless. His mouth hung open and his eyes explored her body, taking in ever inch. He shifted uncomfortably on the bed and she immediately noticed why.

"Problems?" she teased.

"I…I…" *Such beauty. So many curves that I want to explore.*

Her smile relaxed him. "I'll take it slow. There's nothing to be afraid of Thomas, you'll see."

19
Friday October 8, 1976

Sam, Bill and ten other Rangers, aboard the USS Enterprise aircraft carrier, exited the debriefing and headed topside to board a large transport helicopter. That helicopter would take them to the States and from that location back to Fort Benning.

The previous twenty-four hours had been a whirlwind. At Fort Benning the twelve soldiers had been given a half hour notice to prepare their gear before they were to be shipped out. All twelve Rangers sprinted away from morning training to grab their gear. Each of them had a basic "Go pack" ready for missions that could be augmented based on whatever mission requirements were needed. From there they mustered at Lawson Army Airfield where they boarded a cargo plane that, as soon as they were all seated, immediately took off down the runway. That plane landed on a base in southern Florida where the fourteen men then boarded a transport helicopter that ferried them south out to the USS Enterprise.

When they touched down on the aircraft's deck they were then escorted to the mission briefing room. It became very apparent that this wasn't going to be a training exercise. The small groups of Rangers were being tasked with exfiltration of a captured prisoner on the northern coast of Columbia. That prisoner was being secured by Navy Seals that evening. The added security of the Rangers was an extra precaution due to the fact that the prisoner in question was a major drug lord. They were ordered to eat chow and rest. The mission would initiate that evening at twenty-three hundred hours. The Rangers stowed their gear and headed to get chow.

"Nervous?" Bill asked Sam once they sat down and began to eat.

"Not really," he replied as he continued to look around. "If anything I'm nervous about the size of this ship. It's fucking huge."

"That it is."

"But, as for the mission, our job is easy. Get in, secure the beach, wait for the Seals and then get the hell out in one piece. And unless there's a shit storm on the Seal's tails this will be a walk in the park."

Bill nodded as he ate. Other sailors, Marines and Navy personnel were curious about the fourteen Rangers but knew enough to keep their distance. Everyone was well aware a mission was in progress and this wasn't the time for any interservice rivalries to blossom.

"Well, I'm a little nervous," Bill admitted. "This is our first official mission."

"We're going to be just fine," Sam assured him. But internally he was nervous as well.

*   *   *

"Mother One. Mother One. This is Wolfden. How copy?"

"Good copy Wolfden."

"ETA on arrival Mother One?"

"Package has been secured. No casualties. Eight men will be arriving at coordinates in approximately one-hundred and twenty mikes."

"Roger that Mother One. Exfil team is en route; call sign Baby Two."

"Baby Two, copy. Out."

* * *

Three low profile rafts exited the back of the Chinook helicopter and splashed down on the ocean surface. Twelve Rangers jumped into the water right behind them, climbed on board and headed south towards the Columbian coastline as the helicopter headed back towards the carrier. Their destination, fifteen miles away, was the Bahia Honda lagoon.

* * *

Lieutenant Joe Miller signaled the rafts to stop in the calm waters as he began to survey the coastline from a quarter mile out. He didn't detect any movement so he ordered the boats towards the beach. They had only ten minutes left before the estimated rendezvous with the eight man Seal team. All twelve exited the boats quietly by slipping over the edge and sliding into the sea. Together they emerged on the beach. Lt. Miller sent three teams of three out to secure the perimeter while he, and two others, remained prone behind a sand dune where the boats had been beached. Five minutes later the nine men regrouped and waited.

One of the men behind the sand dune had the radio. Three minutes later it crackled to life in the Ranger's ear and he handed it over to the Lieutenant.

"Baby Two. Baby Two. Mother One is inbound in a truck. We have two vehicles on our tail containing an unknown number of tangos. We're two mikes out and under fire. How copy?"

"Mother One. We're in position at the coordinates provided. Bring them in."

"Roger that Baby Two. Good to hear a friendly voice. Out."

The Lieutenant handed the radio back and spoke up. "In less than two minutes we're going to have company. There's no time to setup a proper ambush. The Seals are in a truck with two vehicles in pursuit. Six will engage and destroy from this location while you six," as he pointed at six other Rangers and then at a location in the distance, "move to that other berm and setup a flank. Go!"

Sam and Bill, along with four other Rangers, immediately sprinted to that berm. Sporadic gunfire could be heard in the distance. Not twenty seconds later a large truck appeared out of the jungle in the shadowy distance. A hundred feet behind it two vehicles were chasing it down trying to shoot out the tires rather than taking a chance at hitting and killing their boss. The Seals had used this to their advantage and, even though the truck had been hit a number of times, no one in it had been injured.

The Seals flashed their headlights as they raced towards the beach, much to Sam and Bill's relief. Their truck raced past their sandy berm just fifty feet away and ground to a halt before it hit the ocean. The Seals began to pile out as the Lieutenant, and the other five Rangers, provided security for the truck.

On the road the two fast approaching vehicles lost sight of the Seals and turned on their high beams. The beach lit up, as well as the Seals, their cargo and the five Rangers.

Gunfire erupted from both enemy vehicles and sand kicked up all around the exposed soldiers.

Sam, Bill, and the four others that were hidden behind the sand berm, immediately engaged the two vehicles with their rifles.

In seconds the enemy trucks were shredded by the Ranger's automatic gunfire.

One of the vehicles clipped the other's rear and flipped end over end before it came to a rest.

The second vehicle awkwardly aimed itself right at Sam and Bill's group but abruptly slammed into the other side of their sandy berm.

Two bloodied bodies, from the momentum, flew out and landed next to Sam and Bill.

All gunfire ceased and the fires that had started in the two destroyed trucks were now the only sounds. The fight was over before it had begun.

Within a minute of the Seal's arrival the three rafts were back in the ocean and all twenty soldiers, plus one cargo, were onboard and headed back out to sea. No one spoke except for the Lieutenant who used the radio.

"Wolfden, this is Baby Two. Mother One is onboard and has successfully given birth. All parties accounted for. We're coming home. How copy?"

"Roger that Baby Two. Congrats on the delivery. Cigars all around."

"Thanks for the timely pickup," the Seal team leader said.

The Lieutenant merely nodded as the three boats made their way back towards the carrier.

This was the first time Sam and Bill had experienced combat, as it was described in the after action report. Sam and

Bill didn't overthink the mission too much. They knew they'd probably have to kill at some point in their career, they just didn't know it would be this soon. All they knew was that there were fellow soldiers in harm's way, they needed assistance, and that's exactly what Sam and Bill had provided. End of story.

* * *

Saturday October 9, 1976

The following day, back at Fort Benning, Sam and Bill were discussing the previous night's mission when a familiar face sauntered over to them.

"I heard you boys were knee deep in action."

They stood up and shook hands with Dennis Carter, one of the thirty-two men that had made it through Ranger training with them. Sam and Bill exchanged a quick glance before Sam spoke up.

"We're not at liberty to discuss anything, you understand."

"Well, it's not every day that a major drug lord is captured."

"You heard Sam," Bill added. "No comment."

Dennis put his hands up in mock defense and then sat down at the table. They followed suit.

"Actually, I didn't come over here to talk about that."

"Then what's on your mind Dennis?" Bill asked.

"Right to the point. I like that. Okay, here it is. How would the two of you like to make some extra money on the side?"

"I don't understand," Sam replied. "What exactly do mean by extra money on the side?"

Dennis looked around to make sure their conversation couldn't be overheard. "Selling weapons. There's a surplus of M16's, from the war, that are just taking up space in the Armory. There are people who will pay top dollar for them. This is a one-time gig. Get in, load and get out." He looked at Sam and Bill with great anticipation as if what he'd just told them was pure gold.

"Are you fucking kidding me?" stated Bill. "This isn't a joke?"

Dennis' smile faltered.

"Unbelievable," Sam breathed out. "You're obviously a fucking moron. You want us to help you steal weapons from the military and sell them. Brilliant. Just brilliant. What could possibly go wrong other than spending our lives in a military prison."

"Sooo…what're you saying?"

Bill stood up and towered over Dennis. "Get the fuck out of here you piece of shit. You don't deserve to wear that Ranger Tab. You have no honor."

Dennis and Sam got up from the table as well and Dennis' face was full of confusion.

"I…I thought you guys were cool and that I'd bring you in on a sure thing."

"You obviously haven't thought everything through Dennis," said Sam. "We're obligated to report this conversation."

Dennis' eyes flared. "Fuck you. You wouldn't dare. We're brother Rangers. We have a code."

147

Sam shook his head. "You just lost any right to that code. Maybe you're just too stupid to realize that yet."

Dennis instantly got angry. "I'm warning you. If you tell anyone about this it'll be the last thing you ever do."

And with that he turned on his heels and stomped away leaving Sam and Bill behind. They watched him disappear into the distance.

"Did that just actually happen?" Bill asked.

"I'm afraid so. What the hell is he thinking? What a waste."

"Yeah. What a stupid thing to agree too. That idiot obviously can't be the one behind the idea. Someone must have recruited him."

"Agreed. But who?"

Bill shook his head. "Who knows? All we know is that unless he's full of shit there's a plan to move weapons illegally off this base."

"And that plan needs to be stopped. Let's go."

Sam and Bill began to jog towards their Commanding Officer's building.

* * *

"What do you mean you approached them? Why would you talk to anyone? Are you stupid?"

Carl Hatfield, another Ranger on the base, couldn't believe what Dennis had just told him.

"We need more people for the operation. I thought that..."

"Exactly, you thought and that's the fucking problem. You just compromised the entire operation. I have to report this right away."

148

"What? No, you can't."

Carl looked him square in the eyes. "You fucked up Dennis. All you can hope now is that somehow this problem gets contained."

* * *

"We'd like to speak with Lieutenant Colonel Aleman, sir."

The Lieutenant looked Sam and Bill over with a bit of disdain before he responded. "Do you have an appointment?"

"No sir."

"I see. And what is this in regards to?"

"We'd prefer to talk to the Lt. Colonel about that directly, sir."

"The Colonel is a very busy man, as you can imagine. He doesn't have time for petty nonsense."

Sam restrained himself. "Sir. I assure you that what we need to discuss is far from petty."

Lt. Colonel Robert Aleman's office door opened and he appeared in the doorway.

Sam and Bill immediately saluted and Lt. Colonel Aleman returned it.

"Lieutenant, what's my afternoon schedule like?"

"For a Saturday it's actually wide open today. Plenty of time for a round of golf, sir."

"Very good. Now, why are these two Rangers standing here?"

"Sir, they're requesting a moment of your time."

"Is that so? What about?"

"They wouldn't tell me that sir. They implied it was for your ears only."

Lt. Colonel Aleman looked Sam and Bill over before replying. "Are you Paige and Nicholson that I've been hearing so much about?"

Puzzled looks crossed Sam and Bill's faces. "Sir?"

"I apparently have a few free minutes, gentlemen. I'm intrigued. Please come in."

Sam and Bill walked past the Lt. Colonel and entered his office. He closed the door behind them, walked around his desk and sat down.

"Take a seat."

Sam and Bill complied.

"Now, what could be so important that two Private First Class Rangers need to intrude upon their base commander, on a Saturday no less?"

"Sir," Sam began, "we're here to inform you of a potential base security issue."

"Alright." He leaned back in his chair. "Go on."

"A little while ago we were approached by a fellow Ranger. He tried to employ us in a scheme to steal surplus M16's from the Armory."

"That's quite an accusation to make of a fellow Ranger."

"Yes sir."

Lt. Colonel Aleman stood up and paced around his office for a bit before he eventually sat back down.

"The word on the street about you two, so to speak, is that you're going places."

"Sir?"

"Drill Sergeants talk. Ranger Instructors talk. Word gets back to me. You both must think you're hot shit or something?"

Sam and Bill didn't know how to respond so they remained silent.

"It might surprise you that I've personally looked through both of your files. You each have some impressive scores, talent and recommendations. So, with all that being said, when you come to me and inform me that something as incestuous as the theft of military weapons is brewing on my base, you have my full attention. Now, before we go any further, give me the Ranger's name that approached you."

20
Tuesday October 12, 1976

Three days later, after a day of training, Sam and Bill were the last ones back to the barracks and subsequently were the last ones to hit the showers.

"What'd you want to do tonight?" Sam asked.

"It's still early in the week. I don't know. Maybe we should write a letter back to Tom?"

"Didn't you read his last one? He wants us to call him Thomas now."

Bill shrugged under the water. "Sounds weird. It might be easier to just call him Tommy instead."

Sam chuckled. "Although he might have something to say about that."

"Knowing our boy, he'd better," Bill replied with a smile. "I wonder how college life is treating him? I miss that sonofabitch."

"I hope he finally got laid."

"No shit, right. Course, he's always had a tough time with the ladies, unlike us."

Sam's smile broadened. "Indeed."

"I can't imagine Tom, I mean Thomas, with a woman."

"Stranger things have happened. I only hope the best for him. But, aside from that, I miss him."

"Yeah, me too. Course, he would have never made it through Basic."

Sam nodded. "Tell me something I don't know."

It wasn't long before the shower bay emptied out and left them finishing up by themselves.

"When do you think we'll be called up for another mission?" Bill asked as he rinsed off under the hot water.

"That would be never."

Sam and Bill turned towards the new voice. Four masked men, holding wooden batons, stood between them and the exit. The intentions were clear and they didn't hesitate to attack.

The first man rushed in, baton high, but Sam splashed water in his face, sidestep the baton strike and then used his heel to dislocate the man's knee. The attacker howled in pain as he collapsed.

The second and third attackers, having witnessed the incapacitation, advanced slowly as the fourth moved to flank Sam and Bill.

Bill rushed forward and launched himself in to the air. He took two solid hits to his chest, from the batons, as he tackled the two men. The floor was slippery and all three easily went down in a heap.

Bill widely flung his elbows to both sides which connected with one of the men's faces. A resounding, and very satisfying, crack was heard and that man stopped moving. The other man grabbed Bill squarely around the midsection with his legs and began to squeeze.

Sam crouched down and picked up the loose baton just as the fourth man attacked him. He blocked the baton strike with his own, shot out his left hand and crushed the man's crotch through his jeans. Sam twisted and pulled as hard as he could.

Sam could feel the man's testicles tear and the bellowing scream that followed only confirmed Sam's success. That man fell to the floor and cradled his crotch.

Bill couldn't maneuver his body as the air was being forced out of his lungs. The absolute crushing feeling around his chest was unbearable as he struggled to get loose. His right hand final found a loose baton. He swung it around and connected with something, but the legs around his chest didn't budge.

Sam released his grip of the testicles and quickly closed the distance to the pile of bodies Bill was caught up in. The man saw Sam advancing and blocked the first and second baton strikes to his face. Sam changed tactics and just dropped straight down on the man's chest with both knees, cracking a few of the man's ribs in the process, who then uncoupled his legs. Bill rolled away gasping for breath. At the same time Sam struck the man square in the face which quickly ended the engagement.

A few fellow Rangers appeared in the entryway. "What the hell is going on in here!?"

Sam moved to Bill's side without looking at any of the men from their unit.

"Get the MP's and Medical here asap. Bill and I were attacked." He looked down at Bill's face. "How're you feeling? Anything broken?"

Bill coughed a few times and then sat up with Sam's help. "Nah. Ribs are sore but I don't think they're broken." He looked around at the four downed attackers and then back at Sam. "What the fuck?"

"Yeah."

* * *

Dennis Carter sat in a stockade cell. The other three men who were with him were being treated at the hospital. Dennis had wanted to squeeze the life out of Bill so badly but the fight

155

hadn't gone his way and he was locked up. *How had everything turned so badly so damned quickly? Why would they turn my offer down? It doesn't make any sense.*

The lock to his cell clanged and the door swung open. The MP stepped back and a woman entered carrying a briefcase. She extended her right hand.

"Specialist Hatfield?"

"Yes ma'am?" he replied as he shook her hand.

"My name is Anna Garland. It looks like you're in a wee bit of trouble and I'm here to help you out of that."

Three minutes later she had the information she needed and had exited the building. Two minutes after that Dennis Carter lay dead on his cell floor. Patterns of blood spray covered the walls of his cell from his uncontrollable bought of coughing.

*   *   *

"I have the names, sir."

"Very good. Make sure it gets tidied up."

"I'll do what I can. In the meantime, what would you like done with Sam Paige and Bill Nicholson?"

"Nothing. Let them live for now. In time things will work themselves out on their own. Forget about the shipment from Fort Benning, there's too much heat at the moment. We'll locate another source for our weapon needs."

"Yes sir."

21
Friday October 15, 1976

Sam and Bill stood at attention while Lt. Colonel Robert Aleman sat behind his desk and addressed them.

"You two have certainly made the headlines around here."

"Sir, we…"

He cut Sam off immediately. "Did I give you permission to speak soldier?"

"No, sir."

"Now, as I was trying to say, before I was so rudely interrupted, is that I have quite a conundrum on my hands. You claim one of your fellow Rangers, a Dennis Hatfield, approached and asked you to participate in a large theft of weapons. As soon as I begin to look into your accusation you're targeted in the showers by your fellow soliders, putting three of them in the hospital and one in the stockade. Here's my issue. Dennis Hatfield was found dead in his isolated cell mere hours after the MP's arrested him."

Sam and Bill exchanged glances.

"And no, I do not suspect either one of you. If you wanted to kill him you could have easily have done it in the showers. If anything, you displayed great restraint. I can't say I'd have been able to hold back myself."

He got up from his chair, walked around and stood in front of them.

"Something is happening, right under my nose, and I don't like it. In the meantime, you two obviously have targets painted on your back and I'm not going to idly stand by and watch. No, instead I'm left with the following actions."

Lt. Colonel Aleman extracted pins from his pocket. "Open your hands."

He placed a Specialist pin in both Sam and Bill's open hand.

"I'm promoting you both to the rank of Specialist. You continue to show true courage and dedication to the Rangers."

"Thank you, sir," they both said together.

Lt. Colonel Aleman went and sat back down.

"That was the easy part. The next order I give is going to land squarely on both your shoulders."

"Sir?"

"I can't have you on base anymore, certainly not until the internal investigation flushes out whatever the hell is going on around here. With that said, I have called in a number of favors. You are both immediately ordered to attend four weeks of HALO, High Altitude Low Opening training. Following your successful completion there you will then participate in SERE, Survival, Evasion, Resistance and Escape training for three weeks. If you can successfully negotiate those courses you will be tapped for positions within the Special Forces community."

Sam and Bill both smiled.

"Is this something you both want?"

"Yes, sir."

"Good, but let me clear gentlemen. Your transfers are highly unusual for your current level of achievement and rank. Trust me; these favors weren't easy to come by, so remember that in the future. However, your jackets are proof that I believe you have what it takes to become members of Spec Ops."

He paused and gave them both one final look over.

"Don't either of you make me regret this."

"No, sir."

"Now, get the fuck out of my office. Dismissed."

Sam and Bill saluted, turned and exited.

* * *

The two of them arrived at Fort Bragg, North Carolina the very next morning. They had put the attack behind them and concentrated on the upcoming training.

Week one consisted of an amazing amount of classroom time. They learned about the new type of parachute they'd be using, emergency procedures, repacking and more. All they did was practice, practice and more practice on recovering from malfunctions, entanglements and other deadly issues that could and would arise as they parachuted. They learned how to stabilize their bodies so when the time came to put it in motion they would fall through the air properly. The oxygen tanks were new to Sam and Bill but they couldn't wait to try them out for the first time.

At the end of that first week they were introduced to the wind tunnel. It housed a massive fan that could blow at speeds up to one hundred and fifty miles per hour. It lifted their bodies and allowed them to hover in mid-air. It wasn't long before both of them were able to fine tune everything they learned and simulate freefall flawlessly.

The beginning of week two their training took them to Arizona, at the Yuma Proving Ground. Sam and Bill's days were filled with endless jumps. It was almost as if they spent more time in the airplanes than they did on the ground. For three weeks they practiced multiple jumping variations, from ten thousand feet to twenty five thousand feet using oxygen. They practiced jumping with no equipment all the way to utilizing full gear loads. They practiced cutting away a bad chute, stabilizing and deploying their reserve. They had extensive training around pulling their chutes at two hundred feet and landing safely. They loved every minute of it.

At the end of the third week they were introduced to HAHO, High Altitude High Opening. The idea was to jump out of a plane, immediately pull your chute and then glide for many miles to your target. Much higher jumps for HAHO, around forty five thousand feet, could be done with oxygen and that would allow for a much longer glide time.

Sam and Bill devoured every bit of knowledge they were taught. Their instructors were impressed and during the full month of training knew that Sam and Bill felt very comfortable in the sky. They graduated and were then transferred back to Fort Bragg to undertake SERE training, smiling all the way.

Their smiles would quickly fade.

* * *

"Welcome to your first day of SERE," said Instructor Donald Webb. "For those of you that either don't have a clue about what you've gotten yourselves into, or are just too stupid to remember, SERE stands for Survival, Evasion, Resistance and Escape. For the next three weeks you'll be inundated with a variety of training that will prepare you in case you are cut off, left behind, running from or captured by the enemy. All fifty of you are here because your chosen profession deems that SERE is an integral part of your repertoire, and I agree with that assessment. The Special Operations community can

160

ill afford losing any of you, or the information you possess in your heads, to the enemy, be by bullet, capture, torture or interrogation.

"Survival. The knowledge on how to live off the land; to scavenge and eat what any other human being would consider vile and disgusting.

"Evasion. You will be taught how to successfully evade enemy forces pursuing you. Camouflage techniques, deception trails and traps will come in to play.

"Resistance. You will learn, through trial by fire, how to resist interrogations. What you know must never be revealed or spoken of.

"Escape. To have patience while you gather intel, learn patterns, plan and execute your escape.

"This program is not for the faint of heart, neither are the responsibilities that the Spec Ops community will firmly entrust on each one of your shoulders. But you really don't have a choice gentlemen. In the real world you can either choose to survive, by any means necessary, or you will die. By the end of your time here, with us at SERE, you might just want to die. And just in case there's any miscommunication I'll sum up what I just said. If you fail here at SERE you will not be tapped for Special Ops. You need to let that sink in. Trust me when I tell you that this program will push you to, and then well beyond, whatever limits you think you already have."

Instructor Webb walked away. Sam and Bill shared a quick glance. *What the hell did we get ourselves into?*

"Line up," said Instructor Miles.

All fifty soldiers, of various ranks and backgrounds, formed a single line as instructed. In front of them was a large hutch. Scurrying and hopping around that hutch were bunny rabbits.

"You are required to select a rabbit and name it. You will be responsible for caring for your pet which includes feeding and cleaning up after it."

A number of the men didn't understand. One of them spoke up about it. "Sir. What's this supposed to accomplish exactly?"

Instructor Miles smiled and approached the soldier. The soldier's uniform bore the name Martinez.

"Martinez. I like your spunk. However, your question, albeit valid, is wrong on both counts. First off, I am not an officer. My name is Instructor Miles. Secondly, I didn't realize you were the only one who knows 'exactly' what SERE is all about."

"I don't, Instructor Miles. I was only asking about why you want us to take care of a rabbit."

"I see." He moved an inch away from Martinez's face. "I DON'T GIVE A RAT FUCK WHY YOU WANT TO KNOW MARTINEZ! THIS IS MY WORLD AND YOU WILL DO WHATEVER YOU'RE TOLD TO DO! IS THAT FUCKING CLEAR!?"

Martinez turned white. "Yes…"

"I DON'T CARE! YOU'RE OUT MARTINEZ! YOU WERE OUT AS SOON AS YOU OPENED YOU DUMB FUCKING MOUTH THE FIRST TIME! GET OUT OF MY SIGHT RIGHT NOW!"

Martinez didn't react so Instructor Miles put his hands on his uniform, yanked him out of line hard and threw him to the ground.

"LOOK AT YOU! YOU CAN'T EVEN FOLLOW A SIMPLE ORDER! HOW DID YOU EVER EXPECT TO BE INVITED THE SPECIAL OPS COMMUNITY, YOU MORON!?"

Instructor Miles immediately turned his back on Martinez and headed back to the hutch. He began to hand out a rabbit to each soldier. Sam and Bill finally got theirs and headed towards the empty cages where they would be kept. Each cage had a blank name card that needed to be filled out with the soldier's last name, as well as the pet's name.

"So what the hell do you think this is all about?" Bill whispered.

"I haven't a clue yet," Sam responded. "But I do have a sneaking suspicion that we're in for a really fucked up experience."

"Yeah, I'm getting that same vibe myself."

Bill stroked his rabbit and cradled it in his arms as he walked towards the cage. He placed his rabbit inside, closed the hatch and began to fill out the card.

"Bun-bun," Bill said and jotted the name out.

"Seriously?" Sam kidded as he placed his bunny in his own cage.

"What? It's a cute name. Why? What are you naming yours?"

"Mitsy."

"Mitsy? What kind of a rabbit's name is that?"

"I don't know. It's got to be better than Bun-bun."

* * *

Living off the land was much harder than Sam or Bill ever imagined it could be. They were taught how to locate and dig for water; what plants were edible and which ones to avoid; how to create snares and traps to capture game; make flint knives and other survival skills they would need in the wilderness. Their hunger grew, day by day, as they continued to exert more energy than they could refuel themselves with. They, along with the rest of the class, constantly battled with their willpower on whether to continue to stick it out or not.

In the evenings each soldier was given an allocation of fresh vegetables to feed to their pet rabbit. They were instructed to give all of the food to their pets and not to eat any themselves. Five more soldiers had been kicked out before the end of week two for food violations alone.

During week two evasion techniques were incorporated in to the daily training. Concealment, false trail creation and booby-traps were covered extensively; along with land navigation and how to disguise your tracks. Everyone was starving by this point due to the fact that there was only so much time was allocated for foraging each day, and berries were the most common edible food source.

Teams of six men would be blindfolded, driven by truck to an undisclosed location and then dropped off with empty canteens. They were then given four hours to reach a specific destination, and to do so without getting caught by any of the other teams hunting them. The incentive was easy. If the six man team reached their goal they would be rewarded. If any other team caught them then that hunter group would be rewarded, and that reward was always food. By the end of week two, three additional soldiers had quit. Forty-one soldiers now remained as week three began.

* * *

Instructor Webb stood in front of the dwindling class that
evening. They were gathered around a large fire pit that lit up
the evening sky. "I told that you'd be pushed to your limits
and beyond. So far nine of your fellow soldiers no longer
stand beside you. They didn't have what it takes." He paused
for a few seconds before he continued. "The final week of
SERE has arrived and I know you're all tired, weak and
hungry. There will be many instances, I guarantee it, where
you'll need to dig as deep as you can to continue on, no matter
how you feel and seemingly against all odds. Sometimes
you'll have to do whatever it takes and that doesn't mean you
have to like it. But that's what soldiers do, especially elite
soldiers that you're all striving to prove you can be, both to us
and to yourselves." He walked around some more. "Tonight,
before the final week of training begins, we are going to have a
feast in your honor. Each of you deserve the recognition of
making it this far. It's time to celebrate!"

A number of cheers went up and most of the men began to
smile.

Instructor Miles took over. "Gather around and watch."

Forty-one soldiers did just that so they could all get a good
look at whatever he was about to show them. From within the
folds of his uniform Instructor Miles pulled out a rabbit. It's
large eyes blinked and its nose constantly sniffed the air.

"You hold your rabbit like this," he said as he
demonstrated.

As everyone looked on Instructor Miles quickly twisted
and snapped the rabbit's neck. One of its back legs spasmed

and then its entire body went limp. He produced a knife and proceeded to gut the body, peeling back the flesh and removing the innards. He then skinned the carcass, poked a skewer through it and placed it on the fire pit. A few of the soldiers puked and many more had cringed during the process, including Sam and Bill. The smell of cooked rabbit began to waft over the group.

Instructor Miles stood up. "The majority of you have never killed anyone or anything in your life. As a soldier, and an elite one at that, you will be required to kill, without mercy or hesitation. This is your next test. Tonight you will be eating your pet rabbit or you're out. It's as simple as that. You have ten minutes to kill, gut and prepare your rabbit for cooking. Your time starts now."

Sam and Bill ran back to their cages, opened the doors and removed their pets they'd nurtured for the past two weeks. Mitsy and Bun-bun's big trusting eyes stared back at them.

"Oh fuck man," Bill began, "this is really fucked up. They want us to eat our pets."

"I know. I know."

"This would be a lot easier if we hadn't had to name them."

"Just grit your teeth, like I am and we'll get through this bullshit."

They walked back to the fire pit together with their bunnies cradled in their arms. This was something that neither one of them wanted to do. They sat down and positioned their pets as demonstrated in two hands.

Bill put his mouth next to one of Bun-bun's ears and gently whispered, "I'm so sorry."

166

He twisted his hands in opposite directions and Bun-bun's heart stopped beating as his body fell limp against Bill's body. A small tear escaped the corner of his right eye and slid down his dirty cheek.

Instructor Miles appeared by his side, looming above him. "Problem Nicholson?"

"No problem Instructor Miles," he replied without looking up.

"That's strange, in this light it looks to me like you're crying you pussy."

"Go fu..." Bill began to say as he started to get up. Sam instantly reached over, placed a hand on Bill's shoulder and forced him back down.

"What was that Nicholson? Did you have something you'd like to say?"

Sam slowly shook his head back and forth as he and Bill stared at each other, willing his friend to calm down.

"No, not a thing," Bill finally answered.

"I didn't think so. Bon appetit," Instructor Miles added as he walked away.

"Fuck this shit."

"Take it easy," Sam whispered. "His job is to get a rise out of you and its obviously working. We haven't come this far to quit. Trust me, I don't like this any more than you do."

Sam twisted Mitsy's neck and she collapsed in his hands. Bill winced.

"We do what we have to do," continued Sam. "And I don't know what this next week holds, let alone the next seven years, but I do know we're going to need our strength to face it. Now gut your rabbit so we can have some dinner."

"Brother, that's just cold."

Sam nodded. "Tell me something I don't know. Unfortunately, there's a lesson to be taught and we just learned it the hard way."

"Yeah, okay." Bill nodded. " But I never want a pet ever again. Even if I have kids one day and they want a dog or a cat. Nope. No pets. Ever."

"No shit."

* * *

In the morning Instructor Webb addressed everyone again.

"I hope everyone had a pleasant meal last night but it looks like we lost two more during the process. There are now thirty nine of you left. For this next exercise all teams will be dropped off in random locations. Additional instructions will be given to you there. As for your equipment, each of you is allowed one full canteen, the flint knife you made your first week and the clothing on your back. No food will be permitted. This exercise will last six days, whether you are successful or not. Your goal is to survive and evade capture while following all goals your team is presented with. It all comes down to this ladies. Good luck."

* * *

Sam, Bill, and four others were dropped off in a barren field. They were handed a note and the truck left. The six immediately moved out of the clearing towards the woods. As soon as they were out of sight they crouched down. Sam opened the paper and read it out loud.

"Warning. You are behind enemy lines and are actively being hunted. Your team must traverse the landscape to escape. You have minimal supplies and must live off whatever you can find. You have twelve hours to reach the location below, which is approximately six miles away. At that location a new mission will be presented to you. Failure to successfully negotiate any task, in the allocated time, will result in automatic capture. Hunting parties, as always, may capture you at any time."

A map of the area, with an X on where the six of them needed to be in twelve hours, was included.

"Well, isn't this going to be fun," Bill said offhandedly with a smile. "Course, we'll all be fine if we just work together." He extended his hand out to the other others. "Nicholson."

"Smith."

"Grover."

"Small."

"Barnes."

After all the pleasantries were done Sam put the map down so they could all look at it. It wasn't long before they agreed on their estimated location and the direction they needed to head off in. Bill took point and the group headed off through the woods, carefully watching where they stepped and always scanning their surroundings for any enemies.

It turned out to be a very long day.

*   *   *

Six hours after they started their trek they had managed to travel only three and half miles. The group was making relatively good time but was walking slower than usual to cover their noise level, and because they were all paranoid about getting caught. So far they hadn't come across anything edible and figured they would have to deal with that sooner than later.

Small, who was on point, made the signal to rapidly drop to the ground. All of them hit the earth and blended in with their surroundings. In the distance a few voices could be heard approaching. Ten seconds later a group of twelve soldiers appeared out of the dense woods in front of them. If the hunters hadn't been talking they would have walked right in to them. The hunters walked past as a few of them continued to talk about one thing or another and eventually disappeared.

"Do you think they saw us?" Small whispered.

"Obviously not or we'd be fucked already," Grover replied.

"Noise discipline. Hand signals only," Sam warned as he peered through the bushes. *That hunter group is gone but who knows how many more are out there.*

Sam signaled to Bill to take point again and the group slowly dislodged themselves from the ground and headed back out towards their destination, more paranoid than ever before. Five hours later they were all low on water, hungry but very close to their first goal. They hadn't seen another hunter group since, but they had expected a team to be behind each tree, ready to pounce on them. Everyone was in good spirits but their nerves were definitely on edge.

Bill peeked out from behind his hiding spot and motioned for Sam to join him. He pointed two fingers at his eyes, and pointed them at a spot in the distance. Sam peered out and signaled he saw the same thing. In the distance was a military jeep with two instructors leaning against it. Sam nodded to Bill and the rest of the team, and then made the signal to move out.

"Team checking in," Sam said as the six of them emerged from the woods.

One of the instructors looked at his watch and then made a notation on his clipboard.

"Cutting it close I see." He handed Sam new orders. "Here's your next waypoint. Oh, and be wary out there, I hear there's a lot of soldiers looking for you." The instructor smiled, picked up his radio and reported in.

Sam and the team withdrew back into the woods. The daylight was fading quickly and the team had plenty left to do. First, they looked at their new orders. Their destination was only seven miles away but they only had until noon the next day to get there.

"What does everyone want to do?" Sam asked. "Press on tonight or get some rest and start in the morning?"

Barnes looked over the new map they'd been given. "A couple of miles from here is a large stream. We can hold off on eating but we're low on water. Why not head there and dig in for the night?"

"I concur," said Small. "The moon is already out and we won't last long without water. You never know, maybe we could catch some fish to eat?"

The rest of the team nodded and they struck out towards their new destination. Around midnight, four hours later, they heard the sound of running water. Everyone's canteens were dry and acid churned in their empty bellies. They reduced their speed and cautiously advanced towards the large stream

171

in the distance. They spread out in the bank's foliage, waited and observed for five minutes. Nothing.

Sam signaled to Smith and Grover to proceed. They emerged from their concealment, crept to the water's edge and filled their canteens from the fast moving stream. Within five minutes all six team members had topped off and regrouped.

"Okay," said Sam. "We dig in here until the early morning. We'll try and catch us some breakfast then. In the meantime we need to set up an overwatch rotation."

Ten minutes later five of the men were grouped together in a secluded spot where the stream turned. The quickly fell asleep as Bill watched over the area from the crook of a tree branch ten feet off the ground. The moonlight cast shadows over everything as the constant sound of running water reverberated throughout the night.

* * *

"SURRENDER!"

Sam, Bill, Smith, Grover and Small all jerked awake and looked around.

"YOU ARE SURROUNDED! SURRENDER YOURSELVES NOW!"

Where the hell is Barnes?

"WE HAVE BARNES! WE PULLED HIS SLEEPING ASS OUT OF A TREE SO WE KNOW YOU'RE CLOSE BY! COME OUT AND GIVE YOURSELF UP!"

Fuck!

The sun was up and they were pretty much boxed in. It was only a matter of time before the hunters would locate their hiding spot. Everyone's face told the same story. They were fucked.

"IT'S OVER! YOU'RE CAUGHT! YOU FAILED! THERE'S NOWHERE TO GO!"

From their vantage point they saw a large number of personnel combing the area. They were heavily outnumbered and the only weapons they had were flint knives.

"We have to make a run for it," said Smith.

"Agreed," said Sam. "But we have to split up. Bill and I will take off first. Hopefully they follow us and that will give you three time to escape. There's still a chance you can get to the next rendezvous by noon."

"I don't like it," Grover replied.

"There's no time to debate this." Sam pressed. "Barnes has already been captured. I'm not going to have everyone fail. You guys can make it."

Sam tapped Bill on the shoulder and without another word the two of them sprinted out of their hide and began to cross the large but shallow stream.

"WE'VE GOT SOME RUNNERS! GET THEM!"

Seven hunters began to converge towards Sam and Bill who were now more than halfway across the running water. They made it to the opposite shore just as the seven hunters surrounded them. From their hiding spot the remaining three team members watched as Sam and Bill rushed the hunters. Billy clubs were swung. Sam was clocked in the head and went down. Bill took one to the face, stumbled backwards and then took a second one before he fell to the ground and stopped moving. Canvas bags were placed over their limp bodies and their hands were secured behind their backs.

173

Smith, Grover and Small watched in horror as Sam and Bill were dragged away into the woods as prisoners of war.

* * *

Bill jerked awake. He'd just been dowsed with a bucket of ice cold water. He tried to move but his hands didn't respond. He looked down and realized he was strapped to a chair. His arms and legs were bound by rope and he struggled against them to no avail. His shirt had been removed and all that remained were his pants.

Fuck my face hurts. Why the hell can't I see?

Bill's right eye socket had swollen up. He blinked, with his one good eye and watched the water drip off him. It added to the huge puddle on the floor beneath him.

Movement.

A split second later a fist connected with the side of his face and he immediately tasted blood.

"I want your name, rank and serial number."

Bill didn't answer. *What the fuck is going on?*

The man's fist landed again and Bill's head snapped back in the opposite direction. Blood trickled out of the corner of his mouth and down his chin.

"Your name, your rank and your serial number or this will continue."

Bill half smiled through his pain. "Go fuck your mother."

His face snapped to the side. He spat a huge glob of blood out onto the floor and his smile had faded.

"Tell me what I want to know."

Bill defiantly shook his head and winced as he waited for another strike that never came.

174

His interrogator spoke up again. "In time you will tell me everything. As for right now, let me tell you what we know. Your name is Nicholson and you're part of a six man team."

"I don't know what you're talking about."

"Oh, but we do. We picked up the last three trying to evade us. They're in the pit, along with your buddy Barnes. You know, the same guy who fell asleep in the tree and didn't see us coming."

"Bullshit."

The man moved behind Bill's chair, bent down and whispered in his ear. "You will tell me what I want to know because if you don't...well, let's just say I have all the time in the world to use your body as my playground."

Bill struggled against his restraints violently and the man chuckled.

* * *

Sam's head hurt like never before. The blow he'd received had given him a minor concussion. He couldn't think straight and the beatings he'd received hadn't improved his condition. Initially Sam had been thrown into a small pit by himself. It was so small that he was unable to extend his legs. It was as if every one of his muscles ached and screamed for relief that would never come. Sam had no choice but to grit his teeth and endure the constant pain and agony.

The encampment he was in had been mirrored to look like one of the many POW camps discovered in Vietnam. There were a variety of cages and pits throughout the compound. The place reeked of feces and human excrement. Guards patrolled the area and kicked the small cages each time they walked by, which only added to Sam's immense discomfort. The constant wailing of men resounded throughout the compound in what seemed like a never ending orchestra of human misery.

Sam had remained in a constant state of misery until they had eventually taken him from the pit, placed him in a chair and secured him. He had been drifting in and out of consciousness for over a day now while his interrogation proceeded, from both the pain and the sleep deprivation.

Out of nowhere Sam's entire body strained against its bonds as a man dragged a knife across his chest. The pain he felt was absolutely excruciating. Blood, from the wound, oozed and slowly made its way down Sam's torso.

"Maybe that will jar your memory. Tell me how many men are in your platoon? What were you doing in the woods? What was your mission?"

Sam's face and the majority of his body were covered in bruises and untreated cuts. Blow after blow followed each and every question he refused to answer. It was a perpetual cycle that clearly had no end.

A second slash from the knife opened up yet another gash in his chest. Sam screamed this time, a scream that combined all the raw pain he felt and the anguish of not knowing what they were doing to his friend. *I will not break. I will not break. I will not...*

Sam's head lulled to one side as he passed out once again. This time his interrogator waited a full five minutes before dowsing Sam with a bucket of ice water.

* * *

"I'm impressed Nicholson. You're one tough sonofabitch."

Bill squinted though his one remaining eye slit at his current interrogator. He'd had five or six different men rotate to work on him for the past two days. *I guess they need their rest.* Bill cracked a grin at his own joke, although it was impossible to make his smile out through all the bruising and inflammation.

"You remember your buddy Barnes don't you?"

Bill didn't move or reply.

"No matter. You should know that it didn't take long for Barnes to break. Hell, he spilled his beans after we cut him for the first time. You should have seen how pathetic he was. It was downright embarrassing. One of the things he was quick to tell us is that you and Paige are the best of friends. That was quite interesting to hear."

Don't believe a word he's saying. He's full of shit. You can't break me you asshole, you just can't.

"Needless to say Barnes is no longer with us, and right now you're getting a visitor."

Behind him the door to the crudely constructed single POW room opened. Another chair was placed opposite Bill and a body was forced into it and secured with restraints. Bill could only make out a human blur through his barely functioning left eye.

"What the fuck is this?" he asked.

"I'm glad you asked," his interrogator replied. "Over the past two days it's become very apparent that you have made up your mind not to cooperate."

"Figured that out did you?"

Bill's face snapped to the right from the blow.

177

"And yet, regardless of how many times you are injured you have remained true to your cause. I now believe we have gone about this the wrong way. We've decided not to hurt you anymore." The interrogator waved to one of the other men. "It's time."

Another interrogator removed the canvas hood, and then the mouth gag, from the prisoner facing Bill. Sam's eyes widened when he saw Bill tied to the opposite chair, his face and body badly bruised and bloodied.

"I'll fucking kill all of you," Sam promised.

Bill knew right away that it was Sam. *Oh fuck.* "Hey brother," he squeaked out. "How about we go someplace else for vacation next time?"

Bill's face snapped to the side yet again from the blow. Blood flew out of Bill's mouth and added to the existing spatter on the floor.

Sam was beside himself. "You motherfuckers! He needs medical attention!"

"You're right," replied Bill's interrogator. "And we'll make sure he gets it just as soon as one of you tell us what we want to know."

"Fuck you!" Sam cried out. "Fuck you! Fuck this bullshit! I'll kill all of you!"

"ENOUGH!"

It was Sam's turn to get hit in the face.

The interrogator faced Bill. "I am going to carve up your friend, while you watch, until I get a solid piece of intel from you."

"That's smart," replied Bill. "You want me to watch but I can't even see."

The interrogator plucked a knife off the table and approached Sam. He deftly flicked the blade and opened up another line, this time down Sam's arm who cried out in pain.

"YOU ASSHOLE!" Bill yelled.

"You're right Nicholson, you can't see. But something tells me you can hear what's happening to your friend just fine."

"You sadistic sonofabitch. You're a dead man."

"I've heard it all before. Now, give me a piece of intel or I'll continue cutting him."

"Don't...don't say anyth..." Sam began to say before he was struck in the face again.

"Time's running out Nicholson. What's it going to be?"

Bill didn't respond so the man made another incision down Sam's arm. Sam bellowed out in pain.

"ENOUGH!" Bill screamed.

The interrogator smiled. "Good. Now tell me what I want to know."

The pain Bill had suffered had been extreme, more than he even wanted to experience again. He could go on resisting but his willpower was close to depletion. Bill knew it was over and it was at this very moment that a sense of peacefulness washed over him.

"Sam, I'm sorry, but I would rather die than give them anything."

"Don't you worry about it," Sam replied as a similar realization passed through him. "This will always be bigger than you and me." He turned his head to face the interrogator. "We'll both die before we tell you a goddamn thing."

The man smiled. "I believe you."

* * *

Twenty one men, out of the original fifty, passed SERE.

Sam and Bill spent two weeks in the hospital, but they had learned one hell of a valuable lesson about themselves during the process, and that was a man can only take so much before he will break. They had welcomed death and were no longer afraid of it.

After they left the hospital they were welcomed into the Special Forces community with open arms.

22
Sunday May 22, 1977

Thomas parked his car in the dorm parking lot and headed inside to pick up Samantha for their date. Their time together during the past eight months had been very special. As Thomas climbed the steps to her room he wondered how Samantha would react to his offer. With the college year coming to an end in a few weeks Thomas had planned to ask her if she wanted to do some traveling over the summer and he couldn't wait to bring it up.

He arrived at her door and knocked.

"It's open," Samantha said. "Come in."

He turned the knob and entered. "Hey, I wanted to know if you're interested in that Star Wars movie that's opening..."

Thomas froze in the doorway. On the floor, in the middle of her small dorm room, were blankets and pillows. Lying on top of them, naked and with a seductive look in her eyes was Samantha. However, what had caused Thomas to uncharacteristically pause was that there were two other people with her; a male and a female and they were just as naked as his girlfriend.

"Wha..." he began to say before Samantha cut him off.

"There's no need to be alarmed Thomas. This is Greg and his girlfriend Alicia."

"Hey there," Alicia said softly as she caressed one of Samantha's breasts.

"Hey man," added Greg.

Thomas was stunned.

"Why don't you close the door sweetie?"

Thomas slowly eased the door behind him. He couldn't wrap his head around the fact that his girlfriend was naked with another couple. *None of this makes any sense.*

Samantha got up from the blankets, walked over to Thomas and kissed him. That broke him out of his daze.

"What the hell is going on here?"

Samantha smiled wryly. "Why don't you take off your clothes and we'll stay in tonight?"

"What do you mean?"

"Oh, it's okay. Trust me; you have nothing to be shy about. I've been telling Alicia about you and she can't wait to see what you have to offer her. I just wanted to share this experience with you. It'll be fun."

Rage instantly built up inside Thomas' head and his face became red. "Are you fucking kidding me? After eight months you just happened to think that I wanted to share you with other people? To watch you get fucked by another guy? Does that make any sense to you?"

Samantha's smile faded away. "But you get to have sex with another girl. What's the big deal Thomas?"

He reeled back in shock. "What's the big deal? I love you is the big deal and you just shit all over it. This situation is absolutely horrific. Fuck you."

"Don't say things like that."

"You know what? I thought you were kind, nice and sweet. I fell for you hard. But right now, with all this, I apparently don't have a clue about who you really are or what you're really in to."

"Thomas, you're really bumming me out."

"Right," he replied. "This has to be all about you." He opened the door. "Goodbye Samantha."

"Where are you going? Please don't leave me," she pleaded.

"I don't have a choice. You just stabbed me in my heart."

* * *

Thomas remained in a deep funk as the college year ended and summer began. His world had instantly caved in on itself. He rarely ventured out of his house, and only did as he needed provisions.

A month into summer he saw Samantha and Greg sitting together at the local burger joint. He learned later on that Greg had left Alicia and was now with his ex-girlfriend.

* * *

Ring ring.

Thomas walked over to his phone and answered it.

"Hello?"

"Thomas? It's your grandfather. You're grandmother's out at the store so I thought I'd give you a ring."

He sat down on the couch. "Hey."

"Hey? That's all I get? What's new in your neck of the woods? Your grandmother and I haven't heard from you in a while so I figured I'd check in on you."

"Nothing. Nothing's going on."

"You sound different. Are you alright?"

Shit. "I'm fine grandpa. Are you two going on another trip soon?"

"We are, but don't change the subject. Tell me what's going on. Spill the beans before I come down there and harass you in person."

Thomas sighed. "It's nothing, really."

"Very convincing, but I'm not letting you off the hook that easily. My guess is that is has something to do with your girlfriend. What was her name? Samantha?"

Tears welled up in his eyes. "Yes," he squeaked out.

"What happened?"

Thomas couldn't hold back anymore and through a wall of tears he shared what had transpired. When he was done he remained quiet.

"Thomas? Are you still there?"

"Yes."

"Good. Now listen to me and listen closely. At this point in your life you need to concentrate on one thing and one thing only, and that's college. Trust me when I say women come and go. I'm just glad you're grandmother didn't hear me say that."

"But she was my world."

"I understand how you feel. Breakups and betrayals are part of life. In the future you'll have more time to find someone you'll care about. Someone you'll unconditionally end up trusting with everything. But right now you need to pull yourself together and move on with your life. Do you understand me Thomas?"

"How do I do that?"

"Just make the choice and do it. Get out of your head. Why not go to Venice Beach and walk around?"

"I don't feel like it."

"I don't give a shit," his grandfather replied.

Thomas was shocked. "But…"

"No buts Thomas. I'm going to hang up this phone and then you're going to get your ass off that couch and get your head back in the game. Do you hear me?"

"Yes."

"Good. Now have fun at the beach."

The line went dead. *Sonofabitch. He actually hung up.* Thomas slowly got up from the couch and put the phone back on the cradle. Ten minutes later he had reluctantly showered, dressed and walked out the front door.

23
June 3, 1978

The large cargo plane, bound from South America, landed at the Florida airbase and immediately taxied over to its designated hanger. Soon afterwards the contents of its belly began to unload.

At various other military holdings, throughout the coastal regions of the United States, the flow of cocaine and marijuana continued unabated. Most of these shipments originated from South America. On rare occasions one of the shipments would be discovered and confiscated. But at all of the locations somebody would always be watching over the process, taking note of anything out of the ordinary and identifying problems that needed to be corrected for future deliveries.

The organization's drug trade to the United States, transportation provided by military channels through hard work and connections, was a successful business. But what drove it were the needs of the American citizens, from the poor and destitute needing a release from their pain, to the rich and powerful that were looking for their own escape.

The United States war on drugs had begun, but little did President Carter know that within their own hierarchy the orders to keep the drugs coming in easily outweighed any of his victories.

24
Thursday July 12, 1979

Sam and Bill each kicked the rope out of the opposite sides of the hovering helicopter. A hundred feet below them the rope lines disappeared into the dense South American jungle. Wearing full Tiger camouflage, face paint and carrying ninety pounds of gear and a weapon each, Sam and Bill, along with ten other Spec Ops personnel, inserted themselves via fast rope to the jungle floor. As they each landed they immediately moved off the impact point and took up defensive positions. The helicopter departed and within seconds its sound was replaced by the natural chorus of jungle.

It'd been two years since Sam and Bill had survived SERE school and then tapped into the ranks of the Special Operations community. During that time they had established themselves as solid warriors, both to their fellow mates and the Spec Op community itself. Their missions, in the past two years, had included hostage rescue, advanced recon and targeted terminations, to name a few. As always, they handled themselves and the mission with professionalism and seriousness. When the shit hit the fan they were rock solid and had saved the lives of some of their teammates on one occasion. That classified mission garnered them the rank of Corporal, with the nod that they were each on the fast track to Sergeant.

Since joining Spec Ops their world had changed drastically and the time had flown by. As an elite soldier they continued to train hard every day but it was with a renewed purpose. Sam and Bill knew that if they were going to be tapped for a mission then that mission was going to make a difference, whether it was to save people's lives or take out a bad guy.

This particular mission was Sam's first time to lead and he was proud to accept the reigns.

Each man crouched on one knee, in a semi-circle, weapon trained on any potential danger in the jungle in front of them. Once the helicopter was out of ear shot the primary navigator pulled a laminated map from his side pouch. Using a compass he took a moment and then pointed the team in the direction they needed to travel, and quickly moved off into the jungle to take point. The eleven others silently filed in behind one another at fifteen foot intervals, heads on a swivel while they constantly scanned for danger.

The large cocaine lab had been on the US list for some time and President Carter wanted to send a clear message about his war on drugs. Sam's team had been sent to destroy it.

* * *

"Bravo. Charlie. This is Alpha. What's your status?" Sam said in to the radio he held.

"Bravo. In position."

"Charlie. We need five mikes."

"Roger that."

Bill peaked out from Alpha's concealed spot that effectively hid the four man team just inside the jungle line. A large section of the jungle had been razed, to make room for the drug lab, and Sam had sent his other two teams to the opposite side of the encampment. Various buildings had been constructed far away from where the drugs were being made. A helicopter landing zone had also been setup adjacent to the production area. Without any roads Sam had to assume that this was how the drugs and all supplies were transported in and out of the camp.

Numerous armed men patrolled the perimeter while others oversaw the workers, which included a sizable amount of men, women and children that were underneath large tents. It was unclear whether those workers were engaged in the cocaine production against their will or not but Sam was unwilling to put any innocents at risk during the mission.

"This is Charlie. In position."

"Understood. All teams will lay low and gather intel. You have your assignments. We'll proceed with the mission at zero thirty hours."

Throughout the remainder of the day all teams monitored the camp's activities from their concealed positions. As day turned in to night the workers headed towards the outer buildings. Before long the smell of the evening meal reached the team's noses and some of the security men broke off from their patrols to go eat.

Hours later, as midnight approached, the camp had become deathly quiet. Dim lights dotted the area and the number of security men had dropped significantly. Some of them patrolled the area, but most of them had entered the barracks, which had allowed Sam and his team to know exactly which building contained the workers and the additional security personnel.

Sam's watch hit twelve thirty. They had left their heavy packs behind and carried only their silenced pistols. They additionally brought a hefty amount of C4 explosives that were wired to remote triggers. Sam and Bill, along with the two other Alpha members, crept to the edge of the jungle. The closest two-man enemy patrol was fifty feet away and they were walking towards the production tents with their backs to Alpha. In the distance four more security men could be seen guarding the tents. All twelve of Sam's men had counted the enemies currently awake and on duty, and those guards didn't have a clue regarding the last few minutes of their lives.

With a nod the two other Alpha members, with silenced pistols extended, quickly and quietly closed the distance towards the backs of the roving patrol. Sam and Bill, keeping low, moved away from the jungle and crouch ran towards a shed by the helicopter landing area. They were able to stay out of sight by avoiding the camp's dim lights. The two reached the shed just as the two roving guards heads snapped forward from bullet impacts and their bodies fell awkwardly to the ground.

Bravo and Charlie teams emerged from the jungle, like invisible shadows, and successfully nullified three additional two-man patrols before they continued on with their portion of the mission.

Sam and Bill waited for one of the four tent guards to turn and walk away before they left the cover of the shed and made their way towards him. They had observed that the guards got bored and tended to group together to smoke. In short time Sam and Bill made it to the side of the tent and heard all four of the guards talking. A quick peak around the corner confirmed that the four had their Ak-47's slung over their shoulders and were engaged in a smoke break.

Sam and Bill nodded to each other. To the guards Sam and Bill seemed to materialize from out of nowhere and one of them barely had the time to point in their direction as his eyes opened wide in surprise. Sam and Bill's silenced pistols barked with deadly accuracy. Four cigarettes flew off in various directions as their owners collapsed in lifeless heaps.

The two other Alpha members reappeared and signaled to Sam that they had taken out a total of four guards. Sam nodded and gave them the sign to watch his back. Sam and Bill dug in to their packs and removed a number of C4 explosives. They began to place them throughout the drug production equipment, and added a few extra around the large stack of packaged cocaine that was ready for pickup. They worked quickly and when they were finished they regrouped and headed back to their original hiding spot to wait for the other two teams to check in. One minute later the radio came to life.

"Bravo to Alpha. Mission complete."

"Charlie to Alpha. Ditto."

"Roger that," Sam replied. "Rally on me."

Five minutes later all twelve men were back together and their packs were significantly lighter. The point man led them through the jungle to the top of a knoll that overlooked the camp. Sam couldn't risk waiting any longer in case their actions would be discovered. He pulled the remote detonator from his pouch, armed it and depressed the button. Simultaneous explosions rocked the encampment. The cocaine production, and all of its supplies, evaporated in a massive fireball. The barracks, which Bravo and Charlie had been tasked with, disintegrated along with all the men inside of it. The only structures that remained were the workers quarters and the helicopter shed. The rest of the complex had been obliterated from the face of the Earth.

Sam, and the rest of his team, smiled at their work before they headed off into the jungle towards their appointed exfiltration area.

* * *

"You assured me my operation would not be compromised."

"Carlos, please calm down. My government doesn't always know what it's left and right hands are doing."

"That is no excuse. One of my primary production camps just got blown to shit and all you have to say is 'it's not my fault?' That's bullshit. How are we supposed to do business if I can't rely on my business partner to protect me, like you promised you'd do Bob?"

"Once again Carlos, let me offer my deepest apologies. However, I've just been told that this operation was approved by the President himself. There was no way I could have known about or even stopped it if I wanted to."

"Don't treat me like an insolent peasant pendejo. I lost millions of dollars in product, not to mention men. What steps are you planning to take to compensate me for my loss?"

Raven sighed. He knew he needed this contact. "What would you like?"

"The price of the product you so desperately require just went up by ten percent."

"Now Carlos, you can't be serious?"

"No? Try me."

The line went dead and Raven slowly hung the secured phone back on its cradle.

"Fuck you Carlos, you prick."

He picked the phone back up and dialed another number.

"Code?"

"Two five delta niner," Raven relayed.

"Yes sir, what can I do for you?"

"Tell Serpent that I need the information he possesses as soon as he has it."

"Is this about the South American drug op?"

"You're Goddamn right it is. I just got pressured in to a ten percent hike over that damn operation. Tell him I need a meeting."

"Yes sir."

25
Saturday June 14, 1980

"Congratulations to the class of nineteen hundred and eighty. May all your dreams and aspirations come true."

The USC chancellor stepped away from the podium as a myriad of caps were tossed into the air in triumphant celebration. Thomas clutched his diploma and made his way through the throng of people towards his grandparents.

"Congratulations Thomas," Ed said as he shook his grandson's hand.

"Thanks," he replied with a smile.

Claire hugged her grandson warmly. "We're soooo proud of you." She pulled back. "I know your parents would have been very proud of what you've accomplished as well."

Thomas didn't know what to say to that so he changed the subject as Ed shot a glance towards his wife.

"I wasn't able to confirm whether Sam and Bill could be here. Have either of you seen them?"

"I'm sorry sweetheart but we haven't seen them. Maybe they're around here someplace."

Thomas shook his head. "No. If they were here I'd know about it. They're probably off saving the world or something. They'd better be for missing this. But that's life. Are you two hungry at all?"

Ed and Claire nodded. "We could eat. Why don't we head out and we'll treat you."

Thomas smiled. "Great. And while we're at it you can tell me all about the trips you've been taking."

Claire grinned. "I can't wait to tell you all about them."

"Good. I'll pick your brains on some of the best places to visit as I plan my own world adventure."

"You're planning on traveling?"

Thomas nodded. "Yes. I've been cooped up too long and it's about time I did something new."

"I'm happy to hear you say that Thomas. Your grandfather and I are anxious to see you."

* * *

Two weeks later Thomas' plane landed in London. He had wondered what to do with himself after college, and hearing about the wondrous adventures his grandparents had experienced had prompted him to want to get out and see the world for himself. More importantly, he wanted to see if he could travel on his own, relying on his wits and savvy to get around. Two weeks later, after acquiring the necessary visas and passport, Thomas left the United States.

At first Thomas had become overwhelmed and didn't venture out of his London hotel room. It wasn't until the third day that he managed to get a grasp on what he was avoiding and began to explore. It wasn't long before the sights and sounds of what London had to offer overcame his desire to hide away. Two days later he began to forget what it was like to be alone and after two weeks of driving around England in a rental car was he able to leave his loneliness behind him. That didn't mean he didn't miss sharing his adventures with someone else. All he knew, for this moment in his life, this is what he needed to accomplish by himself.

Thomas took his time exploring the United Kingdom as he eventually made his way north into Scotland. He wasn't on a schedule and when he stopped somewhere he got a room for a few nights and then absorbed what each location had to offer. He enjoyed such magnificent places as Glasgow, Edinburgh, St. Andrews, Montrose, Stonehaven, Aberdeen, Inverness and so many others in the north before he boarded a ferry to Belfast, Ireland. Thomas took another two weeks to drive through Ireland's countryside, taking in both the small villages and the large cities that the country had to offer. Dublin, Waterford and Cork were just a few of the places he was able to visit during his stay there.

Before he knew it Thomas had spent a month on those two islands and he felt the pull to head to France. His first stop was to land in Paris where, aside from celebrating his twenty-third birthday by himself, he spent five days taking in such sites as the Louvre, Notre-Dame, Arc de Triomphe and of course the Eiffel Tower. He traveled to such places as Versailles, Le Havre and the Normandy Beaches as he headed north into Belgium, once again driving so he could really explore the countryside. The major places he stopped was Brussels, Ghent and Antwerp, amongst so many others, before he crossed the border into the Netherlands.

Thomas was constantly awed at the beautiful scenery he drove through. The windmills and fields upon fields of multicolored flowers were absolutely breathtaking. And no matter where he stopped it seemed the people were always so friendly. Before he knew it he had blazed a trail through Rotterdam, Utrecht and The Hague before he finally arrived in Amsterdam. Thomas took his time to explore Amsterdam, with its numerous alleys, canals and streets. Everywhere he walked he discovered something new and wondrous, from various foods to bakeries and sex shops.

It wasn't long before Thomas found himself in the Red Light District, one evening, after a delicious meal at a steak house. Alley after alley contained floor to ceiling windows, and behind each one, lit up by a red light, scantily clad women enticed men who eyeballed them to come in. Thomas was embarrassed and shy as woman after woman smiled at him, followed by a gentle 'come hither' finger motion. He blushed on a few occasions and kept moving. Eventually he ducked into a bar and ordered a beer.

I've only been with Samantha, and that was years ago. Why shouldn't I try one? Don't I deserve some happiness?

He continued to drink as he struggled with his emotions and desires.

I'm on an adventure. I'm here to try new things dammit. This could be my birthday present to myself. I mean, look how far I've come on this trip already.

He drank.

But I'm nervous and afraid. But why? Why should I be afraid? There's nothing to be afraid of.

He downed his drink and headed back out, emboldened and focused.

That night, after the bar, he lost and then found his courage once again. After more thought he approached a beautiful woman, and while full of fear and desire, he finally succeeded. She told him her name was Lisa. She had a striking figure with dark hair and penetrating eyes. Lisa noticed right away that Thomas was shy, but as she began to undress for him his nervousness shed away just as quickly as each piece of her clothing did. For an hour Thomas lost himself in pure blissfulness.

The next morning Thomas had a new bounce in his step and a broad smile on his face. He spent the day visiting museums and taking a canal boat tour. He couldn't wait and tried to kill time by eating dinner as slowly as he could. Time inched by until the clock hit eight and he headed back to the RLD once again. Thomas' nervousness lingered in the back of his head but that didn't stop him from taking his time. In due course he opted to talk to a stunning Thai woman whose name was Mari-Lou. An hour later he felt like a changed man as he headed back to his hotel. He knew he had to leave the city or he may be inclined never to do so.

The following day Thomas flew to Barcelona, Spain and spent a number of days there recouping and taking in the beautiful history. From there he traveled to Zaragoza and then Madrid. Eventually he bid farewell and headed south through Toledo, Cordoba and ended up in Seville. Thomas loved Spain and its entire splendor. Time had no meaning in that country and days past as he traveled from one location to another, writing in his journal about everything he'd discovered. Before long he crossed the border into Portugal on his way to Lisbon, then north to Porto and Braga. He had had a wonderful stretch in Spain and Portugal but he knew it was time to move on.

His adventure continued as the plane set down in Athens, Greece. Thomas spent a week there alone visiting the ruins and taking day trips out to the various islands. He then left and headed to Argos, Tripolis and then Kalamata. If he had to remember anything from Greece it would have to have been the variety of amazing food he'd sampled.

To mix it up a bit Thomas took a boat from Greece to Catania, Italy. Three weeks flew by before Thomas finally ended up in Venice. Along the way he had experienced such places as Naples, Rome, Florence, Pisa and Bologna. But once he arrived in Venice Thomas was taken aback at the pure elegance the city had to offer. The Grand Canal that ran through Venice was breathtaking. St. Mark's Square was spectacular and it was there that Thomas negotiated a Gondola ride through countless back alleyways. He wandered that city for days, getting lost at times but never worrying about it.

From Venice Thomas took a train to Milan. After he explored that city he took the train north to Como and then across the Switzerland border to Lugano. The next day he arrived at Berne and spent a few days there before he headed off to Zurich. Before long Thomas decided to keep heading north, and his first stop was Frankfurt, Germany. He was pleasantly surprised to find the local Germans hospitable and friendly. The beer and sausage were out of this world and even though he didn't want to leave he knew his trip had to continue. Cologne, Dusseldorf, Bremen and Hamburg were his next stops before he landed in Copenhagen, Denmark.

His plane landed in Chennai, India and Thomas slowly made his way up the coast until he got on another plane in Kolkata that was headed to Manila in the Philippines. After five days there he jumped on another flight that took him to Bangkok, Thailand. He made a quick stop in South Korea before he arrived in Nagasaki, Japan. He had no idea how much the Japanese culture would affect him and it was another three weeks before he arrived in Tokyo.

A week later he headed to Brisbane, Australia where he inched his way down the coast to Newcastle, Sydney and finally Melbourne. A month later he made his way to

Invercargill, New Zealand and began the trip north through Christchurch, Wellington and eventually Auckland.

It'd been nine months since he'd left for London and it was time to head back to Los Angeles with multiple journals filled with his adventures. His amazing journey had only touched on the opportunities that each culture had to offer. He was saddened to stop traveling but happy to be home at the same time.

* * *

Thomas had negotiated to continue renting the rental home he'd been in, for the past four years while he traveled, to the delight of the owners who easily agreed to watch it while he was away.

A few weeks after he arrived back in town Thomas knew he needed someplace to call his own and decided to rent something in Venice Beach. It didn't take him long to move and get settled in. It was as that point when Thomas began to re-read his journals and imagined himself in other countries once again.

Before he knew it Thomas began to write his first book.

26
Thursday March 26, 1981

"The line has been secured sir."

"Good. So the conference call is ready?"

"Yes sir. They're waiting for you."

"Very well."

The man known as Raven picked up the secured phone. "Gentlemen, this is Raven. I'll get right to the point with our quarterly update. With your help our shipments continue to arrive from Vietnam and South America unhindered, for the most part. We've had a few setbacks but have learned from those mistakes. Our profits are soaring due to our increased collaboration with various distribution centers. I have more feelers out to expand those options. Also, if I may, I wanted to bring to your attention a new opportunity that has come to light."

"Proceed with your report Raven," the man known as Wolf ordered.

"Yes sir. The Soviets are sparring with the Afghanistan rebels. A large contingency of Soviet forces are already on the ground there. If we play our cards right we'll have the chance to offer military support, covertly of course, in the form of training and weapons. Part of the deal could be to negotiate heroin and opium in return. I don't have to tell the board that expanding into that market would potentially raise our profit margin by forty percent."

"That's a large number," the man known as Bear said. "What are the risks associated with this endeavor?"

"There will always be risks sir," replied Raven. "However, those can be minimalized with the correct personnel and procedures. This heroin venture will not commence until the proper foundation has been put in place."

"Timeline?" Wolf asked.

"Eight to twelve months," Raven replied. "It's better we move slowly on this to ensure all contingencies have been accounted for, not to mention we avoid any scrutiny by planning this correctly."

"Agreed," said Wolf. "You'll let me know what the CIA can do when the time comes."

"Yes sir."

"I concur," added Serpent. "I like what I'm hearing."

"Good," said Bear. "Now Raven, our organization is concerned about loose ends, just as you should be. If the government found out that drugs and weapons were being pipelined in and out of the United States, using CIA, military assets and personnel, the reaction would be far from favorable. Don't you agree?"

"I do," said Raven.

"In the past we've seen you take care of the loose ends swiftly and without mercy. However, in our eyes, you have an old topic that you have yet to rectify, and that troubles us."

"I don't understand. What are you referring to?"

Wolf spoke up. "Our records indicate that Sam Paige and Bill Nicholson were the ones that originally filed the complaint stating they'd been approached to steal and sell weapons. Our records also indicate that a fellow Ranger of theirs, a Dennis Carter, was the man who had made that approach. He was found dead in the stockade, as per your report to us indicated.

As I represent the CIA aspect of this endeavor I must insist that these two loose ends should be tied up."

Raven sighed. "Gentlemen, If I thought those two would be a problem I would have had them nullified years ago. They've been out of the picture for a long time. Nothing's become of it."

"I disagree," replied Bear. "I'm privy to what those two have been involved in. Let me assure you they were onsite two years ago, in a South America op, when that drug camp was blown to hell. Our friend Carlos wasn't too happy with that outcome."

"That was them?" Raven asked.

"It was, and we want you to handle it."

Raven paused. "How do you weigh in on this topic Serpent?"

"Terminate them. No loose ends," Serpent replied.

"Fine," Raven conceded. "I have an inside man within the Spec Ops community. I'll look into what I can do to silence them. I still believe you're all overreacting."

"Just get it done son."

"Yes, sir."

27
Wednesday August 5, 1981

In December, 1978, the Afghan government secured a treaty with the Soviet Union. That treaty allowed them to request assistance as needed from the Soviets. As it turned out the Afghan government, having difficulties with the Mujahideen rebels, requested the USSR to send troops on April 14, 1979. On June 16 the Soviet government sent a number of tanks and men to guard the Afghan government in Kabul and secure the surrounding airports.

On December 27, 1979, seven hundred Soviet troops, dressed in Afghan uniforms, successfully occupied major governmental locations, including media and military buildings in Kabul, as well as the Presidential Palace. The current president was killed and the Soviet Politburo announced over the radio that they were merely complying with the 1978 Treaty of Friendship, Cooperation and Good Neighborliness. Immediately Soviet ground forces entered Afghanistan from the north while additional airborne divisions landed at the airports and deployed troops. By the second week a total of 1,800 tanks and 80,000 troops had occupied the area.

The UN General Assembly passed a resolution that protested the Soviet intervention by a vote of 104-18. As the Soviet troops continued to occupy Afghanistan the Mujahideen rebels fought back. Bloody battles were fought as the Soviets used airborne and ground attacks to destroy the villages, livestock and crops to intimidate the rebels. Attack helicopters, known as the Hind, or flying tank, were used extensively in the use of brute force against the guerillas. It wasn't long before the United States, and other countries, began to supply the anti-Soviet rebels with training and weaponry.

President Ronald Reagan granted the CIA cart blanch towards dislodging the Soviets from Afghanistan. Weapons, mostly AK-47's were continuously brought into the country and distributed to the rebels. It wasn't long before the CIA advisors recommended that arduous training would help to balance the staggering losses the rebels continued to incur. With that mindset groups of elite soldiers were sent to various camps to train the Mujahideen in small arms, tactics and ambush techniques.

* * *

Three helicopters that contained Sam, Bill and ten other Spec Ops team members touched down at a rebel village located in the Panjshir Valley, just ninety three miles north of Kabul. They quickly removed the three crates, and their personal equipment, and then watched as the helicopters reversed direction and flew back through the valley. A few men from the village approached the group.

"Salaam," said one of the men. "My name is Hamid Emal Habibi."

"Salaam," Sam replied as he extended his hand. "Sam Sergeant Paige but you can call me Sam. And this is my second in command, Sergeant Nicholson. Pleased to meet you."

"Bill."

"And we as well," Hamid responded as he shook Sam and Bill's hands. "We welcome you to our village. I will be your translator."

Sam nodded. "If you don't mind me saying so Hamid, you speak English very well."

"I went to school in the states. My father wanted me to have an education and do something useful with my life."

"He sounds like a wise man. Can we meet him?"

Hamid shook his head and his eyes grew sorrowful. "He was killed in a Soviet raid six months ago. It was then that I vowed revenge." Hamid changed subjects. "But that's not your concern. Please, let me introduce you and your men to my elders. After that I'll show you where you'll be sleeping." Hamid looked over Sam's shoulder. "Do those crates contain the weapons?"

"They do."

Hamid signaled and more men appeared. "We'll store them."

Sam shook his head. "Let's take things one step at a time. Introductions first. We'll get to the weapons, and how to use them, in due course."

Hamid waved off the men. "Very well. My apologies for my presumptuousness."

Sam smiled. "Hamid, I think we're going to get along just fine."

Sam and Bill followed behind Hamid towards the main building on the mountainside while the rest of his team picked up the three crates.

* * *

Three weeks later Sam and Bill watched as the rebels practiced various maneuvers. Cover fire, suppression, movement and leap frogging tactics were just a few of the basics the twelve man team had instilled upon the mountain men. At first Sam and his team had been treated with an air of apprehension, mostly due to the language barrier. But as training began both parties soon realized the respect they had for each other. It became very apparent that the poorly equipped Mujahideen rebels, now armed with AK-47's, had a tremendous amount of fight in them. They relentlessly followed Sam's training, running the exercises over and over to weed out imperfections and mistakes. It wasn't long before the rebels overcame their hesitations about the American soldiers and viewed them as fellow warriors.

* * *

Sam, Bill and some others sat around the evening fire. They'd been here six weeks and the rebels had become very competent.

"The men have come a long way," Hamid said.

Sam nodded. "I agree. When does the next group arrive to begin training?"

"Word travels fast here in the mountain country my friend. Those men will arrive as soon as the next shipment of weapons becomes available. Men cannot train without those weapons, no?"

"You certainly have an eloquent way with words Hamid," Sam said. "Wars are not won on talking alone, are they?"

212

"No, they are not," Hamid agreed. "This is our home and we will fight to keep it. Would you not do the same back in America?"

"In a heartbeat," Bill replied.

"Then, and I mean no offense, but may I be so bold as to ask when the next shipment will be delivered?"

"I'll ask during my next communications window," Sam assured him.

"Thank you Sam, for you and your countries support."

"Your father would be proud of the stand you're taking Hamid."

"Perhaps. Perhaps not. My people, on the other hand, hopefully do."

Sam's radio crackled to life. "I've got an airborne contact, south side of the village! Closing fast!"

The Soviet Mi-24 Hind crested the southern ridge at an alarming speed. Its quad gun pods, that hung under its extended wings opened fire scattering men, woman and children in all directions. Sam's men barely had time to engage the threat as a multitude of bullets stitched and chewed up the ground throughout the village during its first pass. The Hind, having passed over the village, could be seen making its turn in the dim evening light.

"Move and get to cover!" Sam cried out. "It's coming back for another pass!"

The immense Soviet death machine finalized its turn and screamed back towards the village. Sporadic AK-47 fire penetrated the night, fired by some of the rebels. Sam and Bill took cover behind a stone wall, while other members of his team fanned out and had found similar locations. The Hind's dual rocket pods opened up and a multitude of ordinance and explosions ripped through the village. Screams emanated from a variety of locations as the Hind finished its second run, its gun pods blazing.

"Target the rear compartment once it flies by!" Bill yelled.

A dozen bodies were strewn throughout the village as the Hind roared overhead leaving a swath of destruction in its wake. As it flew past a sustained barrage of concentrated small arms fire lit up the Hind. Even though the Hind was heavily armored, a trail of smoke suddenly burst forth from the tail rudder. The Hind lurched to one side and immediately disengaged from the fight. Sam, Bill and Hamid watched it disappear down the valley in the distance.

"Fucking hell," Bill exclaimed. "I've never seen one of those in action before. Goddamn!"

Sam turned to Hamid. "Check on your people and I'll check on mine. That damn thing may be coming back."

Five minutes later the ugly reality of war became all too apparent. The quick and decisive Soviet attack had taken the lives of fourteen of Hamid's people, which included three women and two children. The other unfortunate casualty was that two of Sam's men, Lloyd Franklin and Kit Jones, had been killed in the rocket strike. They had died believing in what they were doing but that would never sit well with Sam. Their lives had meant something and their deaths had been completely senseless. It was also the first time Sam had lost men under his command and he didn't like how helpless it made him feel.

28
Friday October 9, 1981

Thomas leaned back in his chair, after he removed the last page from the typewriter, and placed it with the rest of his book. Since he'd been back from his travels he'd continued to work on his newest creation. At first he didn't know what he was writing about but as he kept at it the story, and its characters, revealed themselves more and more. At the end of a month's worth of effort Thomas had figured it out and the final result pleased him to no end.

The book he'd just written was called *The Sandbox*. Initially Thomas thought the storyline was going to take a more serious tone, but after a month of manipulating words and ideas he knew the direction his book needed to take. He thought he wanted to write fiction novels, and it turned out he did, but the stories and ideas he had in his head made more sense as adventures to children. That transformation surprised Thomas and set the stage for his future endeavors. He was going to be a children's book writer and he thoroughly loved and embraced the idea.

* * *

It took Thomas two months to nail down an interview with a local publishing company and Christmas was just a few weeks away. Thomas drove to the company, located in downtown Los Angeles, and waited nervously in the lobby's waiting area. He clutched a copy of *The Sandbox* in his hands and took in everything around him.

What am I doing here? They're never going to go for this. What was I thinking? Maybe I should just get up and get out of here before it's too late?

"Mr. Clark?"

Thomas was startled. He hadn't seen the man with ginger red hair approach.

"Yes?" Thomas replied as he stood up.

"My name is Nick Raynes," he said as he extended his right hand.

Thomas shook it. "Thomas. Thomas Clark."

"Nice to meet you Mr. Clark, I…"

"Please, just call me Thomas. Mr. Clark sounds too impersonal."

Nick smiled. "Would you mind walking with me to my office Thomas?"

"Lead the way Nick."

As they headed to his office Nick continued to make small talk. "So, have you always lived in the LA area?"

"Actually no. I moved down here from the San Francisco area back in seventy five for college."

"Oh yeah? Which one did you attend?"

"USC."

"No shit. Sorry, excuse my language but that's my college as well. Small world."

"Small world indeed."

Nick entered his office and sat down behind his desk. Thomas took one of the two guest chairs. He was still nervous, but not nearly as much as he had been before.

"Listen Thomas. Do you mind if I get right to the point?"

216

Oh shit. He's going to kick me out of here faster than it took to walk to his office. "Please," Thomas said as he cringed internally.

"Excellent." Nick leaned forward. "So here's the deal with your manuscript. We love it and we want to publish it. What do you say?"

Wait. What? "I'm sorry. Did you just say you wanted to publish it?"

Nick nodded. "Is there a problem I should be aware of?"

"No...um...no. I was just expecting, quite honestly, to be tossed out of here."

Nick chuckled and Thomas joined in.

"Listen Thomas. You have what it takes. Your story and its message are solid. We'll need to have it illustrated, of course, but that's all part of the negotiation. The real question is, do you want your book to be held in the hands of children?"

Thomas nodded. "I do. That'd be a dream come true."

"Good, because so do we. What do you say to a handshake agreement before the official one is drawn up?" Nick stood up and extended his right hand.

Thomas smiled, stood up and shook his new friend's hand.

"I see a bright future ahead of us Thomas."

* * *

"That's great news honey," said Claire. "Congratulations. I'm so happy for you."

"Thanks grandma. It still doesn't feel real."

"Give it time dear. Everything just takes time. Speaking of time, are you coming up for Christmas?"

"I can't believe you two are actually going to be in town this year," Thomas kidded.

"Very funny sweetie. Your grandfather and I have more trips planned but every once in a while we have to slow down and rest; recharge the batteries."

"Is that what grandpa's doing now?"

"As a matter of fact I can practically hear his snoring from the other room. He's going to be delighted to hear about your success."

"Well give him my best."

"I will. But back to Christmas. Are you planning on visiting?"

"I think I'm actually going to stay in town this year."

"I understand. Let me know if you change your mind."

"Will do grandma."

"Take care Thomas and once again, congratulations."

* * *

To celebrate his recent success Thomas decided to try something he'd never done before. He drove east on the 210 to San Bernardino. When he hit the Highlands he got on the 330 which took him up in the San Bernardino Mountains. 330 ended in a small town called Running Springs. From there he continued east on 18 headed towards Big Bear.

Thomas had never skied before and had booked a room at the Snow Summit Mountain Resort. For the next three days he had the time of his life. He started off with ski lessons and by the end of the day had mastered the basics. The second day he kept to the beginner slopes and tried a couple of the intermediate runs as he bolstered his confidence. By the third

218

day, bruised and sore from multiple falls, he remained on the expert runs that made his stomach sink but made his adrenaline soar.

Not wanting to head back to his rental in Venice Beach just yet, Thomas decided to explore more of the mountain. He already knew that Big Bear Lake was gorgeous but it was a resort and tourist destination. He headed back west on 18, past Running Springs and followed the signs to Lake Arrowhead. Thomas parked in what could be considered the village downtown and walked around. He immediately discovered that the views of the water were breathtaking.

Everything looked new and Thomas, after reading a few signs, understood why. During 1979 the Lake Arrowhead Village had burnt to the ground. A major renovation took place and the grand opening had occurred earlier in the year. As Thomas continued to explore he realized he really enjoyed the small time atmosphere Lake Arrowhead provided. *I could see myself living here.*

After eating lunch Thomas headed back to his car when he saw another building, nearly completed, that stood just off the water. He walked over and read the information sign.

COMING SOON

BELGIAN WAFFLE WORKS

Featuring Delicious Specialty Waffles

I could also see myself eating breakfast while looking out over the lake. What an amazing and tranquil view.

Thomas drove back east to Running Springs and stopped off to get some gas.

"Can I help you?" an elderly man asked.

"Yes sir. Filler up please."

"You sure are polite for someone your age," the man said as he worked the fuel pump.

"Thank you. So what's it like living here?"

The man removed his cap and scratched his balding head. "It's mostly quiet. We get a lot of traffic that's either headed off to Lake Arrowhead or Big Bear this time of year of course. Other than that it's just a pretty part of the world."

"Is this all of downtown?"

The man chuckled. "Yeah, what you see is what you get. Just a market, bike shop, gas station, rental shops, the post office and that's about all she wrote. Like I said, quiet."

* * *

By the end of February Thomas had found, purchased and moved in to a house in Running Springs. He had decided not to buy in either Lake Arrowhead or Big Bear but rather stay in between in the quiet town of Running Springs. And it wasn't long, after he got settled, that he began to work on his next book.

Thomas knew he was isolating himself up in the mountains, but he didn't mind terribly. He was used to being by himself. He hadn't been able to talk to his friends Sam and Bill in what seemed like forever. Their birthdays had both come and gone during the past October and November and Thomas didn't have a number or an address to wish them each a happy birthday.

I'm better off up here by myself. I can concentrate on my work, ride my bike, go to the Waffle House and ski. It'll be perfect.

220

29
Saturday April 3, 1982

After the Soviet Hind attack on the village in Panjshir Valley, and the subsequent deaths of fellow team members Kit Jones and Lloyd Franklin, Sam's Spec Ops team had immediately uprooted and migrated to another location. The bodies of their fellow soldiers had been flown back to the U.S. while the bodies of the Mujahideen villagers were buried in their traditional ceremony.

Since then Sam and Bill had continued to supply and train the rebels in various locations throughout the valley. If anything, they had a newfound respect for the Afghans and how they managed to live in such bleak surroundings. Food and medical aid wasn't always available. War was the only constant thing they knew and the Soviets were just the latest invaders they had vowed to push out of their land and homes.

The team had been in Afghanistan for nine months and even though they believed in the cause the job was getting old.

* * *

Sam got off the radio and headed back to his men, who were sharing a meal with the rebels, with a sorrowed look on his face.

Bill picked up on it immediately. "What's up?"

"Nothing."

"That's bullshit bro. Talk to me."

Sam spoke up to the group. "We're pulling out in five days and heading back to the states. We'll be relieved by another team. Our tour here in the sand is over."

The rest of the men responded well to the news but Bill didn't buy it. He pulled his friend aside.

"What the hell is up with you? Talk to me."

Sam finally relented. "Dude, my dad died."

"What? Your real father?"

"He's gone."

"How? I don't understand?"

"I don't know anything other than that. They're granting us all leave when we get back and I have a funeral to get to."

Bill put his hand on Sam's shoulder. "Then I'm going with you."

30
Friday April 16, 1982

Sam and Bill walked through the doors of the Walnut Creek, California funeral home looking sharp and professional in their dress blues. They stopped, removed their covers, and then with Sam in the lead they made their way towards his mother and stepfather. Sam's mother saw her son coming and tears began to fall from her eyes. She embraced Sam fiercely.

"Hi mom."

"Where have you been all these years? You just upped and disappeared on all of us. It was so unfair. I'm terribly upset with you."

Sam pulled his mother away. "Today isn't about you. What the hell happened to dad?"

"It was a heart attack," said Jacob, his stepfather. "You should have been there for him."

Sam bristled and Bill stepped in between them quickly.

Bill kept his voice low but firm. "Are you fucking stupid Jacob? Who the hell do you think you are? When my friend's father passed away we were out of the country."

"That sounds like an excuse."

"Why I outta…"

Sam placed his hand on Bill's shoulder. "I've got this."

Everyone in the funeral home watched as Bill moved back and Sam stepped in.

"I don't want you two fighting," Sam's mother insisted.

"Oh, I'm not planning on it. I'm just going to inform the two of you of what my reality happens to consist of."

"We're not interested," Jacob replied.

"Why would you say that Jacob?" Janet asked her husband. "What's gotten in to you?"

"It's okay Mom," Sam said, "but you need to hear this."

His mother and stepdad just stood there while the rest of the room looked on.

Sam continued. "What either of you think doesn't mean a damn thing to me. You have no influence or power over me whatsoever. With that said you probably are wondering where I've been for the past nearly seven years."

"Come on brother, don't..." Bill started before he was interrupted.

"I've been all over the world, killing people so you can feel safe in your bed's at night."

Sam's mother nearly fainted while his stepfather's eyes noticeably widened.

"So all I ask from the two of you is a little goddamn respect. I'm here today for my father, not to deal with the shit either of you want to place at my feet. Do you understand me?"

Sam's imposing tone, confidence and hardened body instantly squelched his parent's wills. He gave them one final look before he left them and made his way to his father's casket. Everyone politely and quickly scooted out of his way. Sam looked down at his father.

I'm sorry pop. I should have been here for you. I angrily pushed everyone away when you didn't approve of my choice to join the military. I should have reached out but I didn't. I just hope at some point you might have been proud of what I've done. I guess I'll never know. Goodbye pop. I'll miss you and I love you.

After the wake later that evening, Sam and Bill headed to a bar in downtown Walnut Creek. They needed a drink and they still needed to decide what they were going to do during their two week leave. They were still wearing their dress uniforms, as they made their way to the bar to sit down, and they noticed quite a few people staring at them.

The bartender approached. "What'll it be?"

"Whatever you have on draft," responded Bill.

"You got it. First round's on the house."

"Thank you," Bill barely managed to say before the bartender walked away. He turned to Sam. "You good?"

"Yeah, I suppose. Parents, right? You can't choose'em and you can't kill'em."

Bill chuckled. "Well, I think you had everybody convinced otherwise I'm sure. Way to lay down the heaviest hammer ever on them brother."

The bartender returned and dropped off the beers. Sam and Bill each grabbed one.

Bill raised his glass. "To parents."

"To parents," Sam responded with a grin.

They both drank a good portion of their beer and then set their glasses back down.

"So speaking of parents," Sam began to say, "I was surprised to see yours weren't there."

"I know. I thought for sure they'd be there."

"Are you going to visit them while we're in town?"

"Probably. Although if your reunion is any indication of what I'll experience, then I'm not so sure."

"I don't blame you. My parent's drive me nuts."

Bill picked his glass back up. "To your dad."

Sam did the same. "To my pop."

They finished off their beers and before they could order another round two more were dropped off.

"Can we start a tab?" Bill asked.

"You can after the next round."

"What do you mean?"

"These came with compliments of the table behind you."

As the bartender headed off again Sam and Bill swiveled in their seats to thank whoever sent them the drinks. To their surprise two gorgeous brown eyed and brown haired women stared back at them. The two women giggled, smiled and motioned them over to their table.

"What'ya think?" Bill asked.

"I think I'll take the one on the left."

They picked up their beers and made their way to the table.

"My name is Bill and this is my friend Sam. Very nice to meet both of you."

"Ladies," Sam began, "thank you for the drinks."

"Oh, it's our pleasure," said one of them.

The other said, "Won't you sit down and join us?"

Sam and Bill did just that.

"I'm Julie," said the one that sat next to Sam, "and this is Kim," who was now beside Bill.

"So you're both soldiers," Kim observed.

"It's funny," Bill replied with a quip, "not everyone gets that from these subtle uniforms."

Kim giggled.

"Your friend's funny," Julie said to Sam. "What brings you out tonight?"

"Well, it's a bit of a conversation killer, but I buried my father today."

"Oh, I'm so sorry."

"Me too," Kim said genuinely. "At least you met us this evening and we can try to cheer you up."

"We're definitely off to a good start," Sam said with a grin.

* * *

Three hours later, and an untold number of drinks later, the four of them were still engaged in conversation.

"So Sam and I grew up in the area. What about you two? How'd you become friends?"

The ladies giggled before Kim answered. "Well, the truth of it is, we're actually sisters. Surprise."

"No shit?" Sam asked. "I didn't see that coming."

"No shit," Julie said. "And we're from Ohio. But that's not the biggest secret we have."

"Shhhh, don't tell them," Kim insisted with a huge smile on her face.

"What? What's the secret?" Bill asked.

"Okay fine," Julie said as she put up her hands in mock defeat. "You forced it out of me. My sister and I love men in uniform. When you both walked in we couldn't help but get your attention."

"How absolutely horrible for us," Sam kidded.

"Indeed," Bill added. "Terrible."

* * *

As the bar closed the four of them had already switched to coffee. On the sidewalk both Bill and Kim, along with Sam and Julie, shared their first kiss. For the next two weeks they saw a lot more of each other and by the end of those two weeks they had officially began to date.

31
Saturday May 15, 1982

"I'm excited to see what you have for me today," Nick said.

Thomas smiled. "I hope you like it," he said as he handed over his latest work.

"Well Thomas, if it's anything like your first book then I can't wait."

Nick opened the binder and read the title. *The World to Tom.* He looked up at this new friend and client. "What's it all about?"

"I don't want to spoil it for you. Give it a read and then we can talk about it."

"Before I start I wanted to ask how you're enjoying your new home in Running Springs."

"It's been great. I still need to make a run up to my grandparent's house and retrieve my things, but aside from that it's just what I need. It's quiet, secluded and since the snow's gone I've been riding my new bike around the mountain quite a bit."

"I'll have to come up and visit sometime."

"You should. There's this great waffle house that sits right on Lake Arrowhead. Its views will blow you away."

32
Wednesday June 4, 1982

"I see that your projections were right on the money," praised Bear.

"Yes," Wolf, the CIA side of the operation added. "The heroin pipeline has significantly boosted our revenue. Good job Raven."

"Gentlemen, thank you, but it's a group effort. Without your backend support this endeavor would never have been this successful."

"Keep up the good work Raven and we'll all retire to a tropical paradise," said Serpent.

"You could very well do that right now sir," Raven hinted.

Wolf and Bear laughed. "True, but why should we stop now? More has always been the backbone of American life."

33
Friday March 4, 1983

"It's hard to believe it's been almost eight years," Bill said as he and Sam drank a beer and reminisced about their time in the military.

Sam nodded as he took a swig. "Eight years seemed like an eternity way back when. But shit, look how fast the time flew."

"Yeah, but not at first, that's for sure. The endless amounts of grueling training we had to endure."

"More like suffer." Sam smiled. "Hell, if it wasn't for me your sorry ass would never had made it through."

Bill chuckled. "You can tell the story any way you'd like, but we both know I was the one who pulled your ass out of the fire more than I can remember."

"Oh, it's going to be like that is it?"

Bill raised his beer for a toast. "Brothers for life. We look out for each other."

Sam echoed, "Brothers for life," and they both drank.

They were quiet for a minute before Bill spoke up again.

"So, speaking of eight years, did you get your re-up notice too?"

"That I did."

"Thoughts?"

"I have mixed feelings actually," Sam replied.

"What do you mean?"

"Don't get me wrong, I love the Army and I think we're incredibly fortunate to be part of the Special Ops community."

"But...?"

"But," as Sam lowered his voice, "wouldn't you rather call the shots rather than be told what to do and where to do it?"

Bill thought about it and then nodded. "Ideally, yes. But we're involved in Spec Ops. We deploy where the powers that be need us."

"Exactly my point. We may be on the cutting edge, ready to take the fight to wherever it needs to be taken, but the reality is that we're just tools for someone else to use. Yes, we enjoy our work and put everything we have into the missions, but ultimately we're pawns in a much larger game."

"Jesus Christ bro, that's a lot to tear off and chew."

"Okay Bill, how about this. Did you enjoy our nine month training regimen in Afghanistan?"

"It served its purpose and we trained those rebels well."

"You didn't answer my question. Did you enjoy being sent out there for nine months without even being asked if you wanted to go?"

"But that's our job. We go where they want us to go."

Sam sighed, took another sip and just stared at Bill.

"Fine," Bill said as he relented. "No, I didn't enjoy it. Yes, it was one hell of an experience, but it felt like we had been taken out of the action and stuffed someplace far away." He paused. "What's the point you're trying to make here?"

"I've been thinking that instead of re-upping we go into business for ourselves."

"What, like mercenaries or something?"

"No no no. Nothing like that. I'm talking about a business venture. Think about this. What if we started a company? People in need would come to us for protection needs. We would decide what we wanted to get involved in. We would decide how to do things the right way. We would keep people out of harm's way, and we would be the ones calling the shots rather than being the ones taken the orders."

"A business?"

"Yes."

"You and I?"

"Of course."

"Are you kidding me? I don't know shit about running a business and neither do you."

"That doesn't mean we can't learn," Sam pressed. "Listen, we have six months left but we have to put our papers in much sooner than that. What'ya say?"

"I don't know brother. This is so out of left field. How long have you been thinking about this?"

"A couple of weeks now."

"And you thought about finally telling me about it now?"

"I'm just running it past you." Sam took another swig. "Listen brother, I could see us taking our military career to great heights, but we're always going to be limited by someone above us deciding if we're good enough to move up the ranks. We joined the Army to get away from our parents, to make a point that we won't be told what to do. Well the joke's on us. We're told what to do every day and I'm not thrilled that I just figured that out."

Bill made a face. "Alright, I'll give you that point."

"So instead of living our lives by someone else's rules we could live them by our own ideals."

Bill began to slowly nod his head.

"No more hidden agendas. No more bullshit egos. It'd just the two of us running the show.

"And what did you say we'd be doing again?"

"I've been brainstorming that and currently I'm thinking that we'd run a protection service."

"Nice. So we'd be shaking local businesses down for payouts," Bill joked.

"Ha ha. I'm still working out the details but obviously I need your input on this."

"It's a lot to take in, but you have a way with words my friend. Now, on a totally different topic, we should talk about Julie and Kim."

"Okay. What's on your mind?"

"We've been dating them for just about a year now."

"Your point?"

"Nothing, except for the fact that I really like Kim. And quite frankly I don't see her becoming a military wife, if things with her went that far. The short time we've spent with them, on our time off, has been amazing."

Sam nodded. "Yes it has, and I miss that."

"Well, look at us. A couple of mid-twenties bastards that just got all mushy. I guess what I'm saying, and maybe it's not off topic as I thought, is that I miss them."

"Yeah, me too."

"Maybe your business idea isn't that far off the mark as I thought. We would start it up on our own and become our own bosses. The sisters wouldn't be able to resist having us around all the time, now would they?"

"We can only hope. I'm glad you're contemplating the idea now brother. I was worried you wouldn't see the merit in it."

"It took a moment for me to catch on. But you know how we are, we're brothers for life."

"Brothers for life."

"I have an idea. Let's give them a call."

Sam drained his beer. "That's a great idea."

* * *

Julie hung up the phone after her fifteen minute
conversation with Sam. Kim had gone first and couldn't get
the smile off her face after talking with Bill. Julie joined her
on the couch in the apartment they shared in Walnut Creek.

"What are you grinning at?" Julie said to needle her sister.

"Oh please, like you didn't thoroughly enjoy your talk
with Sam either."

"I just wish we saw them more often."

"Me too. I miss Bill more than I want to admit and it
sucks that we never know where they are or what they're
doing. All they've ever told us is that they're in the Army and
can get deployed at any time. But that doesn't make a lot of
sense. We're not even at war with anyone."

"It bothers me as well," responded Julie. "What worries
me the most is not knowing where they are or if they're in
danger."

Kim nodded. "That's it exactly. I mean, don't get me
wrong, the times we've spent together have been wonderful.
Is it selfish of me to want more?"

"No. We both want more. I just don't know what to do."

"I...I need to tell you something. I think I'm falling for
Bill big time sis."

Julie smiled. "And here I thought you were going to tell
me something I didn't already know."

"Bitch!" Kim laughed and threw a couch pillow at her sister. "And don't think I didn't notice how you get when you're in Sam's arms either. You have no secrets from me."

Julie tossed the pillow back. "Okay okay. So it officially sucks that we've fallen for these two soldiers."

"And how. I guess we'll have to give it some more time and see if anything changes for the better."

"I like that. Now, it's Friday night and although we're not single it doesn't mean we can't go out and have some fun. Do you want to go dancing or check out a movie?"

"We're not tied down yet," said Kim as she smiled. "Who says we can't do both?"

34
Sunday September 11, 1983

"They didn't seem terribly happy with our decision."

"No, I don't believe they were," Sam replied.

"Do you think we made the right decision?"

"Only time will tell. But we have to believe in what we're pursuing."

"It's not that. If anything these past six months have really solidified my need to get our company up and off the ground. It's just a knee jerk reaction to saying goodbye to all the guys we know. That was harder than I thought it was going to be."

"Yes," Sam agreed. "That was difficult."

Sam and Bill had just boarded a flight that was headed to San Francisco. The commander of their Spec Ops group had personally asked them to reconsider their decision to leave. He repeatedly told Sam and Bill what valuable members they were and the contributions to the community had been top notch. Although his words meant the world, both of them remained unswayed and signed the final release papers.

The commander picked up the phone and ordered all present Spec Op operators to immediately gather. He personally walked Sam and Bill outside where they faced the men they had served with. A large single line had been formed and the two men, now ex-military, said goodbye to each man they called brother. Their walk down the line had not been an easy exit.

* * *

239

"Sir, have you heard the news about Sam Paige and Bill Nicholson?"

The man known as Raven lowered his Sunday newspaper. "Tell me."

"They're officially out. They signed their exit papers and are on a plane headed to the west coast."

"That's interesting. I wonder why they decided not to re-up. Leaving the Spec Ops community isn't something a soldier just walks away from; it's very unusual. Continue to keep tabs on them."

"Yes sir."

* * *

The following Saturday Sam and Bill hosted a BBQ in their backyard. It had been a whirlwind week. After arriving back in town they had literally surprised the hell out of their girlfriends when they knocked on their apartment door, and both Julie and Kim squealed in joy when they opened it. An hour later, after the two couples came back up for air, Sam and Bill told them all about leaving the Army and that they were going to start a business. They two women couldn't have been more thrilled and immediately were onboard with the idea.

Sam and Bill had socked away a good deal of money over the past eight years, having really only spent it on buying drinks during their down time. They quickly rented a house in Walnut Creek, close to Julie and Kim, and soon after began to make the dreaded phone calls, to their parents, to invite them to their barbeque that weekend. Sam and Bill offered to fly out Julie and Kim's folks from Ohio as well, not only so they could meet them for the first time, but in hopes to quell any parental infighting that historically was destined to occur. They knew it was going to be a long afternoon.

"Hi mom," Sam said as he hugged her, "I'm glad you could make it."

"Well, it's not every day that you get a call from your son letting you know that he's back in town. What's this all about anyway? And whose house is this?"

"All in good time. Please come in."

Janet walked inside and Jacob, his stepfather was right behind her.

"Jacob," Sam said as he extended his hand. "I'm glad you could make it."

Jacob paused as a puzzled look washed over his face and then vanished. He shook Sam's hand. "Your call was unusual. How are you?"

"Not bad actually. Why don't you come in and join the fun already in progress."

Jacob walked in and joined the group. Bill's parents had already arrived and the atmosphere was already tenuous. Bill's mother Louise and stepfather Reggie had been the first to show up, closely followed by Bill's father Stuart and his new wife Michelle, who appeared to be at least ten years younger. Louise hadn't wasted any time and had begun to berate Stuart openly.

"So, is this the tramp you cheated on me with while we were together? I can't believe you brought her here. How much more despicable can you become?"

"It's always a pleasure to see you too Louise," Stuart replied. "And of course you as well Reggie. I always enjoy being around the man that couldn't have children of his own so he decided to raise my son instead."

241

"How dare you," Reggie retorted.

"And we all know how well that turned out now don't we," Stuart continued. "My son couldn't wait to get out of your house. It was my house but I lost that right during the divorce, isn't that right Louise?"

"Go to hell. You're no saint so stop preaching like you were the victim. That rhetoric has gotten old and tiring over the years. Grow up already."

Sam and Bill had stood off to the side and watched the fireworks begin.

"You sure you don't have a grenade I can't borrow?" Bill whispered to Sam.

"To borrow? How would you give it back once it's been used?"

"Good point."

"Besides, even if I did have one I wouldn't give it to you until my parent's arrived."

"My apologies. I can't wait for them all to get together. This is going to be the best day ever."

Ding dong.

"Oh good," Sam said, "speak of the devils. Oh, and the grenade is in my top drawer under my socks." Sam headed to the front door, greeted his parents and invited them in.

"Everyone," Sam's voice boomed. The bickering came to an immediate halt. "You remember my mother Janet and my stepfather Jacob."

The normal handshakes and 'how-do-you-do's' were exchanged. Sam took drink requests and before long everyone had a stiff drink firmly in their grasp hoping like hell it would help them forget this day ever happened. Bill, in the meantime, brought out some appetizers and then lit the coals on the grill. Sam and Bill were elite soldiers and had faced and overcome many perilous encounters; but they both knew without question, that family always created the most volatile situations that could never be won.

Ding dong

Oh thank God. Sam and Bill headed to the front door and gladly opened it this time. Julie and Kim couldn't help but to kiss and hug their men. They then turned around and introduced Sam and Bill to their parents, Mary and Eric Roads.

"Sir, it's a pleasure to meet you," Sam said as he shook Eric's hand.

"An honor sir," Bill added as he took his turn.

"So polite these two," said Mary as she looked her daughters. "And I can see why both of you talk so highly of them. I mean, check out their muscles alone."

"Mom!" Julie and Kim said in unison, a little embarrassed.

Sam and Bill smiled at their girlfriend's discomfort. They knew right away they were going to get along just fine. Mary gave Sam and Bill each a hug and then winked at her daughters who only rolled their eyes.

"Please come in," Sam said.

"Yes, and join the chaos we call family," Bill said under his breath.

The six of them came inside and Bill closed the door. *Here we go.* He rejoined Sam as all eyes became focused on the two of them and the four strangers that stood behind them.

Sam spoke up. "Everyone, I'd like to introduce our girlfriends, Julie and Kim, as well as their parents that flew in from Ohio today, Mary and Eric Roads."

"Girlfriends?" Janet and Louise asked at the same time as they stood up.

"When did this happen?" Sam's mother pressed.

"For over a year now," Sam replied.

Bill jumped in. "Now, before everyone loses their shit I will remind you all to play nice. Sam and I invited you all here to inform you of three specific things."

"Which are?" Bill's mother asked.

"We're going to get to that. Now, while Sam and I get a new drink order going, please make Julie and Kim, and their parents welcome."

Sam and Bill took a quick inventory of the groups refreshment needs and disappeared into the kitchen.

"Holy crap that's exhausting," said Bill.

"Yeah. I'd almost rather be back at SERE instead of here."

"No shit brother. I'm afraid we're in for one hell of a ride this afternoon."

* * *

The group had migrated to the backyard and sat down at a couple of picnic benches. Bill worked the hamburgers, hotdogs and chicken on the grill while Sam delivered the food requests as they became ready. In short time all twelve of them were enjoying a late lunch as empty beer bottles and drained glasses were continually replenished. Sam and Bill sat next to Julie, Kim and their parents. The other six barely contained themselves at the other table. Sam eventually stood up and got everyone's attention.

"First off Bill and I would like to say thank you for attending our gathering, especially at the last minute. As Bill mentioned before, we have three topics to tell you about. The first you're already aware of, but I can't help but mention again. We were lucky enough to meet Julie and Kim on the tail end of a sad day, the day I buried my father."

Julie took Sam's hand in hers and squeezed it in support.

"Bill and I were overseas when I got the message that he had passed. The funeral was anything but a celebration, because it was an embarrassment that I won't soon forget."

Sam's mother, Janet, bit her tongue while his stepfather bristled somewhat.

"However, that evening after the wake Bill and I went out for drinks, and that's when we met these two lovely angels. We are privileged that they have stayed with us for the past sixteen months even though we've been deployed for most of that time. Needless to say it hasn't been easy on them, or on us.

"With that being said, I want to take this time to also thank Mary and Eric for their bravery. They hadn't met Bill or myself until today, nor did they really understand what they were subjecting themselves to by meeting our families today. And just in case anyone is unclear on what I'm inferring I'll come out and just say it. Yes, Bill and I have dysfunctional relationships with our parents. It is what it is. But aside from that we wanted you all here today in the hopes that breaking bread together might begin to mend some fences."

Sam and Bill were actually shocked that no one had interrupted Sam yet.

"The second topic should actually bring a smile to your faces. After eight years in the Army Bill and I decided to leave."

"Are you telling your mother and me that you quit?" Jacob insinuated.

245

"I don't understand," began Louise. "I thought you loved the Army. You certainly joined it to punish us so why quit now?"

"What did you do in the Army anyway?" asked Reggie, Bill's stepfather. "You were always so secretive about it. Course we didn't hear from you for years anyway. It was like you wanted us to worry on purpose."

Bill whispered to the girls and their parents as he stood up to join Sam. "Welcome to our family. Aren't you glad you showed up?"

Bill put his hands up to quiet them all down. "Yes."

"What does that mean? Yes to what?" asked his mother.

"Yes," Bill said again. "Yes that Sam and I joined the military to get away from you crazy people. I mean look at how you're all acting. How do you think the Roads think about you all? I would be judging the absolute hell out of each one of you."

"How dare…" began his mother.

"Mom. Shut it. Dad cheated on you and is rubbing it in your face. The man you married to get back at him is not my father even though he desperately wanted to be. Sorry Reggie, it just doesn't work that way. And dad, you're pretty much an asshole for cheating on mom. But you know what, we're all family whether we like it or not, so suck it up.

"Now, to answer your pointed questions, yes we quit. And before you ask why I'll tell you, which brings us right to topic three. Sam and I are starting our own business."

Jacob spoke up with a spiteful tone. "But you two never went to college. What hope do you two have on running a successful business?"

Sam took a deep breath and then let it out in the hope of regaining some of his inner strength rather than pull his stepfather from his seat and toss him around like a ragdoll.

"You're right Jacob, Bill and I never went to college. But you know what? For the past eight years we've done nothing but learn, train and absorb information. You all want to know what we did in the Army so I'll tell you."

Everyone seemed to lean forward in anticipation.

"Bill and I have been all over the world to various hotspots. We were sent there to take care of business, and not with a pen."

"What are you saying? What does he mean not with a pen?" asked Janet.

Bill spoke up. "He means we handled situations with a gun. We killed bad people."

Both their mothers audibly gasped.

"No, I don't' believe it." Louise stated. "My boy would never murder anyone."

"Sammy," his mother said with a sad face, "please tell me it isn't true. You would never do anything like that."

"Oh for Christ's sake you two," said Bill's father, Stuart. "What the hell do you think soldiers do in the military? They certainly don't sit around playing cards all day."

"But...but I thought you just joined to get away from me," said Bill's mother. "I don't understand why you would want to take other people's lives. That's not who you are."

"Enough," Sam stated. "It's not that black and white. We went and did what we were ordered to do. That's how the military works. But here's the important aspect you need to keep in mind. We're out now. No one can order us around again. We're going to be our own bosses."

247

"Sam. What's the business?" asked Eric, a newcomer to the conversation. "My daughters are obviously enamored with the two of you and are ecstatic that you'll be here for them. With that said, I'll ask it again. What's the business?"

Everything stopped. The bickering. The harsh looks. The condescension. Everything. They all hung on what Sam was about to say.

"Bill and I have decided to open a VIP protection service."

"What is that?" Jacob asked.

"There are threats all over the world, both real and imagined. We'd been providing protection for groups or individuals that pay for it."

"I still don't completely understand," said Sam's mother.

"Okay, I'll explain it a little differently. Say someone important comes to the Bay Area. As an example let's say it's one person who requests our service. We would provide that client with armed security while they were conducting whatever business or activity for a negotiated fee."

"Like mercenaries?" Reggie inquired.

"No," Bill replied. "Mercenaries are hired to fight other people's wars. What Sam and I would be doing is only protection. It's a preventative service."

"But Sam said armed security," Reggie pressed.

"That's true," Bill replied. "Any threats need to be met with a proper response."

"I don't like it," said Louise.

"Me either," added Janet. "It's too dangerous."

Sam and Bill both chuckled.

"What's so damn funny?" Stuart asked.

Bill answered. "Sam and I cannot talk about what we've seen, been through or had to do for our country. The point that

I will painfully try and get across to all of you is that this business we're going to start up, it'll be a walk in the park compared to what we've been through already. You have no idea, and more importantly you'll all sleep better at night not knowing what we know."

"Okay," said Eric. "I can see you're both very passionate, but let me ask you this. Jacob has a point about you two not having gone to college. I understand that you know you can do the job, I clearly get that. But there is more to a business than just doing the job. There's a lot of groundwork to getting it up and running. Location, permits, equipment, clients and capital come to mind immediately. I mean no disrespect, but where are you with all that?"

Sam and Bill shared a long look.

"We're currently working on that aspect," responded Bill.

Sam nodded. "I won't lie. It's a bit overwhelming and there's a lot to do, but I know Bill and I can learn the ropes and make it happen."

Julie and Kim got up from the table and hugged their men.

"I believe in you," said Kim.

"And I believe in you too Sammybear," added Julie. "We're just glad you're out of the military and we'll have you to ourselves from now on."

* * *

Two hours later both Sam and Bill's parents finally left. They had forgotten about their personal issues with each other while the topic surrounded their boy's news. On the heels of their folks Mary and Eric followed.

249

"It was a real pleasure meeting the two of you," Mary said sincerely. "Your parents, on the other, hand…well, good luck with them." She smiled as did Sam and Bill.

"Very nice to meet you both as well," Eric said as he shook both their hands. "If my girls believe in you then that's a good sign. We trust their judgment."

"Thank you sir."

"Yes, thank you sir."

"Good luck," Eric said as he and Mary began to walk away.

"The business is going to be fantastic," replied Bill.

"I'm sure it is," Eric said over his shoulder. "I was actually referring to our daughters. Good luck with them."

"Daddy!" Julie and Kim exclaimed together.

Sam and Bill chuckled.

"I like your old man," said Sam.

"And your mother's really nice," Bill added.

"We know," Kim joked. "I'm sure they'll be traumatized for a bit. Your folks are a little intense."

"They held their own," Julie said. "They just want us to be happy. I can't say the same thing about your parents though." She laughed and they all joined in.

"Don't we know it," Bill replied. "You sure you both can't stay?"

"We'd love to but we picked them up from the airport. We're taking them over to a hotel so they can rest and then we're spending the day with them tomorrow before they head back out."

"Tell them thanks for coming."

"Oh, we'll do more than that," Julie said. "As soon as we leave the topic will be focused on both of you and your families."

"Hours of delight," Kim added with a smirk.

"Then give me a kiss and get out of here," Sam insisted.

"Me too of course," added Bill.

They watched Julie, Kim and their parents drive away down the street before they headed inside and began to clean up.

"It could have been worse," stated Bill.

"Much worse. I do know one thing though."

Bill nodded knowing exactly where Sam was going. "We have a lot to learn and a short amount of time to do it."

"Exactly."

35

Saturday December 1, 1984

"Well look who we have here," Bill said with a smile as he stood up from the park bench.

Sam got up as well as their old friend crossed the grass and approached them.

"How in the hell are you Tom?" Sam asked while he gave him a huge bear hug, smiling from ear to ear.

"It's Thomas now, thank you very much. And holy shit, look at the two of you. When did you figure out your bodies could grow muscles?"

Bill and Sam laughed.

"Fuck you too," Bill said and gave his friend a hug. "And you go by Thomas now? Really? Shit, too many changes for me. I'm outta here."

Bill pretended to walk away before Sam hit him in the arm which made Thomas smile. It was as if none of them had spent the past nine years apart from each other.

"Ouch...fucker."

"Get your ass back here and take a seat."

They all sat down at the table and just stared at each other for a long time.

"I can't believe we're all twenty seven," Thomas said. "It's just hard to swallow. Where in the hell has the time gone?"

"No shit," said Bill. "But getting our band back together has been long overdue."

"It has," Sam added. "You know that we've been back for over a year now Tom...I mean Thomas. We called your grandparents and we left a number of messages on your machine. What's with the cold shoulder?"

"Honestly?"

"After the shit we've all been through together as kids?" Bill said. "Yeah. We should only be opening our mouths if we're honest."

Thomas sighed. "Okay. Listen. I was pissed off that my best friends didn't make it to my college graduation. I guess I wanted to snub you both for a bit. I feel like crap about it and I want to apologize. I'm sorry."

"Shit," said Sam. "That was back in June of eighty four wasn't it?"

Thomas nodded.

Sam and Bill looked at each other.

"We were..."

"Indisposed at the time," interrupted Bill. "I know that doesn't make it right." He stopped himself. "What I actually mean to say is, I'm sorry brother."

"Me too. Sorry. We would have been there if we weren't deployed at the time."

Thomas nodded. "Thanks. I just miss you two assholes is all. High school ended and we just went our separate ways. Well, I went one way and you two stayed together."

"Are you saying you were jealous of that?" Sam asked.

"Yeah. I'll admit it. But at the same time I was happy you had each other to lean on with whatever you had to go through."

"Bro," Bill started, "you have no idea. The shit we've been through has been epic."

"I'm all ears."

Sam shook his head. "We can't. Maybe someday we can talk about it. You need to understand that what we've been through is classified. It's the 'lock us up and throw away the key' type of work."

Thomas' eyes widened. "No shit. So what I'm hearing is that you become more than Rangers."

Sam and Bill shared another glance.

"We can tell him," Bill insisted. "It doesn't have anything to do with a mission."

Sam thought about it. "Yeah, I suppose we owe him that much."

"Good." Bill turned back to Thomas. "Dude, this information can't go further than this table. We've all been best friends since the third grade so I'm not fucking around with this secrecy. Swear you won't repeat what we're about to tell you to anyone else?"

"You're serious?" Thomas asked.

"Deadly serious," Sam replied. "You need to swear, I shit you not."

What the hell? "Okay. I swear on our friendship. Satisfied?"

"That'll do," Sam assured him. "Bill?"

"Got it. Thomas, you were absolutely correct. Becoming Rangers was hell for us, in both mind and body."

"It can't be explained in words," Sam added.

"No, it really can't. But that's only part of it. We were tapped to join the Special Operations community."

"Shut up," Thomas replied. "So you're telling me you guys are like ninjas? You stealth in, get the job done and then get out?"

"Something like that," said Bill.

Holy shit! Thomas' brain was on overdrive. "I hate to ask…but…does that mean you've killed people?"

Sam and Bill leaned back, looked at each other and then nodded at Thomas.

"Wow. I…I don't know what to say or think about that. Was it difficult?"

Sam held up his hand. "While I understand where your question is coming from you need to understand that we're not going to talk about that, period."

"Sorry," Thomas replied. "I didn't mean…"

"It's okay brother," Bill interjected. "We could say it's just part of the job or that it comes with the territory. It doesn't mean we enjoy that aspect. Now, how about we change the subject?"

They were all quiet for a bit before Sam opened his mouth.

"So you're living in southern California now?"

Thomas nodded. "I am. I rented a place during my four years at college, as well as when I went abroad for nine months. Then I moved to Venice Beach for a bit. I sold my first book and then…"

"Wait a second," Bill said as he stopped his friend. "You sold a book? Why in the hell are we hearing about this just now you sonofabitch? That's awesome!"

"Thanks."

Sam smiled along with Bill. "Well look at you Mr. Author. What was your book about?"

"It's a children's book. It's called *The Sandbox*."

"Fuck you and the horse you road in on," Bill said as he chuckled. "Seriously?"

"Yeah."

Sam spoke up. "And here I thought you'd be writing novels with all the short stories you used to come up with back in the days."

"It was weird," Thomas answered. "I got back from traveling and just had so much inspiration to suddenly draw on. It just came out."

Bill got a puzzled look on his face and asked a question. "So this book paid for your house in whatever town you're living in now? I forget the name of the place."

"Running Springs. And no, not exactly. I completed my second children's book a year and a half ago entitled *The World to Tom*."

"And that paid for a house?" Bill repeated.

"Not exactly," evaded Thomas.

"What do you mean not exactly?"

"So what have you two been up to for the past year then?" Thomas asked turning the tables. "I haven't heard about any jobs. Fill me in."

Bill and Sam gave Thomas a strange look but let the topic slide for the time being.

"Well, funny you should bring that up," said Sam. "Instead of staying in the military Bill and I decided to leave and start our own business."

Thomas was intrigued. "What kind of business?"

"A VIP protection service."

"And what does that entail?"

"Think of it as an armed escort. A bodyguard service."

"And there's a need for that?" Thomas asked.

Bill answered. "There really is. High value clients come to the Bay Area on business all the time. We'll offer a local

257

service that provides the necessary security for that individual, or group, during their time in the city."

"And that service comes with a price tag I imagine?"

"A large one. But to the clientele we'd be providing the service to it'd be peanuts."

Thomas nodded. "So that's up and running right now?"

"No," Sam said with distaste. "Over the past year Bill and I have laid the groundwork. We scouted locations, had architectural plans drawn up, greased the local wheels for a variety of permits, etc etc."

"And?"

"We've come up short on investors."

"Really short," Bill added. "There's mixed feelings out there. Some people think our service isn't necessary. Others think it's a good idea but aren't willing to blindly jump in."

"I don't get it. How have the two of you paid for anything? Oh, never mind, I just figured it out. I don't mean to pry but at what point are eight years of Army paychecks going to dry up?"

"See," Bill said, "he gets it."

"Thomas. Bill and I have another six months before this whole project collapses in on itself. Our day to day living expenses isn't what worries us. It's the permits and everything else we need to do."

"I'm sorry to hear that guys."

"You and us both," Bill replied. "It really sucks. We're so close and then we can't seem to get around this damn investor wall."

Thomas leaned back. "Do you mind if I tell you a story?"

"What?" Bill replied.

"A story?" Sam asked.

"Yes, a story. It's something I've been holding in for nine and a half years now."

Sam and Bill shared a glance. "Okay. Sure, by all means."

"After our high school graduation my grandfather took me down to Loard's ice cream parlor."

"Oh man, I used to love that place," said Bill.

"Anyway, I thought he took me there to celebrate. I was wrong."

Sam and Bill leaned in a little.

"What happened?" Sam asked.

"The weirdest, and yet the most incredible thing ever. The end." Thomas sat back.

"Oh come on," Bill exclaimed. "Don't pull that same 'the end' bullshit you used to do back in the days. Spill it motherfucker. What happened?"

Thomas leaned back in. "It's time for both of you to swear secrecy to me, I shit you not."

"You're not kidding are you?" Sam asked.

"Does it look like I'm kidding?"

Sam and Bill instantly realized Thomas wasn't messing around.

"I swear on our friendship," Bill pledged.

"I swear on our friendship," Sam pledged. "Now give."

"My grandfather handed me a letter. In it contained an amount of money that my father entrusted to me before he passed."

"Holy shit bro. What was it…like thirty grand or something?"

"I'm going to go with fifty grand," guessed Sam. "But I don't know why all the secrecy over fifty gee's."

259

"Twenty two point seven," Thomas told them.

"Pfft. I win," said Bill. "I was closer to twenty three thousand with my guess."

"Whatever," Sam said to Bill.

Thomas shook his head.

"What?" Sam asked.

"Twenty two point seven million. Twenty two point seven million dollars was the amount."

Sam and Bill's mouths opened and didn't close for a few seconds.

"Dude, he's just messing with us," Bill finally said. "Twenty two million my ass."

"No. I said twenty two point seven million," corrected Thomas.

His friends were skeptical and their faces showed it.

Sam asked the obvious questions. "And your father, rest his soul of course, was able to come up with this insane amount of money how? I mean, you were ten when he passed, so the year was like nineteen sixty seven or before when he set this all up for you?"

"I guess," Thomas replied.

"If this is for real, where did he get that much money?"

"I don't know. I asked my grandfather the same question. Apparently, before my father passed away, he and my grandfather had a conversation about that. My father was vague. To this day neither my grandparents, nor I, know what my father did for a living or where the money came from."

Bill's skepticism was eroding. "This isn't a joke, is it?"

"No. I'm actually not full of shit. Listen, earlier you were pressing on how I was able to afford a house in Running Springs off a single book sale, right?"

Bill nodded.

"Well, let's back up first. College wasn't cheap. I had a rental house for five years because right after I graduated I traveled all over the world for nine months. How'd I pay for all of those expenses without a job?"

"You're totally serious right now?" Sam said as he looked his friend dead in the eyes.

"Totally. Now, before either of you say another word let me say something. I don't want you to ask for the money so I'm going to offer it first."

"Thomas, I..."

Thomas held up his hand. "Shut up for a damn second."

Sam and Bill closed their mouths.

"You two are my best friends and I want you both to be successful. I have a house in Running Springs and I write books. I like it up there. It's quiet, peaceful and nobody really bothers me. I don't need much and I don't lead an extravagant lifestyle. I am going to give you fourteen million dollars to start your business."

Sam and Bill were absolutely stunned. Their eyes started to glisten.

"Now, before you say no I'm going to tell you to shove it up your ass. You're taking this money and you will start your business with it. The only thing I ask is that I remain a confidential and silent partner. I don't want to be involved in how you run your business." Thomas smiled. "I'll just take a dividend check now and then."

"I...I don't know what to say," Sam stammered.

"Me either. Fucker has me speechless."

"All I need to hear is a yes," said Thomas. "Let me help you do what you obviously want and love to do."

Sam and Bill wiped their eyes and then turned towards each other.

"What ya think?" Sam asked.

"I'm not sure yet. Do you think fourteen million is enough?" Bill kidded.

"Yeah, I don't think it is."

"We should roll him right now, take his wallet and get the full twenty two mil he obviously carries on him all the time."

"I agree."

"Fuck you both," Thomas said and began to laugh.

"Fuck us?" Bill mocked. "No, fuck you Mr. Moneybags. All this time and you come clean like ten years later. What's that all about?"

"I understand," Sam said. "He didn't want us to treat him any differently than we usually do. Besides, we were off doing our own thing as it was. The fact that he's telling us now, and quite frankly saving our ass, means that much more. To answer your question, yes, we'd love to welcome you in to our business as a silent partner."

Sam extended his hand and Thomas shook it, followed by Bill.

"Well that felt too damn formal," Bill said. "Now what?"

"You guys want to get some dinner?" asked Thomas.

"Who's paying?" Bill joked.

Sam hit him in the shoulder. "We are of course."

"Right, that's what I meant to say," Bill said as he rubbed his shoulder.

They all got up from the table and Sam walked around to his friend and gave him a huge hug.

"Thank you brother. This means the world to us."

"My pleasure."

"Brothers for life," Bill said as he came around the table.

"Brothers for life," Sam repeated.

"Yes, brothers for life," said Thomas.

They all started to walk towards the parking lot when Thomas spoke up.

"So what's the name of your business anyway?"

"Shit," replied Sam, "we haven't come up with that yet."

"Well, Thomas' first book was called '*The Sandbox*'," Bill said. "Why don't we call our business SANDBOX? You know, in all caps."

Sam and Thomas chuckled.

"Works for me," Thomas replied. "Takes me back to how we all met."

"And look, we're together again today," said Sam. "I like the name but I really like the fact that the gang is back together."

"Me too," agreed Bill. "And we know you live down south but promise us we'll see more of you now that we're back in the same state."

"I promise," Thomas said.

"Good," Sam said as they arrived at their vehicles. "Let's go celebrate."

36
Friday January 4, 1985

"We're so proud of you," Julie beamed as she raised her glass to toast Sam and Bill.

"Yes, very proud," Kim added as she lifted her drink.

The four of them finally found the time to go out and celebrate now that the business was off the ground. Since their meeting with Thomas, a month ago, Sam and Bill had worked tirelessly to complete the necessary negotiations they had already set in motion. With such an influx of money at hand they had ran up against very little resistance to obtain the necessary permits and signoffs. Their biggest battle had been with the San Francisco and Marin city councils to obtain permits for carrying, transporting and utilizing weapons in public. Under the table deals were made so that when SANDBOX was up and running the company would take the time to train both cities SWAT teams.

Overall it had been a relatively painless endeavor and the property they had purchased in the Marin headlands had just broken ground the previous day, which is why they were taking the time to celebrate. To stay close to the new complex, and to stay on top of any issues that may arise, Sam and Bill rented a house in Marin. They also asked Julie and Kim to move in with them and the two sisters agreed to it immediately. The business was taking a lot of Sam and Bill's time, but the women knew where they were and that they were out of danger. It always made them feel good to know that their men came home every night.

"To SANDBOX," Bill toasted.

They all drank and then went back to work on their steaks. Kim ate a bite and then poised a question.

"So you guys have been hitting the pavement looking for investors for a while now. Which group finally realized you're worth backing?"

Sam and Bill shared a quick glance before Bill replied.

"As of this moment we're unable to disclose that information."

"Why? I don't understand."

"That particular group has invested fourteen million dollars in to our venture. They wish to remain anonymous. You understand."

Kim just about choked on her next forkful. "Fourteen million dollars! Seriously? That's a ton of money."

"So you're rich now?" Julie inquired.

Sam shook his head. "It doesn't work that way. The money is to setup the company's foundation."

"So you'll have to pay it back?"

Sam nodded. "That's how it works."

"So whatever group gave you fourteen million dollars has a lot of money invested in you and they believe you're going to reap that much and more in the business?"

"Weird, right?" Bill said off hand.

Kim was still wrapping her mind around it. "You two are going to have to do a lot of business to come up with millions."

"Yeah," Bill replied, "but it's going to be one wild ride as we're doing it. Who knows what lies ahead of us in this business. In time we'll have the whole world at our fingertips."

"So I hope you don't mind me asking," Julie interjected, "but what kind of company name is SANDBOX anyway?"

Sam and Bill smiled.

"It's a throwback to our childhood," Sam replied. "Thomas, Bill and I used to play in the school sandbox all the time."

"And the name holds a special value to both of us."

"Speaking of Thomas, when are we ever going to meet him?" asked Julie.

"One of these days for sure," Bill responded. "We finally caught up with him last month for a short visit before he headed down south again."

"And you've all been friends since childhood?"

Sam nodded. "Yeah. We've been through a lot together, especially playing in that damn sandbox during recesses."

Bill laughed. "Indeed. We had fun making castles and towns before we'd destroy them. Good times in that sandbox."

"But why call your business SANDBOX?" Kim asked. "Does it mean something other than it just being a childhood memory?"

"Yeah, does it stand for something?" Julie added.

"Our mission statement is what clients will be concentrating on," Sam said. "We don't need each syllable in the word SANDBOX to actually stand for something."

"Well hold on a sec," Bill said. "Maybe they have a point."

"Really?" Sam retorted. "You really want to try and make something tangible out of SANDBOX?"

Bill shrugged. "I don't know. Maybe. It'll be fun. Give me a minute." Bill's eyes stared in to the distance.

"So what's the next step?" Julie asked as she looked back at Sam.

"With the business?" Sam inquired.

Julie nodded.

"Well, we'll oversee the actual construction of our initial office building. Later on down the road the idea is to add a training area and a motor pool. We don't want to bite off more than we can chew right now. But if this business takes off the sky could be the limit."

"And marketing?" Kim probed.

"We have some feelers out in the community. We don't want to push too quickly without having our foundation and backend ready to tackle any clients that come our way. Right now Bill and I are researching small arms so we can make a purchase. We also need additional equipment like Kevlar vests, vehicles and such."

"I've got it," Bill blurted out. "What about **S**ituations **A**lways **N**ecessitate **D**ecisive **B**lueprints or **O**peration e**X**tremes?"

"Let's call that a work in progress," Sam replied with a smile.

"Fine. Oh, and I heard about this Austrian company that came out with an advanced synthetic polymer handgun a few years ago."

"What's that?" Kim asked.

"It means a portion of the handgun is made out of plastic."

"That sounds like science fiction," Julie stated.

"Maybe. The weapon is called a Glock seventeen and it takes nine-millimeter rounds. So far the reviews of it are very positive."

"Look in to it more. If it pans out I want a dozen of them ordered. But that still leaves us needing rifles and sub-machine guns."

Julie put her hand up. "Hold it you two. Why don't we drop the business talk at the table and just enjoy a meal out together. Would that be too much to ask?"

"No, you're right Jules. We just get carried away."

"And Suburbans," Bill quickly added. "I like Suburbans."

Kim chuckled. "Boys and their toys."

"But I like our toys," Bill replied as he played along.

"I'll show you something else later if you're a good boy then."

"Okay then," Bill asserted with a grin. "No more business discussion at the table. This is serious adult time. Besides, I don't want to miss out on getting laid later."

Kim hit him in the shoulder. "Behave!"

"And if I don't will you put me over your knee?"

Sam choked on his drink and they all began to laugh. While Bill and Kim continued having fun, Julie tuned them out, took Sam's hand in hers and gently squeezed it. *I'm the luckiest girl in the whole world. I feel so safe when I'm in his arms.* He smiled at her.

"Something on your mind?" he asked her.

She softly shook her head. "No, just taking in the moment. I love you."

Sam smiled. "I love you too."

* * *

Wednesday February 6, 1985

"Mr. Books." Sam extended his right hand as he approached the man, who was in his mid-forties, whom they had contracted to protect for the day. "I'm Sam Paige. You're expecting me."

"Indeed." Scott Books stood up from the table, where he'd been eating his breakfast, and shook Sam's hand. "Won't you please join me?"

"Thank you." Sam sat down opposite Mr. Books as he took another look around the sparsely populated restaurant at the top of the Transamerica tower in the very heart of San Francisco. He didn't pick up on any immediate threats and refocused his attention back on his client.

"Would you care for something to eat or drink?"

"No, thank you," Sam replied.

"Very well. Mr. Paige, you led me to believe you and your partner would be, shall we say, watching out for me today."

Sam nodded. "My associate Bill Nicholson is providing a second layer of security as we speak."

"I see. And what are you providing Mr. Paige?"

"The first layer."

Mr. Books nodded as he took a sip of his coffee. "Just so we're on the same page, Mr. Paige," he said with a slight smile at his pun, "I've done my research on your company, and on the two of you."

Sam didn't move, blink or give any indication that what he'd said bothered him whatsoever.

"And I conclude you both have the necessary skills and background that I require, hence why you're sitting here in front of me now. The reality, however, is that apparently I'm SANDBOX's first official client. My research shows that your office construction isn't even finished. What conclusions should I make from that?"

Sam stared at Mr. Books intently. *This guy is testing me, trying to push my buttons. Are all high level execs with money and power this cocky? I guess we'll find out.*

"Has your schedule changed from the one you've provided us Mr. Books?"

Mr. Books appeared a little put off that Sam didn't want to engage him in his mind game, but he covered that up immediately.

"No. My itinerary remains the same." He paused for a few seconds. "Out of curiosity, what are you packing?"

"Sir?"

"Convince me that you can protect me."

Christ. Here we go again. We've already done this dance over the phone, but oh well, he's the one paying our bill so I might as well indulge him.

"Under my suit, which is what you requested, I have on a Kevlar vest. As for weapons I carry a Glock Seventeen, an extendable baton and a six inch steel knife. You will be transported in one of our lightly armored Suburban vehicles. If the shit hits the fan the windows and doors are bullet proof. The Suburban also houses an armory that contains Heckler and Koch MP Fives and CAR Fifteens, along with smoke, flashbang and other devices.

"Now, SANDBOX has been contracted to protect you. If a threat does present itself we will neutralize it while keeping you safe. If that means we take a bullet meant for you then that's what we'll do. Does that answer your question, sir?"

Mr. Books smiled. "Thank you Mr. Paige. I appreciate your patience with me. Quite frankly I'm used to dealing with subordinates who hang at every word and jump at every command I give. I have power and I have money. But that's not the case with you, is it? You have power, that's for sure. I can see it in the way you conduct yourself. You could reach across the table and kill me in seconds I imagine, but that's where the money portion of this equation comes in to play. I have it and I'm using it to procure your services."

"When you word it like that you make it sound like we're just guns for hire. Let me assure you we're not mercenaries Mr. Books. We're not here to kill for you. We're only here to protect you; to keep you breathing. Nothing more." Sam paused. "And while you were vetting us we were vetting you in return. You are Scott Books, founder and CEO of some up and coming tech company that you started in your garage years ago. You have an appetite for success and tend to do whatever it takes to obtain it. Because of that you're not terribly adored, which leads me to understand why you have received a few credible death threats before your visit to San Francisco."

Mr. Books clapped a few times. "Bravo Mr. Paige, bravo. I see that you're not going to cow down to me and I respect that. You literally hold my life in your hands and I'm well aware that I'm paying you for that luxury. With that said," as he looked at his watch, "if we don't leave soon I'll be late for my first appointment. Shall we?"

Sam nodded as he stood up and spoke into his left wrist. "We're on the move."

"Roger that," came Bill's voice in Sam's ear. "Lobby's clear."

Mr. Books' first meeting lasted an hour and the ride to it
had been uneventful. His second meeting was located in a
building on Second Street and it wasn't until it had concluded
that things went awry.

"How's it look?" Bill heard in his earpiece as he continued
to case the lobby as he'd done for the past hour.

"Looks clear. Bring him down," Bill replied.

"Roger that. Taking elevator one."

"Understood."

Bill continued his rounds through the lobby as he
scrutinized and accessed each and every person who entered it.
He assigned everyone a threat level at a glance based on their
facial expression, how they walked and how they held
themselves. The three beefy men that just entered the double
doors from the street set off all of Bill's alarms.

"Hold. Potential trouble," Bill nonchalantly whispered
into his left cuff. Sam didn't respond. "I repeat, potential
trouble." Nothing. Bill looked up at elevator one and saw that
it was on its way down. *Damn radios.*

Bill watched the three men out of the corner of his eye as
they approached and sized them up as brawlers. They wore
street clothes and they all had very determined expressions on
their face. He didn't notice any bulges that would indicate
they carried any weapons on them, aside from their powerful
fists. Bill, dressed in a suit, didn't get a second glance from
any of them as they passed by and fanned out by the four
elevator doors. They looked up and watched the lights move.

"I don't know which one he's in," said one of the men, "but his schedule shows his meeting just ended. He should be in the lobby very soon."

"And then we'll have a talk with him," said another as he smiled and smacked one large fist into his other palm.

"We've got trouble," Bill whispered once more with no response.

The lobby was empty aside from the three men and Bill. The four elevator lights constantly moved and two of them were on a freefall to the lobby. Bill casually walked over and joined them.

"Cover that one and I'll take this one," the same man said to the other two.

The other two moved to the other elevator as Bill opened his mouth by elevator one.

"I take it your suit must be at the dry cleaners."

The large man glanced over at Bill. "Fuck you."

"I see," Bill responded. "You here for a meeting then?"

With the elevator lights seconds away from the lobby the large man turned and took one menacing step towards Bill.

"Fuck off before I end your shitty life."

Bill pretended to cower as he backed a few steps away. "Okay okay. Take it easy."

"Run home to mama you pussy," the man added as he turned back to the elevator. All three men laughed.

The whooshing sound cut through the air like butter as Bill's baton connected with the back of the large man's legs, who then screamed and crashed to the floor. The other two men turned just as Bill brought his baton down on the man's head, knocking him unconscious.

The remaining two rushed Bill.

The doors on elevator one opened just as one of the men sailed past it, hit the hard floor and did not get up.

Sam instantly placed himself in front of his client just as a third person yelped from a dislocated shoulder. Sam pulled his pistol out as he watched Bill kick the man in the face, knocking him out as well.

"We're clear!" Bill yelled. "Move him!"

Sam briefly witnessed the panicked look on Mr. Books' face as Sam pulled him out of the elevator and towards the front doors.

Bill smacked the second man he'd thrown with his baton and then quickly searched his pockets as Sam moved their client with purpose across the lobby. Seconds later, with all three adversaries incapacitated, Bill ran past Sam and checked the outside for any additional threats. Seeing none he opened the back door of the Suburban just as Sam and their client appeared through the double doors. Sam pushed Mr. Books into the back seat and climbed in after him as Bill rushed around to take the driver's seat.

"Go!" Sam pressed.

Moments later Bill pulled out of the parking spot and gunned the vehicle down the street.

"What the hell was that!?" Mr. Books demanded as he straightened out his suit Sam had manhandled.

"Three men were waiting for you in the lobby, sir," Bill stated.

"Impossible!" their client responded. "My schedule is confidential. The only ones that have it are you two. Maybe you set this whole thing up to extort me for more money."

Sam and Bill rolled their eyes as Bill handed back what he'd found on the man he'd searched to Sam.

"What's this?" Sam asked.

"Something I found on one of them."

Sam began to open it but Mr. Books snatched it out of his hands. "Let me see that."

He opened it and his eyes opened wide. He looked down at his own itinerary. "What? I don't understand. How is this possible?"

"What is it?" Bill asked from the driver's seat.

"It's....it's my private schedule for today, down to the last detail, much more so than the one I gave you. No one but my executive admin has access to this information."

"Well, sir," said Sam, "it would appear as if you have an internal problem to handle, doesn't it?"

Mr. Books' body had stopped shaking and was quickly replaced with anger.

"Goddammit!" He folded and pocketed the piece of paper inside his suit jacket. "I suppose I owe both of you an apology. I've always taken the threats I get with a grain of salt but apparently I shouldn't take them lightly at all." He paused as he collected himself. "Thank you both for your quick actions today. Consider your invoice balance doubled for your troubles. Now, take me to the airport. And please be quiet on the way, I have a lot to think about."

"Yes, sir."

* * *

After they safely watched Mr. Books enter the secured section of San Francisco International, Sam and Bill headed back to short term parking and climbed into the Suburban.

"So what happened Bill?"

276

"I tried giving you a heads up a few times but apparently the radios we have don't work in elevators."

"No shit. Damn. I'll look in to some other models. But aside from that, good job identifying and then nullifying the threats. Those were some big boys."

"Tell me something I don't know. But the goods news is that they went down even harder. It was a good workout. Overall I don't care for the suit though."

Sam nodded. "It is what it is. Expect to be in them more often than naught in the future."

"I know. Just something I have to get used to is all. You okay?"

"Yeah. You?"

Bill thought about it for a few seconds before he smiled. "Right as rain. We did good today and we doubled our money. Hard to say no to that. Although, for this job, we could have used more men."

"Agreed. However, with SANDBOX's office still under construction we're going to have to limit our jobs to ones we can handle ourselves for the time being. We don't have the facilities to house men yet and until we do we'll have to build our reputation all on our own."

Bill pulled back on the 101 freeway heading north. "Well, if we have more days like this then you can definitely count me in."

Sam smiled. "Me too."

*   *   *

Saturday March 23, 1985

"Where are you taking us?" Julie insisted.

"You do know that it's cold out, right?" Kim added.

"Relax," Bill said as he tried to soothe the sisters. "We're going to take you someplace special. Now just sit back and enjoy the ride."

"Oh it's sooo infuriating when you don't tell me what's going on," Kim said. "I could beat you with my bare hands right now."

Julie chuckled. "But I know how much you like to beat him sis. In fact, Sam and I can hear you through the walls. Cry Brer Rabbit some other time."

Bill laughed while Kim's face turned red.

Julie turned to Sam in the driver's seat. "But seriously, where are we going Sammy Bear?"

Sam gave her the 'are you kidding me, you just called me that' look and then looked back at the road. "Bill and I decided we're going to take you both on a picnic. We've been busy with the business quite a lot lately and we feel we haven't spent enough time with you. That is, unless you both wanted to do something else?"

"No no no," they said in unison and then laughed.

"Thank you. This sounds wonderful," Julie said.

"Where are we going?" Kim asked.

"We figured we'd take a little hike up Mt. Tamalpais, find a grassy area overlooking the valley and go from there."

Kim kissed Bill and then cuddled in next to him.

* * *

After thirty minutes on a trail they came across a small grassy hill. It was perfect and both Julie and Kim ran up to the crest of the knoll while Sam and Bill continued to lug the basket between them.

"Nervous?" Sam asked.

"Does a bear shit in the woods?"

"I'll take that as a yes."

"You should. And no foreplay. Let's just get this out of the way. The anticipation is killing me."

"Agreed."

They reached Julie and Kim who were looking out over the horizon.

"This is the perfect spot. Look how far we can see."

While the two sisters continued to gawk at the view Sam and Bill setup the large blanket and then began unpacking the picnic basket. Before long all of them had sat down and were enjoying the scenery.

"It's warmer than I thought it was going to be," Kim stated.

Julie nodded. "Thank you both. This is wonderful."

"Yes," Kim added. "Thank you for taking time out from your busy schedule. It means the world to us."

Sam and Bill smiled.

"Champagne anyone?" Bill asked.

"Oh, yes please. What's the occasion?"

As Bill prepared their drinks Sam answered the question. "Well, our business is successfully off the ground and we wanted to share that with both of you. Without your support Bill and I probably would have come to blows by now on a few decisions we had to make. But thanks to you you've kept everything in perspective and we can't thank you enough."

279

Bill handed a glass to Sam and then held one up in his hand.

"Kim. You mean the world to me and I consider myself the luckiest man alive to have found you."

"Julie. You keep me balanced and life would be forever diminished without you by my side."

"What's going on with you two? Kim asked.

"Yeah," Julie added. "You guys are starting to freak me out."

Sam handed the champagne glass to Julie and Bill handed his to Kim. They hesitantly took them and then the sun hit both glasses at the same time. Reflections appeared at the bottom of each glass.

"Are you kidding me?" Kim said with glee.

"No way!" Julie said.

Both sisters smiled at each other and then drained their glasses. Out of each of their mouths they produced their stunning engagement rings. Without a moment's hesitation they slipped them on their fingers.

"Yes!" the sisters cried out in unison.

"But we haven't even asked you the question yet," Sam said.

"Well hurry up and ask us," Kim urged them, "because we're not taking these off!"

Sam and Bill smiled, gulped and asked the question together.

"Will you marry me?"

Julie and Kim tackled their men and kissed them passionately. Eventually they came up for air.

"So is that a yes? Bill asked jokingly.

"Ooooo! I'm so going to beat you later!"

"I love you Kim."

"I love you too," she replied.

"I love you Jules."

"I love you too Sammy Bear."

Afterwards they all enjoyed a fantastic picnic on top of the grassy hill. It was a day that neither of them would ever forget.

37
Sunday May 4, 1986

"Proceed with the update Raven," Serpent instructed.

The phone call had been encrypted so Raven began his presentation.

"Yes sir. Our profits have continued to rise during the past four years with the addition of our heroin pipeline out of the Middle East."

"We are very pleased with your progress," Bear from the military side of the business replied.

"Indeed," the CIA contact Wolf added.

"I'm going to push your promotion through," Bear continued. "In a few months you'll give up your bird, Colonel, and be handed a General star instead."

Bob, aka Raven, had been waiting patiently for this promotion for years. "Thank you sir."

"You deserve it Raven," Serpent said. "Now, back to your update."

"Of course, sir. As I was saying, our profits have soared and we've all reaped the benefits. There continue to be a small number of mistakes that occur somewhere along the delivery chain. Those incidents have caused a small percentage of our product to be seized in transit. However, as these incidents pop up I continue to handle them with a certain amount of permanent finesse."

"We like your style," Wolf said.

"So, with that being said I propose to expand our market to China. I have had feelers out for some time now in regards to the opium that country produces. In the near future, and if the council so wishes, I will introduce everyone to my main contact, codename Tiger."

"Do you have any concerns that need to be addressed at this time?"

"No, sir. I would merely like permission to move from the tentative phase to our first actionable delivery."

"Permission granted Raven. Keep us informed."

38
Friday June 13, 1986

"Thomas, why don't you plan on coming up to the Bay Area and visiting us sometime soon?" his grandmother asked over the phone.

"I'm keeping myself pretty busy."

"Writing? What else do you do up there in the mountains?"

"I ride my bike and I've started a garden out front."

His grandmother sighed. "I hate to say this Thomas but it feels like it's been forever since we've seen you."

"It has been a long time," his grandfather said in the background.

"You see," Claire continued, "you even have Ed talking to himself."

Thomas chuckled.

"So what do you say?" she pressed.

"I don't know. Maybe I'll come up to visit in a few weeks. Sam and Bill are getting married next month on the fifth."

"Well that's better than nothing. You know your grandfather and I aren't getting any younger. When are you going to find someone special, settle down and give us grandchildren?"

Thomas didn't reply.

"Alright. Thomas, you know you can't stay up in the mountains forever. It just doesn't seem healthy. We're worried about you is all we're trying to convey."

"I like it up here," he replied. "I feel safe."

"Oh sweetie. I know life hasn't dealt you a good hand but becoming a shut 'in isn't the answer. People need interaction with others to survive. It's just how life works."

Thomas gripped the phone a little tighter. "That's easy for you to say. You have grandpa to lean on."

"And you have us to lean on."

Thomas shook his head. "It's not the same. You don't understand. I miss them both so much. It's just not fair. None of it is fair. I have to go."

The line went dead and Claire slowly replaced it back on the receiver.

"What happened?" Ed asked.

"Our boy is having a difficult time is what's happening."

"Did he say something? Anything?"

Claire sighed and sat down on a kitchen stool. "If I had to guess I'd say maybe he's beginning to remember what happened that night."

Ed shook his head. "No. He never needs to find out what really happened to his father. That would destroy him. Besides, it's a part of history that we don't like talking about."

"I know. It's disturbing and it's unfair. We'll never know why Michael did what he did. What I do know is that we took on Thomas. He became our responsibility whether he wants to acknowledge it or not. And right now I'm worried about him."

* * *

"Damn this place looks good," Bill exclaimed as he and Sam inspected SANDBOX.

"This place is going to be amazing. A couple more weeks and it'll finally be complete. And, with the extra funding

286

Thomas gave us I'm glad we built out the motor pool and indoor shooting range at the same time."

Bill smiled. "Our dream is really coming together."

Sam put his hand on Bill's shoulder. "Damn straight. I think we really have something special here."

"We'd better have. We've spent the last year doing contracts on our own. I can't wait to hire out some operators and take a break."

"Tell me about it. We've been running ragged. Our expectations have been shattered and business couldn't be hotter."

Bill nodded. "Who knew? But here we are reaping the benefits of our hard work. It feels good brother."

"Yes. Yes it does."

"We'd better get back home. I know Julie and Kim have more wedding chores that they've added to our 'to do' list."

Sam chuckled. "Whipped already, eh?"

Bill playfully knocked Sam's hand off his shoulder. "Oh please, like you're not?"

"Okay okay. Truce. But you're right, we'd better get back. The wedding is right around the corner and we still need to talk about our bachelor party."

"Oh yeah. We should call Thomas up and make sure he's attending the wedding. That bastard's been up in that mountain house of his for years now and he still hasn't met our future wives."

Sam nodded. "Yeah, at this point it's like we're talking about an imaginary friend."

"I don't see why he wouldn't come to our wedding."

"Neither do I," Sam replied. "But that doesn't mean we don't put the full court press on him. I miss our friend."

"So do I brother, so do I."

39
Friday July 4, 1986

Sam and Bill got out of the limo right in front of Larry Flynt's Hustler Club, which was located on San Francisco's Kearny Street. It was the night before their wedding and both of the twenty-eight year olds were looking forward to this last hurrah before tying the preverbal knot.

"I feel bad for lying to Julie and Kim about what we had planned tonight," said Sam.

"We didn't lie exactly," Bill replied. "We told them we were heading out on the town to have some drinks. We just didn't happen to mention where we were going to have them."

"Yeah yeah. Details. I'm just saying it feels a little shady."

Bill put his arm around Sam's shoulders and dragged him towards the front door.

"Listen, you need to relax a bit. We're not going to cheat on them. There's no harm in sitting back and watching topless women at work. If anything we're feminists for patronizing this establishment."

Sam gave Bill an odd look but that soon materialized in to a smile.

"You sly talking devil. Too bad Thomas isn't here to partake in our bachelor party."

Bill nodded. "I talked to him earlier and he said the flight up had been cancelled and he was getting another one. I didn't push it. As long as he makes it to our wedding tomorrow everything will be good."

Bill opened the front door, ushered Sam inside and followed behind.

"Gentlemen," a very attractive redhead said as she greeted them. "My name is Summer. How may the Hustler Club service you this evening?"

Throughout the establishment there were a number of platforms that displayed women in various stages of disrobing.

"Uh…" Sam stammered as he took it all in.

"What my friend here is trying to say, Summer, is that we're here for our bachelor party. My name is Bill Nicholson and this is Sam Paige."

"Very nice to meet you Mr. Nicholson and Mr. Paige. Will the rest of your party be joining you shortly?"

"It's just the two of us I'm afraid."

Summer's sexy smile broadened. "Well then, more for each of you. May I entice you to try one of our VIP rooms?"

"What's that entail?" Bill asked.

"It's a private, luxurious room. In it you'll be guaranteed to receive all the attention your bodies can endure."

"For a special night like this that sounds perfect."

"I'm glad to hear that. Please, follow me and I'll show you the way."

Sam grabbed Bill's arm. "What are you doing?"

"Trust me. This is exactly what we need. We're getting married tomorrow. Loosen up a little. Everything will be just fine."

Bill took off after Summer. A few moments later Sam reluctantly followed Bill towards the rear of the establishment.

Summer pulled a thick velvet curtain back to reveal a private room. It contained a pole, raised up above the floor with six comfortable leather chairs surrounding it. All three of them walked in and Summer pulled the curtain closed behind her.

"Gentlemen, please make yourselves comfortable. I'd love to bring you both something to drink. What can I get you?"

Bill spoke up as he sat down in one of the seats. "We'll start with a couple of beers and four shots."

"Excellent. I'll start a tab. May I have your credit card?"

"Of course." Bill fished an American Express card out and handed it over.

"Thank you Mr. Nicholson. Now, before I bring you your drinks I think your bachelor party needs to officially get under way. Ladies."

The curtain opened and three gorgeous women, wearing very enticing lingerie, slowly filtered into their private room.

"Holy shit," Bill whispered under his breath.

Summer introduced their new company. "Gentlemen, I present you with Eve, Ginger and Candy. Enjoy."

"Oh, now we're in trouble," said Sam.

Summer couldn't help but giggle as she watched their reactions. "I'll leave you in their capable hands while I retrieve your refreshments."

40
Saturday July 5, 1986

The Continental flight landed on time at 1:45 p.m. at San Francisco International. Dressed in jeans and a polo shirt Thomas wasted no time in retrieving his carry-on and exiting the plane. He knew he didn't have a lot of time before the wedding started as he headed to obtain a rental car. Twenty minutes later Thomas left the airport as he drove north on 101. Cutting west over 380 he continued north on 280 towards San Francisco. 280 became CA-1 and Thomas followed the signs along 19th Ave towards the Golden Gate Bridge. Traffic was lighter than Thomas remembered, but then again, it had been years since Thomas had driven through San Francisco. He was glad he took 19th rather than taking Van Ness through the city. He knew he'd saved time.

The weather was absolutely beautiful, and the view equally stunning, as Thomas crossed the Golden Gate bridge. He drove through the tunnel at the top of the hill and eventually exited at Spencer Ave. Thomas made his way down to the water and found a parking spot close to the Spinnaker. The time was 2:57 p.m. He got out, grabbed his carry-on and headed towards the restaurant. At the door he identified himself and was shown where Bill and Sam were waiting.

"Holy shit Thomas, we didn't think you were going to make it," said Bill who came up and gave Thomas a hug.

"Good to see you too bro," Thomas replied.

"Well well well, look who decided to show up." Thomas turned around and saw Sam with a huge grin on his face.

"Come here." Sam bear hugged Thomas. "Really good to see you."

"Wouldn't miss it for the world," Thomas barely managed to breathe out. Sam let go.

"We missed you last night Thomas," said Bill. "A few us of visited the Hustler club for our last free night. As the best man you should have been there bro."

"Sorry about that. I got hung up."

"Leave the man alone Bill, he has a right to squat up on that mountain of his, all alone, and miss out on all the grinding that took place last night," said Sam. "Of course if you mention a word of that to our future wives I'm afraid no one will find your body." Sam smiled.

"Speaking of women," Bill interjected, "I don't believe you've met ours. We'd introduce you but the ceremony is starting soon, and with the bad luck and all. Hurry up and change."

Thomas changed in to his suit that he'd brought and was ready to go in a few minutes. The guests were gathering so Bill and Sam headed out to greet them. Thomas went looking for the brides. After a little investigating Thomas found what room they were in and politely knocked on their door.

"Yes?"

"Hi. My name is Thomas Clark. I'm the best man. May I come in?" Thomas said through the door. The door cracked open and a myriad of women, of various ages, were inside.

"Please come in Thomas. My name is Kim Roads," she said letting him in and closing the door behind him. "My sister Julie is the other bride to be."

"Pleased to meet you both."

"We've heard a lot about the mysterious Thomas Clark," said Julie. "Let us get a good look at you." Both of them were in their wedding gowns. The final touches to their primping were taking place around them.

"Go ahead and do a spin for us," said Kim.

"A spin?" he asked.

"You know, a spin," Kim repeated twirling her finger in the air to illustrate. Thomas blushed.

"How cute," said Julie. "No wonder the boys love him so much."

"We're just kidding Thomas," Kim said smiling. "Bill asked us to mess with you a bit. It's very nice to meet you too."

I'm going to kill him. Thomas relaxed. "So you're sisters?"

"Guilty as charged," Julie replied. "Twin sisters to be exact."

"This is quite a production then."

"A double wedding, you mean?" Kim inquired. Thomas nodded. "Actually, it's what we've wanted since we were little girls. The only hard part was meeting the right men. I think we got really lucky there."

"Bill and Sam are two of the nicest guys I know. But I'm a bit biased since I grew up with them."

"How long are you in town Thomas?" asked Julie.

"I leave tomorrow."

"Oh, that's no good. You'll need to change that. Bill and Sam haven't seen you in a long time. You can't skip out that quickly. We'll talk about it later tonight. Sorry to chat and run but we're about to head down the aisle."

"That we are," confirmed Kim. "Thanks for coming by Thomas." Kim opened the door and Thomas walked out. *Wow, those two are a handful.*

Thomas made his way back to the main area and the view hit him. The entire room contained floor to ceiling windows. Angel Island, Alcatraz, the Bay Bridge and San Francisco were all visible within this room. *Nice location guys.*

"Hey Thomas." Bill walked up to him. "Sam's still schmoozing the guests. Did you meet our ladies?"

"Remind me to kill you later," Thomas replied.

"Heh heh. Sorry about that, I couldn't resist."

"They're great Bill. Congratulations."

"Thanks Thomas. We're really glad you're here. It's been too long." Bill paused. "Anyway, the ceremony is beginning soon. We'll talk later bro." Bill took off to collect Sam.

Thomas made his way up to the altar and took his position. He nodded to the two bride's maids as he settled in. He gazed out over the crowd and realized he didn't recognize many of the people that were attending. *I remember Sam's mother, as well as Bill's mother and father. Wow, it's been ten years since I hung out at their houses. That really seems like an entire lifetime ago.*

His thoughts were interrupted as Sam and Bill suddenly joined him.

"You ready for this best man?" Bill kidded.

"Here, you'll need these," Sam said as he handed two wedding rings to Thomas. "Try not to lose those in the next few minutes," he added playfully.

"You guys are hilarious," Thomas replied.

"We try," Bill said. "But seriously, thanks for being here."

"You make it sound like I was going to miss this."

"Well," said Sam, "the idea did cross our minds. You have been MIA for a while now."

"Point taken you assholes. Now, can we all concentrate on the fact that you're both about to get hitched for life please?" he joked.

"Oh, you'll pay for that one my friend."

Before anyone else could add to the conversation the wedding music began to play. All three of them stopped quibbling and everything immediately became serious. The audience rose as a cute little girl began tossing flower petals onto the floor as she made her way down the aisle. Afterwards, with a daughter on each arm, Julie and Kim's father appeared with the two beautiful brides. They slowly made their way down the aisle until their father handed each one off, with a handshake and a hug, to both Sam and Bill before he took a seat next to their mother.

"Friends. Family. We're gathered here today..."

* * *

The wedding was amazing. The sunlight was perfect and backlit the ceremony. Both Kim and Julie glowed.

"I now pronounce you man and wife. You may kiss the bride." Sam and Bill did just that.

* * *

The reception that followed was spectacular and Thomas couldn't be more happy for his best friends. Everyone was having a good time and in the distance the sun was beginning to set. Thomas drank from his glass as he looked out over the bay. *This is truly amazing. To think we grew up together, and now look where our lives have taken us. I miss hanging out with them but I'm happier knowing they have someone special in their lives.* He turned around as he was tapped on the shoulder. The two brides, along with who he assumed were their parents, had appeared behind him.

"Hi Thomas," said Julie.

"You two make stunning brides," Thomas said. "I don't think Sam or Bill really know how lucky they are yet."

"Oh shush," Kim replied.

"Thank you," said Julie. "My sister and I wanted to introduce you to our parents, Mary and Eric Roads."

Thomas shook Eric's hand and gave Mary a hug.

"Very nice to meet both of you."

"Likewise," their father replied.

Mary spoke up. "It's my understanding that today is the first time you met our daughters. Is that true?"

"I'm afraid that fault lands entirely on my shoulders Mrs. Roads."

"But how is that possible?" their mother insisted. "It's been four years since they started dating. How does the best man manage to avoid that situation?"

"Mother. Please. You're embarrassing us," Kim pleaded.

Thomas put his hands up. "Mr. and Mrs. Roads. Julie and Kim. You're absolutely right. I owe you all an apology. I live in a small town in the San Bernardino Mountains and I make my living as a writer. I have an awful tendency to seclude myself from society as a whole. It works for me but, truth be told, you caught me looking out over the water and wishing things were a little different. Now, I don't mean to be rude, but please excuse me, I'm going to go check in on Sam and Bill."

Thomas left the four of them as he walked away. *Wow. That was weird.*

"Thanks a lot mother," Julie said. "That was a little heavy handed."

Thomas located both grooms and bee lined to them.

"How're you two holding up? Can I get you anything?"

Sam and Bill put their arms around Thomas.

"Best day of our lives bro," said Bill, "and we couldn't be happier that you were a part of it."

"My sentiments exactly," Sam added.

"Well you all have put on one hell of a wedding, that's for sure. Great job."

"Our wives did most of the work. Bill and I have been busier than we thought over this past year."

"Very busy."

"So you're saying that SANDBOX is going to be successful?" Thomas asked.

"You don't know the half of it. Thanks to your generosity we were able to build out everything all at once rather than piecemeal it. In a few weeks, right as we get back from our honeymoon, we'll be able to take possession and start to hire staff."

"It's a dream come true," said Bill. "Thank you."

Thomas smiled. "Anything for you guys, you know that. Maybe I can drop by sometime and you can give me a tour?"

"Anytime," Sam replied. "Anytime. Now, as much as we could stand here and catch up with you all night, I'm afraid we have a million guests, which we don't know by the way, that we need to meet and greet. We'll catch up with you later."

"Thanks Thomas," said Bill. "You did a great job today."

And with that Sam and Bill left Thomas standing there and began to mingle. Thomas watched them go and smiled. *You two are going to be just fine.*

* * *

Monday morning, the newlyweds, after spending a good portion of Sunday catching up with Thomas, headed out on their honeymoon to Hawaii. They spent two weeks island hopping and having the time of their lives.

The four of them couldn't have been happier.

41
Friday August 1, 1986

Sam and Bill had spent the past week installing furniture in their new office building as well as setting up the motor pool, armory and a million other things on their to do list. They were busy and desperately needed help. It was time to hire some much need assistance and add some operators to SANDBOX's roster.

They had met with a few perspective candidates to fill the executive admin role, which they had agreed was the initial position that had to be filled immediately. The first two applicants had been young, ambitious and well out of their depth because neither of them had experience in running a business before. Although Sam and Bill were desperate, to a degree, they knew they absolutely needed the right individual to be the forefront of their company. It wasn't long before the third candidate had just sat down across the table from them. She was older, perhaps in her late fifties, and she seemed very at ease.

"Thank you for coming in today Mrs. Constance," Sam said.

She smiled. "I haven't gone by Misses in years. I'd love it if you'd just call me Roberta."

"You got it Roberta," Bill replied. "Now, before we begin, we wanted to clarify that you know exactly what position you're applying for."

Roberta raised her hand slightly and politely cut Bill off. "I come from a family that's been in the military Mr. Nicholson."

"Bill."

Roberta nodded. "My ex-husband retired from the service with the rank of Major. I traveled the world with him from station to station, raising our two boys along the way. As life would have it, our sons ended up joining the army.

"To answer your question more directly, Bill, this position requires both front and back end management, organization and attention to detail. You offer VIP protection to high-end clientele, both to individuals and groups; although at this time you've been limiting yourself to individual jobs. To bolster your bottom line you're going to need headcount, and from the looks of this building alone you're ready to start that process immediately.

"Let me assure you that I can and will provide you with the utmost professionalism, soft or tough as nails attitude that each particular situation requires. I am well versed in organization and will keep both of you focused on what you need this business to grow in to."

Roberta's words hung out there for a few moments before Sam spoke up.

"I see that your work history is limited to the past six or seven years."

"That's correct. My husband and I divorced seven years ago after our youngest son was killed during a training exercise, or at least that's what the military told us."

"I'm sorry to hear that."

"Me too," Bill added.

"Thank you. The age differences between our two boys had been significant. More to the point, our second, Christopher, hadn't been a planned pregnancy. Anyway, our oldest, Mike, didn't come back from Vietnam and it was tough on all of us for a long time. When Christopher decided to enlist my husband and I were furious, but he wanted to honor his older brother's memory. There was nothing we could do about it." She paused for a few seconds and looked away as her eyes began to glisten. "Seven years ago we received word that Christopher has been killed during a training exercise. His funeral was closed casket."

"Roberta, you don't have to…"

"It's okay, really. Please, let me finish."

Sam nodded.

"My husband took early retirement and began to drink heavily. In order to support us I took a job as a checker at Safeway. Two years later I had risen to become the assistant manager. He, on the other hand, continued to drink. I filed for divorce and moved out of the house."

"I'm sorry to hear that."

"Mr. Paige. Mr. Nicholson. I have been through hell and high water because of the military. But I'm still here, stronger than ever. When I saw your executive admin position I knew I had to have it. From what I've seen so far you're going to need a firm hand as your continue to negotiate the ups and downs of growing your business. You're going to hire quite a number of personnel and you'll need someone to not only mother them, but keep them in line at the same time.

"I can help run and expand your business. More importantly I need to. Let me demonstrate that I have what it takes. I owe it to you, I owe it to myself and I owe it to my boys."

Sam leaned forward. "You realize this job isn't for the faint of heart."

"I do."

"Our plans are to ramp up very quickly, hiring approximately twelve to eighteen operators. That means a ton of paperwork, from hiring packages, medical coverage, paychecks and anything else that comes along."

"I look forward to it."

"Our job requires us to work long and impractical hours, seven days a week, depending on our client's needs."

"I'm at your disposal. I want to be an integral part of your business and I know I won't let you down."

Bill smiled. "You don't frighten very easily."

She looked them both in the eyes. "Try me."

Sam and Bill exchanged a quick glance and their eyes said it all. They turned back and they both extended their right hands.

"Roberta, welcome to SANDBOX."

"Tomorrow," Bill said, "we'll get you situated. Sam and I have some solid leads on personnel we'd like to pursue, along with a growing list of potential operators that have responded to our ad already."

"If it's all the same to you, I'd like to get started right away. Just show me to my desk and I'll organize everything you need from there with my own system. I'll have this place running like a well-oiled machine in less than a week."

It was Sam's turn to smile. "Roberta, I think we're going to get along just fine."

Roberta smiled as she followed them out of the room. "You two remind me of my boys."

"I hope that's a good thing." Bill said.

"It's comforting. But remember, you give me any sass and I won't hesitate to put you over my knee," she said with a grin.

Bill started to chuckle.

"And as for you," she said pointing a finger at Sam, "I'm watching you like a hawk. Don't think you're safe from me either."

Sam put up his hands as he gave up. "Okay okay. Truce."

* * *

Three weeks later Sam and Bill took their first four employees out for a training run. Three black Suburban's raced down Howard Street in the middle of the night. Alan, Pete, Jeff and Darrell were ex-military and prime SANDBOX candidates. They were welcome additions and had already passed all training obstacles, including team live fire scenarios that Sam and Bill had thrown at them. Tonight was one of their final tests to validate they could work well as a cohesive unit. Sam and Bill were in the first Suburban, followed by Alan and Pete in the second leaving Jeff and Darrell in the third.

Sam spoke into the radio. "This is Alpha. Bravo, take the lead."

"Roger that Alpha. Bravo taking the lead." Alan pulled into the passing lane and surged ahead of Sam and Bill.

"Keep it tight gentlemen," Sam urged.

Charlie closed the distance to Alpha's rear bumper as Bravo took the lead and pulled back in front of Alpha.

"Good," Sam said. "In a block take a left on Fifth, and then half a mile down we're going to enter the 80 freeway heading east, which will take us over the Bay Bridge."

"Roger that. Taking a left," Bravo replied.

"Wilco," Charlie echoed.

At Fifth Street the three Suburban's squealed around the empty corner and accelerated towards the freeway onramp. In no time at all the three vehicles were cruising at high speed over the Bay Bridge.

"Nice job everyone," Sam said. "We're done for the night. Back off and reduce speed to fifty-five. When we hit 580 head north and take an alternate route back to the compound. Alpha will take the lead."

Sam relaxed as Bill passed Bravo's vehicle and retook the front position.

"What'ya think?" Sam asked his partner.

"I think we're well on our way. We keep this up and you know we'll need to eventually expand the business outside San Francisco."

"I was thinking the same thing. People and companies require protection in a variety of locations. But first thing's first. We'll see where this takes for now while we look for new opportunities in the future."

42
Monday February 2, 1987

Julie knocked on Kim's front door and seconds later it opened.

"Oh good, I was hoping you'd be by in time for lunch."

Julie chuckled as she stepped inside. "Sure sis, like we don't do this every day."

Kim closed the door behind her sister and smiled. "Sue me for having some fun. Let's head inside."

"What're we having?"

"It's a surprise," Kim teased.

The two women made their way to the kitchen and Julie sat down on a barstool at the end of the center island.

"What can I get you to drink?" Kim asked.

"Iced tea."

"I was lucky enough to make some yesterday during a rare sunny afternoon. It's been hard to make it naturally outside this winter, but not nearly as difficult during our winters in Ohio."

"That's for sure."

"Speaking of, what do you think the 'rents are up to these days?" Kim asked as she handed Julie a glass of iced tea and began to prep lunch.

"Same old thing I suppose, work and antiquing on the weekends."

"We should have them out again. The last time we saw them was at our wedding nine months ago."

Julie thought about it. "Well, it'd give us something to do other than hang around and clean house every day."

Kim nodded. "I know what you mean. We were used to working and now I feel like a kept woman. Bill told me I never had to work again if I didn't want to."

"Sam told me the same thing. But the truth is, if we didn't see each other every day I think I'd go crazy living alone in that house while Sam was at work."

Kim finished up making a couple of roast beef sandwiches, handed one over to her sister and sat down next to her.

"I agree. And I've been thinking about going back to work but I've been also kicking around something else."

"Which is?" Julie asked as she took a bite of her sandwich.

"Starting a family."

Julie smiled. "Apparently we've been thinking along the same lines. We're twenty-six years old and time is ticking. Besides, if we had kids at the same time we'd be able to raise them together."

Kim swallowed. "I'd like that. I think we'd be great moms."

"So do I. I think the issue now is to convince our men."

"I think I can handle that just fine in the bedroom. Bill can't help himself with me."

"Shush you," Julie blurted out. "Like I want to know about my sister's seduction techniques."

"Oh please. We had our routine down to a tee back in the days."

Julie smiled. "Oh yeah we did. Remember that one time with that air force pilot?"

"Jules!" Kim exclaimed as she wadded up her napkin and threw it at her sister. "We swore never to bring that up again."

Julie laughed as she batted away the incoming projectile. "And believe me I know why you didn't want to bring it up. You were a freeaaaak. You ended up giving me nightmares that night and there were only three of us there."

"Shut up! I don't know what you're talking about nor do I recall any such threesome."

"Keep telling yourself that sis. I know the truth. I also know that your husband is reaping the benefits of your ill-begotten youth."

"You weren't that innocent either."

Julie raised an eyebrow. "Oh, so you do recall that night. Interesting."

Kim laughed out loud and Julie joined in.

"Those were the days," Kim finally said. "But look at us now. We tied the knot and haven't looked back since."

"Nope. We really found two great guys."

"Yeah we did."

"What I don't get," Kim began, "is how their friend Thomas fits into the overall picture."

"Yeah, it's a little weird," agreed Julie. "I mean we spent the day after our wedding getting to know him but he seemed really reserved. Maybe guarded is a better word."

"That's it exactly. That day, and even now, I've been trying to wrap my head around the fact that they were all best friends and did everything together."

"No shit. Two jocks and a writer."

"You mean two jocks and a nerd, right?" Kim corrected.

"Hey now. I was just trying to be nice."

"Well don't you worry about that. I'll be the asshole spokesperson for the both of us."

"You're right. Some things will never change sis. You can take the girl out of Ohio but you can't take the Ohio out of the girl."

"Oh you're dead now sis," Kim said as she pretended to start a fight with her sister.

"Bring it on! You've got nothing!"

"Oh, that's rich. You could break a nail or something and I would never hear the end of that."

Julie chuckled. "Pussy."

Kim opened her mouth in mock surprise. "Mama didn't raise no inbred, potty mouth whores. You better clean up your mouth that everyone knows is only good for one thing and one thing only."

Julie began to giggle uncontrollably. "Shiiiiit sis. I really think I'm going to pee my pants."

"Well not in my kitchen," Kim teased. "I just cleaned it."

That sent Julie into another bought of laughter and tears rolled down her face. "I...I...can't....can't breathe."

Kim laughed alongside her sister. Once they had collected themselves the two of them finished up their lunch and spent the afternoon talking about their plans to expand their families.

43
Thursday March 3, 1988

Thomas looked up as Nick Raynes walked through the front door of the Waffle House in Lake Arrowhead. He waved his friend and agent over to the table. They shook hands as Nick sat down and joined him.

"It's good to see you Nick."

"You too Thomas. How've you been? You keeping busy up here in the mountains?"

Thomas grimaced. "Right to the point, eh?"

"I'm afraid so. What the hell happened to you? You had two strong children's books get published and then nothing. I've been pestering and cajoling you for years for something new. I've got the publisher all over on my case about it. They're seriously considering dropping you altogether. The only thing that's keeping you in the game has been me. What gives?"

Thomas took a long drink of his coke and put it back down.

"I don't know."

"That's not an acceptable answer."

"I know Nick."

"Is it writer's block or something?"

Thomas shook his head. "It's not that. I've been writing short stories for a while now."

"I don't understand then. Are you out of the children's book genre?"

"Maybe. Yes. No."

Nick rolled his eyes. "Which one is it? You're not making this easy."

"Sorry." Thomas was quiet for a few moments. "I think it's just that I haven't focused on writing as of late."

"No shit."

"What I mean is, I've been filling my time with other activities."

"Such as?"

"Gardening. Bike riding. Hiking."

"I get it. You like the outdoors. But here's what I don't understand. You are an amazing story teller. Your first book, *The Sandbox*, hit it out of the park. Do you remember what it was about?"

"Don't do this."

"It's about some kids who build, create and destroy things in their sandbox. Then, one day, they get transported to a faraway place and end up in a large sandbox. Together they realize they can build anything they can dream up and end up fighting off a huge sand monster that attacks their sand town.

"Your story was full of imagination and dreams and became an instant must have."

"I remember."

"Then you came up with your second book, *A World to Tom*. It was a pop-up book that followed the story of a young boy, Tom, and how he viewed the huge world around him from his perspective. Each page took the reader to a new location along with the narrative, from the boy's point of view, embellished on the fact that he saw everything a bit differently than everybody else. He described the enormous and overwhelming height of the Eifel Tower, and on that page a huge Eifel Tower popped up."

"I get it."

"Do you? What happened to that person I knew?"

"I'm still right here. I haven't changed."

"Bullshit man. Come on. Do you really like it up here that much?"

"Most of the time I do. I putter around the house and the garden. I catch a new movie here and there, or rent a VHS tape. I like my quiet life."

"Fine," Nick relented. "But that doesn't fix the problem does it?"

"No, I guess it doesn't."

"So what do you want to do about it then? Should I tell them you're done?"

Thomas shook his head. "No. Just give me some time to get my head on straight and get back to work. I'm sorry I've put you in this position."

Nick leaned back. "I made the trip up here to look you in the eyes, but to tell you the truth I'm fine either way. As your agent I only make money when you write something and you're not my only client. You are, however, my friend. Speaking of money, how are you holding up for funds?"

"I'm okay."

"You sure? The money from your first two books is still coming in but…"

"I'm good Nick, really."

"Okay. No harm no foul. I was just asking. Is there anything I can do for you?"

Thomas cracked a grin. "You make it sound like I'm an invalid or something."

"Shit. Heh. You're right. Sorry. It's just that Susan and I worry about you up here." Nick's eyes got sad for a moment but Thomas caught it.

"Maybe I should be asking what I can do for you?"

"What do you mean?" Nick replied as he tried to deflect.

"Oh come on. When you mentioned your wife's name you got a little sad. Is everything okay with you two?"

Like I can tell you that just the other day I walked in and caught my wife in bed with another woman. No, I don't think so. Nick waved his hand. "It's nothing. Married stuff. Why don't I walk you back to your car?"

Nick got up before he could react. Thomas dropped some money on the table to cover his drink and followed Nick outside to the parking lot.

Nick was looking around somewhat confused. "I'm not seeing your car. Did you ride your bike here?"

"It's over here." Thomas made his way to a new 325i BMW and opened the door.

Nick looked at it in awe. "Nice. It makes sense now. And to think I thought you needed help with money."

"I told you I had it covered."

Nick nodded as he inspected the BMW. "That you did. So when did you pick this up?"

"A couple of weeks ago."

"It looks new."

"It is."

Nick waggled his finger at his friend. "There's something you're not telling me, but I have a strange feeling you wouldn't share it with me even if I asked, so I won't." He looked back at the car. "Nice choice though. How's it handle?"

"It's amazing. It corners these mountain roads like a dream."

"I bet." Nick walked around to the driver's side and up to Thomas. "Just so we're clear, you're planning on getting your head back in the writer's game sooner than later, correct?"

Thomas nodded. "You have my word."

Nick smiled. "Good. But I want your word on paper so get in this awesome piece of technology, drive yourself safely back home and get to work for me."

Thomas chuckled. "You got it buddy." They shook hands.

"Take care Thomas."

"You too Nick. Give my best to Susan."

"I'll tell her you said hello, and when I do I'm sure she'll want to have you over for dinner."

"I'll drive to LA for it."

Nick began to walk away. "You bet your ass you'll drive to LA," he said over his shoulder.

Thomas smiled and sat down in his new car, turned it on and drove back to his house.

* * *

"So are you getting excited or what, proud papa to be?" Bill said as he razzed Sam.

Sam beamed. "The doctors say our daughter will poke her head out in late May. What about you asshole? I'm not the only one with a pregnant wife."

"Fair enough. I think we're a month and a half behind you two. Early July is our estimated due date."

"Right around our wedding anniversary. That should make it easy to remember your daughter's birthday at least."

"I think it's the other way around. I'm more worried about forgetting our anniversary," Bill kidded.

"Shit, don't let our wives hear you say that or you'll be sleeping on the couch," said Sam.

"I live there already."

"Oh?"

"Let me ask you this. Does Julie ask you to go to the store in the middle of the night for the weirdest cravings?"

Sam stopped what he was doing. "You too?"

Bill nodded.

"Just the other night she sent me down for relish and hot dogs because she HAD to have them."

"This is some weird shit we're being subjected to brother. What the hell have we gotten ourselves in to?"

"No shit," Sam replied. "But, on the other hand, I wouldn't want to go through it with anyone else but Jules."

"Except that Kim and her are tied at the waist, so whatever they're going through we're both experiencing at the same time."

Sam nodded. "Yeah. But I'm really looking forward to holding my baby daughter."

"Me too. I just hope I give my kid a better family environment than what I had."

"I'm on the same page. But hell, if we can handle the shit we've been though then I know we can handle raising kids."

Bill smiled. "I guess we'll find out soon enough."

Roberta suddenly appeared in their office. "Sorry to interrupt but I need signatures for these additional new hires.

Also, I have some new contracts that have come in that need your review."

It'd been nearly two years since SANDBOX officially moved into their Marin office and hired Roberta. She had turned out to be everything she had claimed to be, and more.

"Thanks Roberta," Sam said. "We'll review and get them back to you."

"You ready to quit yet?" Bill jokingly asked.

"You wish. Without me this place would crash and burn." She turned, and as she walked away said, "Maybe I should ask for a raise?"

"And maybe you'd get it," Bill replied as she disappeared.

Sam sifted through the pile of prospective jobs she'd brought in. "No rest for the wicked."

"Too much work? You telling me you want to throw in the towel now too?"

Sam smiled. "Like either of us could ever give this up."

"Ain't that the truth."

44
Wednesday March 16, 1988

Laura Bond opened her office door and let the couple. "Please, have a seat."

"Thank you," Nick Raynes replied as he sized Laura up.

Susan, his wife, sat down on the couch. Nick followed suit but didn't sit terribly close to her. Laura noticed this in as she closed the door behind them. She made her way back to her desk, picked up a pad and pen and sat down in one of the chairs. She observed Nick and Susan examining her office and took the time to observe their body language and demeanor. Laura immediately noticed that Nick seemed agitated and somewhat embarrassed. Susan, on the other hand, kept her feelings closer to her chest. *She has an excellent poker face.*

"I like your taste in books," Susan said to break the ice.

"Thank you," Laura replied. "Are you in to detective, mysteries and serial killer stories yourself?"

"Sometimes, when I get the chance to read, I pick up something in that genre."

There was a pause as Susan and Nick settled in.

Laura took that opportunity to introduce herself. "As you know my name is Dr. Laura Bond. You must be Nick and Susan Raynes."

"That's right," Susan replied.

Laura smiled to put them at ease. "What can I do for you today?"

Nick shifted uncomfortably. "Uh…my wife and I have some marital problems."

"I see. And you're both here to work this out together?"

319

"I am, but I'm not sure about her," Nick grumbled.

"That's not fair," Susan countered.

"Fair? Oh please. I'm the one who walked in on you fucking somebody other than your husband. Don't talk to me about fair Susan."

"You didn't even want to hear my side of things," Susan retorted.

"Your side? It's pretty obvious. You want someone other than me."

"No, it's not like that at all."

Laura interjected. "Why don't we take some time and catch our breath. What I'm hearing is that you're feeling hurt Nick."

"Yes, I am. Betrayed is a better word."

"Okay. You're feeling betrayed." Laura looked at Susan. "And Susan, you're frustrated that Nick won't listen to you."

"Yes."

"But why should I?" Nick countered. "I wasn't the one cheating."

Susan had enough. "Our marriage has been rocky for the past couple of years. You haven't been paying any attention to me. What'd you expect me to do?"

"I don't know! Maybe talk to me about it rather than betray me."

Laura put her hand up. "I'm hearing anger from both of you, which is to be expected. You should also be aware that it's perfectly normal in a situation, such as this, where trust has been broken." She paused for a few seconds. "Let me ask you both this question. Do you still love each other?"

Nick and Susan cautiously looked at each other.

"I haven't stopped loving her since the day I met her all those years ago at USC."

"Nor I you."

Nick's face changed. "Then what the hell happened to us Susan? Why? Why did I have to walk in on you two and have my heart torn out of my chest?"

Tears began to roll down both of their cheeks as Laura looked on.

"I felt ignored by you Nick. Unappreciated. But that's not the complete truth."

"You're telling me there's more?" Nick asked as he wiped his face.

Susan nodded. "And I don't even know where to begin. I'm embarrassed to bring it up."

"This is a safe place," Laura said with a soothing tone as she handed Susan a tissue. "Whatever you say in this room stays here. Remember, you're here for each other, to start mending the trust that has been broken."

"Fine." Susan breathed in and exhaled as she gathered her strength. "I...I have needs."

"Needs? Are you kidd..."

"Nick," Laura said as she cut him off. "We're in a safe place. She has wanted you to listen to her for a long time now. Please give her that opportunity."

Nick sat back and crossed his arms as Susan continued.

Susan nervously looked at Nick and then turned back towards Laura. "Like I was trying to say, I have needs."

"What kind of needs are we talking about?" Laura probed.

"Sexual needs. But maybe they're more like desires or fantasies."

"And do you believe these needs led you to, what I've come to understand is, and affair with another man?"

"What?" Susan replied. "No. No, never."

Laura didn't follow. "But correct me if I'm wrong but didn't your husband say that he walked in to find you in bed with someone else?"

Susan nodded.

"It was her girlfriend Tracy," Nick blurted out. "I walked in and the two of them were all over each other."

The light bulb went off in Laura's head. "Ohhh, I see. Please, forgive my misunderstanding." She looked at Nick. "And how did seeing your wife with another woman make you feel?"

"Honestly?"

"We're working on your relationship and how you communicate. The two of you are only going to start healing if you're honest with each other."

"Okay. Fine. I felt betrayed, disgusted and aroused all at the same time. How's that for being honest?"

"Very good," Laura said.

"You were aroused?" Susan asked.

"You're joking, right? What red blooded man doesn't like to see two women go at it? It just happened to be you and Tracy."

"I...I'm sorry. I just didn't know how to talk to you about all this."

"So you just went ahead and did it anyway? How's that make it right?"

Susan lowered her eyes. "It doesn't. And I'm sorry to say it wasn't the first time."

Nick froze. "What are you saying?"

"Tracy and I have been together more than once."

"Ugh," Nick responded. "Christ Susan, that doesn't make me feel any better."

"I need you to know that I don't want you to leave me over this."

"Well what the hell am I supposed to do about it, just let you have sex with other women and be okay with it?"

"No. But I have a question that I've been afraid to ask you even before I started sleeping with Tracy."

Nick gave her an odd look. "What question? And why would you be afraid to ask me anything?"

"You're right I shouldn't, but let me ask you anyway."

Nick and Laura waited patiently as Susan gathered her courage.

"The question I wanted to ask you was whether you'd ever consider a ménage a trois?"

"A threesome?" Nick clarified.

Susan nodded. "I know it sounds weird, and certainly unconventional, but I've wanted to bring another woman into our bed and share her with you for a long time now."

Nick was stunned.

"Please, say something," Susan pleaded. "I didn't want it to be this way between us. I love you and I made a mistake for not trusting you."

Nick sat up. "So what you're saying is that you want me to have sex with you and other women?"

Susan winced. "Do you hate me? Is that too weird?"

Nick visibly relaxed. "Holy shit Susan. I've been worried over practically nothing. I thought I had done something and that's the reason we haven't been talking, or messing around in the bedroom."

Susan was surprised. "You're..you're not mad?"

"A little bit, sure, but in light of what you've just said I'm incredibly relieved. You're not pushing me away and, on top of everything, you want me to have sex with other women right alongside you."

"I know. I'm a freak."

Nick shook his head. "I've loved you since I saw you for the first time. You're not a freak. You're just human. The reality is that this is going to take some getting used to on my part but I should be thankful that you didn't want to bring another man into our bed. I'm thrilled over that."

"So you're okay with this?"

He nodded. "More or less at this point. I wish you had asked me much earlier rather than how I found out about it. But now that we're finally being honest with each other, well, I like where we're suddenly at."

"Me too."

Laura smiled. "I'm proud of both of you. Why don't we take this time and pause. I think with a few more sessions you'll regain the necessary groundwork to successfully move forward with your lives, and needs, together."

Nick and Susan stood up and hugged each other.

"I love you," Susan said.

"I love you too freak," Nick joked.

Susan smiled and they turned towards Laura. "Thank you Dr. Bond."

"You're welcome. But all I think I did was supply a safety zone for you two to talk things out. With that said, how does Friday afternoon sound for your next session?"

"Ouch. The weekend commute back to LA would be brutal afterwards," Nick replied. "Do you have something on Monday instead?"

"Oh, I didn't realize you two had traveled all the way to San Bernardino to see me. There are plenty of psychologists in LA. Why travel this far out for therapy?"

"We didn't want to take the chance and run in to someone we knew," Susan replied.

Laura nodded. "I understand. Monday afternoon at two is open."

"Thank you Dr. Bond, we'll take it," Nick replied. "And would you happen to have a card I could have?"

"Certainly." Laura took one off her desk and handed it over.

"Thanks. You've helped us so much already. This first session has been a huge relief off my shoulders."

"Glad I could facilitate."

45
Thursday May 19, 1988

"Breathe honey," Sam urged as he brushed his wife's sweaty hair back from her face.

"Don't you think that's exactly what I've been doing!?" Julie yelled back.

Doctor Hampton cracked a grin at Sam's discomfort as he was under the sheet where Sam or Julie couldn't see him at the moment. A couple of hospital nurses tended to other birth giving duties while he performed the actual delivery. Dr. Hampton raised his head up, so both Sam and Julie could see him, and spoke in a reassuring tone.

"Julie. I need you to push down hard. She's almost here."

"It hurts!"

"I know it hurts but you have to work with me right now. Push Julie push!"

Julie bore down and gave it everything she had.

"Very good. Excellent. Here comes your daughter!"

An immediate relief washed over Julie as their daughter entered the world. Sweat poured down her body. A small spank later and they all heard their baby daughter take her first breath. A moment later the doctor placed her on Julie's chest, her little hands opening and closing.

"She's beautiful," Julie managed to say.

"Like mother like daughter," Sam said as a tear made its way down his cheek.

Julie and Sam looked into each other's eyes and smiled.

"You did it," Sam managed to say.

Julie corrected him. "No, we did it."

327

A nurse gently picked their daughter up and said, "I'm just going to get her cleaned up and dressed. I'll be back momentarily."

Sam kissed Julie."

"I'm proud of you Jules."

"It was a team effort. But next time you get to be pregnant."

"Only if you agree to go to work and protect the clients who hire us," Sam joked.

"I don't know which job is worse."

Sam chucked. "I assure you giving birth takes the cake every time."

The doctor smiled as the nurse came back into the room and gently handed their daughter back to Julie and left.

Dr. Hampton spoke up. "Congratulations. She's beautiful. Have you two decided on a name for her?"

Sam looked down at his two beautiful girls and smiled. Julie smiled back.

"Amanda. Her name is going to be Amanda Paige."

* * *

Saturday July 2, 1988

"Don't you dare try and talk me through this," Kim commanded.

"Are you kidding me," Bill replied. "You'd probably end up tearing my taint off or something."

Dr. Hampton chuckled at their banter. "And to think you and Julie are twin sisters."

328

"Fraternal twins," Kim said between labored breaths. "What's your point doc?"

"Nothing in particular other than you both have acted completely differently during childbirth."

"And?"

The doctor shrugged. "And nothing. You both made me laugh in your own way and that's a good thing." He turned to one of the attending nurses. "Get ready."

"Yes doctor."

"What's happening?" Bill anxiously asked.

"Kim, one more push, if you please."

"I can't believe I wanted a child," Kim whined. "This kid, it's ripping me a new one."

"Oh, it is, but we'll get that stitched up for you."

"Stitched up?" Bill hesitantly asked.

The doctor only smiled once again. "Last push. You can do it."

Kim strained and a moment later was rewarded with the sound of their crying baby girl.

"Well done," Dr. Hampton praised. "Nurse, would you take her and clean her up please? Thank you," he said as he handed her off. He turned to Bill and said with a grin. "Did you care to observe the stitches in action?"

Bill's face turned ashen as he got a little queasy. "You're a horrible doc, doc."

"Oh I know. I was just playing. You did great Kim."

"Thank you."

"I'll leave you two alone."

"About time," Bill said in an attempt to get even.

"Honey?" Kim asked.

Bill looked down at his wife. "Are you okay? Can I get you something? What is it?"

"First off, relax. Everything's fine. I just want a drink of water."

"Sure...sure." He held the glass while she sipped out of the straw.

"Thanks."

"That was intense," Bill spit out.

"I know. I was right here when it happened," Kim retorted.

"I meant..."

"Relax. I know what you mean you silly man."

The nurse returned with their baby girl and carefully handed it over to Kim. The doctor peaked in from the hallway.

"And my favorite person has returned," Bill joked. "What's up doc?"

"Touché. On a more serious note, have you decided on a name for your daughter?"

"Sarah," Kim replied. "Sarah Nicholson."

46
Tuesday January 17, 1989

Raven picked up the secure phone line. "This is unusual timing, dad. What can I do for you?"

"Shut it all down immediately," Serpent ordered.

"I don't understand," Raven replied in surprise. "Why? What's happened?"

"Portions of the operation have been discovered."

"Portions?"

"A significant amount of product has been compromised during a random inspection."

"How significant?"

"Game changing."

"Dammit. And you're telling me it was random? That can't be right. I have people who ward off these inspections on the payroll."

"Suffice it to say I've gotten word that a secret congressional investigation is now up and running."

"Wait a minute. Something doesn't add up. How long ago was this discovery made?"

"A week ago."

Raven was furious. "One week and you're just now coming to me."

"I thought I could take care of the problem. I was wrong."

"No shit. I could have handled this. Now I'm a week behind in damage control. And on top of that you tell me there's a congressional investigation underway. What the hell were you thinking?"

"Remember who you're talking to Goddammit."

"Yeah yeah. Let's deal with your bruised ego later. Right now I need as much information as you can provide me and I'll start that off with an easy question for you. Which congressman is spearheading the investigation?"

"Congressman James White," Serpent grumbled at his son.

"And what agencies are currently involved?"

"The DEA, FBI, CIA and the military. This is going to become public very quickly."

"We'll see. Now, it's going to take some time to shut everything down. You do realize we're going to make some serious enemies by dropping our supplier's cold turkey?"

"That's unavoidable at this point. Self-preservation comes first."

"Trust me," Raven said, "I completely agree, but I've spent years putting this together and I'm furious that I have to walk away from it." He paused as he collected his thoughts. "But, this doesn't mean we should get out of the business altogether."

"I told you to shut it down," Serpent demanded. "And take care of the Congressman."

"And I'm going to do just that, I was merely thinking out loud. Now, if you'll excuse me, I have a network to disassemble."

Raven hung up the phone.

"Damnit."

* * *

Thursday January 19, 1989

The congressman's assistant knocked on his office door.

"Sir?"

No response. She tried the doorknob and found it locked.

"Sir, are you alright?" she asked through the door.

Nothing.

She headed to her desk, opened a side drawer and removed a spare key she'd been given years before. She walked back to his door and unlocked it.

"Congressman?"

As the door swung open she noticed that James White was slumped over his desk. His assistant flipped on the office lights. She saw an open bottle of Jack Daniels next to him, along with a glass that was clutched in his hand. She stepped closer to him.

"Sir?

He didn't stir as she put a hand on his back and gently tried to shake him awake.

"Congressman?"

He refused to wake up.

She bent over to get a better look at his face. His eyes were wide open and the edges of his mouth contained white dried froth. It was at that moment that she let out a terrifying scream.

* * *

"It's been handled," Anna said over the phone.

"Good," Raven replied. "It's time to disappear for now. I'll have a few jobs for you in the near future."

"As you wish."

334

47
Friday January 20, 1989

Thomas reread the latest revision of "The Little Brown Chair" that he'd typed on his new IBM 486 computer. His conversion from using a typewriter to using a computer had taken some getting used to be, but he enjoyed the fact that he'd never have to use whiteout again.

I think Nick will really enjoy this one. At least I finally started writing again. I had practically forgotten all about that chair of mine until I walked into my second bedroom months ago looking for something I'd stored. Strange how my favorite childhood chair inspired me all of a sudden, but I'll take it.

Thomas got up from his desk, in his upstairs master bedroom, and headed down to the kitchen. He poured himself a glass of milk and looked out through the window at his poor snow covered garden.

I can't wait for winter to be over so I can be back outside again. I guess I could ride my bike but I know I'd hit a patch of black ice and be done for.

He drained the glass, rinsed it in the sink and left it. He then walked back to the family room and perused through his extensive VCR tape collection.

What to watch, what to watch.

Thomas decided against *Above the Law* and *Young Guns* and finally latched on to *Die Hard*. He pulled the tape out of its case and immediately noticed he hadn't rewound it after his last viewing. *Dammit, I suck.* He inserted into the VCR, hit rewind and took the time to go and make some microwave popcorn.

<u>48</u>
Saturday January 21, 1989

"Where's our meeting taking place again?" Bill asked.

"Fernwood Cemetery, right here in Mill Valley," Sam replied.

"You know this is a weird location to meet a potential client, right?"

"Roberta took the call and made the appointment. She said we'd recognize him."

"Still. A cemetery? Creepy."

Sam nodded. A minute later he pulled into the parking area and cut the engine. The cemetery was heavily wooded and provided ample cover and concealment.

"You packing?" Sam asked.

"Yes."

"Vest?"

"Always."

"Good. Let's go."

They exited the Suburban and made their way towards the center of the small cemetery. As they approached they immediately noticed five men. Four were spaced out around the perimeter while the fifth man, dressed in a military uniform, stood on the paved walkway while he watched Sam and Bill advance towards him.

"What the hell is this shit?" Bill whispered.

"Steady."

"I don't like it."

"Me neither."

Sam and Bill approached their proposed client.

"Gentlemen. It's been a long time."

Suddenly Sam and Bill recognized who they were meeting and instantly dropped their guard. They closed the distance and stopped a few feet away from their old Ranger base commander, Lt. Colonel Robert Aleman. From the star on Aleman's shoulders he'd risen in the ranks, over the years, to a Colonel and now a one star General.

"General sir," Sam said as he shook his hand. "Congratulations on the promotions. It's been a long time."

Bill shook his hand as well. "Sir. Good to see you."

"I'm pleased to see both of you as well."

"What are you doing here?" Sam asked.

The General motioned them towards a picnic table close by where they all sat down. The four men on the perimeter shifted slightly.

"I've been following your careers since I sent you away to join Special Operations."

Sam and Bill looked at each other and then back at General Aleman.

"Sir?"

"The truth is that I was unhappy with your decision to leave the teams when you didn't re-up."

Bill spoke up. "And you decided to visit and tell us that out of the blue a couple of years later? That doesn't add up General."

"I had bigger plans for the two of you."

"Plans?" Sam asked.

"Let me ask you this," the General started. "Why were you two singled out to join such a privileged community as Spec Ops?"

338

"Because we earned it every step of the way," Bill countered.

"That's part of it, absolutely. But neither of you had had any real combat experience, or the necessary service time in the army to qualify. There were plenty of soldiers ahead of you in line but you managed to jump in front of them. How do you explain that?"

"I don't like where you're taking this conversation," Sam growled. "What the hell are you trying to say sir?

"Nothing quite yet."

"To me it sounds like he's implying we owe him for our success," Bill stated.

"Is that what you're saying General?" Sam added.

"In one word, yes. I told you years ago that I'd come to you in the future. Well, here I am."

"We're clear of the military by choice and we don't owe you a damn thing. How dare you try to insinuate otherwise."

General Robert Aleman raised his hand. "You're right. I apologize for coming as strongly as I did. I merely brought you out here today to propose a collaboration between myself and your company."

"What type of collaboration?" Bill inquired.

"But before I get in to those details I wanted to pick your brains on some of your past successes."

"Out of respect for our past, and your rank, you may proceed," Sam said.

"Thank you. Ten years ago, in seventy-nine, both of you were part of a twelve man team sent into South America to disrupt a major drug manufacturing camp."

"No comment," Bill responded.

The General smiled. "It doesn't matter. I know you blew that camp to hell. What you don't know is how much it cost me."

"Cost you?" Sam asked. "What the hell are you talking about?"

"Those drugs you destroyed were mine."

"You're not making any sense, sir," Sam said as he rose from the table.

"Join my organization."

Bill and the General also stood up.

"It's simple," continued General Aleman. "You both owe me and you will join me."

Sam and Bill shared a quick glance and their faces said it all. *What the fuck is going on?*

"Join you to do what exactly?"

"Isn't it obvious?"

"Not at all," Bill said. "What are you asking us to do?"

"I want you to help me smuggle drugs into our country of course."

"Have you completely lost your mind sir?"

The General continued unphased. "It's all coming apart. All my work. Years of meticulous strategizing and planning. It's made me rich. Hell, it's made us all rich. But I don't want it to just end. If I do they'll come after me, they'll all come after me."

"You've been running drugs through military channels for years, sir?"

The General nodded. "Yes. And I want both of you onboard. Don't you see? That's why I made sure you received the necessary training all those years ago. I was grooming you to join Spec Ops. You'd have unprecedented access all over the world to bring my product back to the States unhindered."

"You're insane," Bill said. "If you knew us at all you'd know we'd never be a part of something like that."

The General chuckled. "You're right of course, but I had to try. You know, maybe my superiors were right about you two."

"What are you talking about?" Sam asked.

"They wanted you two dead years ago but I decided to kept you alive instead. I could have reached out and had you eliminated at any point. I really had great hopes for you two. You should have come onboard willingly. The things we could have achieved together. But now, now I don't have a choice. I can't allow you to leave and tell anyone what I've told you."

Sam and Bill had heard enough and reached for their weapons.

Two shots rang out from the trees and those bullets hit Sam and Bill square in their chests. They both toppled backwards and landed on the grass, stunned for a few moments.

Bill's gun landed near him while Sam's had fallen underneath the table.

The General's four men began to approach from all sides, weapons out, as the General stood over them. Bill tried to reach for his but the General stepped on it before Bill could retrieve it.

"You understand that I have to eliminate any potential witnesses. And, since you two never thanked me for making you who you are today, I'll have to punish you for that as well."

Sam and Bill were in pain but their eyes focused on General Robert Aleman. His eyes screamed insanity.

"Once you're dead I'm going to go to your houses and kill your wives and your baby girls."

Bill kicked out his right leg, caught the General in his knee which sent him sprawling to the ground.

Bill grabbed his gun just as a second round hit him high in the chest, which knocked him back down.

Sam rolled towards his weapon, under the table, and grabbed it just as two rounds kicked up dirt around his face.

Bill winced through his pain, focused and fired off three quick rounds towards one of the advancing men. One of the bullets caught the man in the upper leg and he crumpled to the ground.

Sam immediately rose up off the ground, and at the same time grabbed the picnic bench as he did. The table turned on its side and Sam used his left arm to keep it from falling over as he used it to temporarily shield Bill and himself from two of their attackers. Sam saw one man going down from Bill's shooting so he leveled his shaking right hand at the second man and fired off four rounds in his direction.

A multitude of bullets impacted the other side of the table.

Bill saw the second man drop from a chest wound as he scrambled to join Sam behind the table. A third bullet grazed Bill's chest and the space he'd just occupied was torn to shreds as he maneuvered behind the table.

"You okay? Sam quickly asked as he saw the two distinct holes in Bill's vest.

"I've been better," Bill replied with a shortness of breath.

The table's wood began to splinter from the continuous barrage of gunfire of the remaining two men.

"It's now or never," Sam said.

"Go right. I'll go up."

Sam moved to the far right off the table, still holding it upright with his left arm, and exposed a portion of his body.

Bill popped up from behind the table and unloaded on the left attacker just as Sam shot at the man on the right. Moments later the last two attackers fell over.

"Nice shooting," Bill said.

"You t.."

A round caught Sam in his back and he and the table he held pitched forward.

Bill instinctively swiveled, put his sights on the man he'd shot in the leg, and pulled his trigger twice. The man's body jerked from the double impacts and lay still.

Bill hastily verified the other three men weren't moving and then went to Sam's side.

Sam breathed out as he rolled over on his back. "Fuck that hurt."

"How bad?"

"I don't think it penetrated the vest," Sam replied. His eyes suddenly went wide. "Where's the General?"

"Fuck." Bill stood up and scanned the area. The cemetery was empty. "He's gone."

"Shit. Help me up."

Bill pulled his friend to his feet. "We need to search these fuckers and then call this in."

Sam shook his head. "There's no time. We need to get home right now!"

49
Saturday January 21, 1989

Sam screeched the Suburban to a halt just outside Bill's house. The two of them quickly exited and withdrew their side arms. After taking a quick look around, and not identifying anything unusual, they headed towards the front door. Bill tested the door and it was locked. He pulled out his keys as Sam watched his back. Two seconds later Bill turned the handle and they entered aggressively as Bill swept left and Sam went right. Everything was in place and there were no signs of a struggle.

"Kim!? Kim, where are you!?"

No answer. Sam caught up with Bill back at the front door.

"Sarah's not here either," Sam said. "They'd better be at my house."

Sam turned and left as Bill closed the door behind him and then ran to catch up to his Sam as they headed next door. Sam tried the door knob and it turned easily in his hand. Bill appeared behind him and together they entered the house.

Immediately they heard their two wives, in the kitchen, chatting away. After clearing the front entryway they rushed into the kitchen, weapons at the ready.

Julie and Kim screamed in shock, which in turn caused their two babies to start crying.

"Are you both alright?" Sam asked.

"You scared the hell out of us," Kim angrily said as she picked up Sarah.

"Yeah, what the he..," Julie started to say just as she noticed Sam and Bill wore Kevlar vests. "Are those bullet holes?"

Kim whirled around, took in the scene and saw that both of them had been shot.

"Oh my God," Kim exclaimed. "You've been shot!"

"We're fine," Bill replied.

Kim began to cry. "No you're not! You've been shot!"

Bill pulled Kim and Sarah close to him. "It's going to be okay. I'm fine. Really."

"Sam? Sam, I don't understand," Julie said through teary eyes as she traced the holes in Sam's bullet proof vest. "Why did you burst in here like this? What's going on? What aren't you telling us?"

"I don't have time to explain right now," Sam retorted.

"That's not an answer," Julie insisted.

"We need to get all of you out of here right now and over to SANDBOX."

"Why?"

"Dammit Julie. This is for your own protection."

"Don't lie to me Sam. You've been shot. What's going on?"

Dammit! "Jules, do you trust me?"

"Yes, of course, but what does that…"

"Then we need to move right now. Bill and I have a job to do and we can't tell you about it."

"Are we in danger?" Kim hesitantly asked.

"Possibly. That's why we need to get everyone to SANDBOX right now, no questions asked."

"Let's go Kim," urged Bill.

Julie and Kim gathered what they needed to take care of their babies and followed Sam and Bill outside to the Suburban. As they climbed in Sam and Bill watched the road intently until their wives were seated and had firm grasps on both daughters. Sam started up the vehicle and headed out towards SANDBOX.

"What's going on?" Julie insisted. "Why did you get shot?"

"The less you know the better, trust me."

"Fine. What's going to happen then?" Kim asked.

"We're going to secure you at the office where you'll be protected. After that Bill and I have someone to track down."

"Absofuckinglutely we do," Bill added.

"But I don't want you to leave me," Kim pleaded.

"Neither do I," Julie said.

"We don't have a choice Jules," Sam countered. "This is what we do and this issue has to be taken care of."

50
Saturday January 21, 1989

Roberta assured Sam and Bill that their families would be safe before the two of them regrouped alone in their office.

"Where do you think that bastard is now?" Bill asked between clenched teeth.

"I intend to find out. I need to make a few phone calls."

Twenty minutes later Sam placed his phone down. "Got him. He's staying at the Hyatt Regency."

"Who'd you call to find that out?"

"Let's just say I still have some contacts within the Army. I called someone at the Pentagon and they tracked down his itinerary."

"Nice. But who's to say the General's still there?"

"I'm about to find that out. Just in case he is we're going to need some backup."

"Roger that."

Sam dialed the Hyatt while Bill hit Roberta's extension.

"Yes Bill?"

"Are there a couple of available operators on campus right now?"

"Alan and Pete are currently practicing on the range. Darrell is watching over your families at the moment. I can pull him if you need the extra help."

"No, leave Darrell where he's at. Tell Alan and Pete that we need them tactically geared up and ready in the motor pool ten minutes from now."

"I'm on it," Roberta replied.

Bill hung up just as Sam did.

"He's still there. The woman I talked to said there were a few scary and intense looking men in the lobby."

"I've got two guys that will meet us at the motor pool."

"Good."

Sam and Bill headed out of their office back towards the lobby.

"Maybe we should get the local police involved."

Sam shook his head. "We need to keep this as low profile as we can. If we get the police involved then we won't be able to get General Aleman all to ourselves. It'll become a circus."

"So what's our plan of attack?"

"Surprise."

They walked outside and headed to the armory, switched out their damaged vests for new ones and then geared up for a tactical assault. They decided against the powerful CAR-15 assault rifles and decided to go with the 9mm MP5's instead to minimize potential bullet penetration. Afterwards they met Alan and Pete, ready to go, by the vehicles.

"What's up boss?" Alan queried as Sam and Bill approached.

Sam spoke up. "We were just attacked by our old Ranger battalion commander, General Robert Aleman and four of his men. He threatened to kill our families."

"What?" Pete reacted. "Are they safe?"

Sam nodded. "They are, thankfully. During the attack we took down his men but the General escaped during the firefight. We're heading after him. Problems?"

Alan and Pete both shook their heads no.

"Good. You're designation Bravo. Bill and I are Alpha. Mount up."

350

Ten seconds later two black Suburban's left SANDBOX and headed south towards the Golden Gate Bridge.

Bill drove the lead vehicle as Sam spoke into his mike.

"Bravo, how copy?"

"Good copy, Alpha."

"We're headed to the Hyatt Regency down on the Embarcadero. Currently the General is onsite but that could change at a moment's notice. When we arrive we'll park and take the front entrance while you observe the rear."

"Roger that," Bravo replied.

Bill looked over at Sam and then back at the road.

"Are we up for this?" Bill asked.

"What do you mean?"

"There could be some serious fallout from what we're about to do, that's all I'm saying."

"He threatened our families. On top of that he admitted to smuggling drugs in to this country for over a decade using the military pipeline. That doesn't sit well with me. What about you?" Sam countered. "Are you up for this?"

Bill smiled. "No issues here whatsoever. I just needed to check on where your mind's at. This rogue General...we're taking him down."

* * *

Bill parked in a temporary spot, just off Market Street, across from the hotel. Bravo did the same on the adjoining Drumm Street. Endless amounts of people, braving the winter winds that constantly whipped amongst the skyscrapers, were on the streets.

"Bravo, in position."

351

"Roger that. Keep your eyes peeled."

"Wilco."

"There are a lot of civies out," Bill observed. "We can't have this thing turning sideways on us in the middle of the street. A firefight in downtown San Fran is too risky."

"Agreed."

Sam pulled a large rectangular device from the backseat and placed it in his lap.

"When did you pick that up?" Bill questioned.

Sam pressed a latch and the phone's receiver released.

"A couple of weeks ago actually. Having a portable phone available seemed like a good idea."

"That thing is huge. Hopefully they'll make mobile phones smaller in the future."

"No shit."

Sam called the hotel and asked for the same person he'd spoken to before.

"What do you mean he just checked out?" Sam asked with unease.

Bill's earpiece came to life. "Alpha, we've got a potential target, plus three, that just came out of the side exit. Again, we count a total of four. The General just sat down in the rear right seat."

Sam had already hung up the phone and hurriedly replaced the large portable cell phone behind his seat.

"Roger that." He turned to Bill. "Start it up. We're live."

"Targets have just entered a vehicle. It's a brown Cherokee four runner." Bravo paused for a few seconds. "Target vehicle just flipped a bitch and took a right on Sacramento Street heading west. We're on him."

"Following behind. We see the target in the distance. Don't get too close but stay close enough not to miss any lights they go through."

In the distance Bill watched the Cherokee take a left on Battery Street heading south.

"Battery turns in to First Street," Bill said out loud. "I'm guessing he's probably going for the Bay Bridge."

Sam nodded. "Bravo, surge past the target and make your way to the Bay Bridge onramp."

"Will do."

Sam and Bill watched the other Suburban dart pass the Cherokee as they approached Market Street. Bill closed the distance behind their target just as all three vehicles braked as the light changed to yellow and then red.

"Options?" Bill asked.

"I'm working on it," Sam answered.

The light eventually cycled to green and Bravo continued their fast pace towards the bridge entrance while Sam and Bill stayed as far back as they could from the Cherokee. A minute later their target crossed over Folsom Street.

"Alpha, we just got on the freeway."

"Roger that. Stay in the center lane and just drive the speed limit. Wait for my orders."

"Understood."

"The moment of truth is coming up," Bill said. "Will they or won't they get on that bridge."

The Cherokee, at the last minute, transitioned from the right lane to the center lane and merged with a second lane of cars onto the Bay Bridge.

"Good call," Sam said.

"It's what I do," Bill replied.

Ten seconds later Bill followed suit and entered the lower deck of the Bay Bridge heading north towards Oakland.

"Bravo, what's your location?"

"Alpha, we're approaching the Yerba Buena Island tunnel," Bravo replied.

"Roger that. I want you to enter the tunnel and come to a dead stop in one of the two center lanes."

"Will do. You know that's going to piss a lot of people off, right?"

"Just be ready," Sam replied. "I'll call whether they're going to pass on your left or right side."

"Roger that," Bravo responded.

"Ballsy idea," Bill stated.

Sam gripped his MP5 sub-machine gun tighter. "Let's just hope that it works. Now, if you don't mind, close the gap between us."

Bill pressed down on the accelerator and the Suburban surged forward.

Bravo entered the tunnel, turned on the its hazard lights and came to a stop. Blaring horns sounded as angry drivers veered around the now immobile and dangerous obstacle. Traffic immediately began to slow down and a line of cars soon formed up behind the Suburban, all trying to merge either left or right to get around it.

"Alpha, traffic congestion has begun. We're in the second lane from the left."

Sam smiled. "Thank you. Stand by."

* * *

"What the hell is this?" General Aleman queried from the back seat as the Cherokee began to slow.

"It looks like an accident, sir," replied his man behind the wheel. "It must have just happened. I can see a stationary vehicle in the distance. We'll pass by it shortly."

* * *

"Bravo. Target is coming up on your left. I'm going to want you to pull forward to block them in while we come in from behind."

"Roger that. Rules of engagement?"

"I don't want to make this a messy takedown," Sam replied. "Do not fire unless fired upon. I want the General alive and his vehicle disabled. If we can make that happen without any casualties, then that's how it's going to go down. Fast and efficient."

"Understood. I see the Cherokee approaching our left side. Ten seconds."

Bill sped up and accelerated to pass the final car to maneuver behind the Cherokee. "This is going to be close."

He swerved into the left lane directly behind the General just as Bravo's Suburban lurched forward and pulled to the left. Both lanes were immediately blocked.

"Wake them up," Sam ordered.

Bill rammed the back of the Cherokee with considerable force that jolted all four men inside.

The two men from Bravo smoothly exited their Suburban and pointed their MP5's at the front passengers. Sam and Bill followed a split second later and covered the rear.

"HANDS! HANDS!" one of the men from Bravo yelled.

The other Bravo member took his knife and wasted no time as he punctured both front tires.

The man who sat next to the General opened his left rear door and attempted to get out. Bill quickly advanced, reversed his grip on his sub-machine gun and brought down the stock on the man's face, knocking him out.

Sam, with his left hand, opened the right rear door and stuck his MP5 in the General's surprised face. Sam only got a quick glimpse of the two angered men in the front before he forcibly yanked General Aleman out of the Cherokee.

Sam pushed his captive up against the side of his Suburban as Bravo continued to cover the other two men. Sam slung his MP5, produced a pair of handcuffs and secured the General's hands.

Bill, at the same time, pulled the unconscious man's body out of the way and swiftly eyeballed the Cherokee's backseat. A briefcase lay on the floor. Bill retrieved it.

As Sam placed the General in the back of the Suburban, Bill and the other two SANDBOX team members extracted the last two men, disarmed and then secured their wrists. Bill then collected the unconscious man's sidearm and cuffed him as well before he stood up and gave the all clear signal.

"LET'S GO!" Sam yelled as he climbed into the passenger seat next to General Aleman.

Bravo quickly got back into their Suburban as Bill retook the driver's seat and tossed the briefcase on the seat next to him. He backed up a few feet and then pulled in behind Bravo as they both accelerated away from the scene.

"Rally back at the office," Sam said over the mike.

"Roger that," Bravo replied.

General Aleman struggled against his cuffs to no avail. "You have no idea how big of a shit storm is going to come crashing down on you. I have assets everywhere. There's nowhere you can hide where I won't be able to get to you or your families."

Sam wasn't buying his demeanor. "Honestly Robert, you make me sick."

"You will address me as General."

"In your dreams Bob," Sam scoffed. "You don't deserve the respect that title gives."

"I earned that rank," he spat back.

"And how's that, by smuggling what must have been a shitload of drugs from all over the world into America? You must be so proud."

"And rich," the General added with a smile.

"Ahh. And there's the heart of it all; what really matters. Money. Selling out your country just so you could be rich. Pathetic."

"It doesn't matter. You're both dead men."

"You're going to need to rethink the position you currently find yourself in," Bill said from the driver's seat. "The bottom line is that you shouldn't have threatened our families. That won't stand."

"So what," the General said.

"I'd be more than happy to put a bullet in the back of your head and bury you in an unmarked grave you treasonous prick."

"Bill, you just don't have the balls."

"Try me," Bill coldly replied.

"And what can you really prove anyway? Nothing. At this point it's just your word against mine."

"Maybe," Sam countered. "But who knows what leads we'll find in your briefcase."

The General's eyes widened for a brief second. "I'll be protected. I have contacts that won't let me see the inside of a cell."

"I hope you're right. I mean, can't imagine what will happen once the pieces of the investigation fall in to place? You have to figure anyone you thought would support you will run for the shadows, and then point their finger in your direction to protect their own interests."

"Yeah," Bill added. "You're pretty screwed."

"Go to hell," was the last thing the General said as both Suburban's made their way back to SANDBOX.

<u>51</u>
Tuesday January 24, 1989

"Raven has been taken into custody and placed in solitary," Bear stated. "It's only a matter of time before he tells the interrogators everything."

"We'll continue to scrub our tracks and then go dark," Wolf replied. "We have to distance ourselves from this situation."

Serpent spoke up. "I'll look in to the alternate contingency that my son brought to our attention."

"Agreed."

* * *

Thursday January 26, 1989

Sam and Bill passed through Pentagon's security and were led to General Frank's office. The Lieutenant told them the General would be ready for them in five minutes.

"This has rapidly turned in to one hell of a clusterfuck," Bill whispered.

"No shit," Sam answered. "The jackpot of information we uncovered in Aleman's briefcase was downright ludicrous."

"After we made that phone call it certainly didn't take long before the Military Police showed up at SANDBOX. Where do you think Aleman is now?"

"Fuck if I care."

Bill nodded. "Hopefully in a deep hole someplace."

"What gets me is why the Pentagon flew us out here to chat."

"I think we're about to find out," Bill said.

The Lieutenant stood up from his desk, motioned to Sam and Bill, and then opened the doors to the General's office. "He'll see you now."

Sam and Bill walked in as an imposing two-star stood behind his desk. The General immediately sized both of them up as they entered his office. As the doors closed behind them Sam and Bill reverted to their old ways and both snapped off a sharp salute.

"Sir."

"Sir."

"At ease sergeants and take a seat," the General said as he returned their salute.

Sam and Bill sat down on the opposite side of his desk.

"My name is General Franks and I'm overseeing the investigation you two have heavily contributed to."

"Why are we here sir?" Sam asked.

"Straight to the point, I respect that. You're both here so I could look you in the damn face while we had this conversation. I needed to see what type of men you really are, aside from what these thick dossiers on my desk have described about each of you."

He extended his forefinger and placed it decisively on the large file folders that rested on his desk.

"Gentlemen, we have a situation that needs to be resolved and I've come to the conclusion that I won't be able to bully either of you in order to get my way."

"Bully us, sir?" Bill asked.

"Mr. Paige. Mr. Nicholson. You're both men of integrity, which is painfully obvious. So let me break down the situation at hand as plainly as I can for you. Currently there is a secret congressional investigation, which was being run by Congressman James White, until he was found dead of apparent natural causes a week ago. That investigation revolves around the smuggling, and importing, of illicit drugs into the United States using our military pipelines as the mules. Once this leaks out the press will have a field day and the world will view the U.S. Military, along with President Reagan, as weak and susceptible. Are you with me so far?"

Sam and Bill nodded.

"Good. Now, enter you two and General Robert Aleman. He has a distinguished military service record. However, at the same time, he is justifiably guilty based on the evidence you presented us with."

"Where is General Aleman now, sir?" Sam inquired.

"This is off the record and I'll deny ever having said it. He's being held someplace no man would ever want to find themselves. Now, on to exactly what I need from the two of you. I need you to keep your mouths closed."

"I don't understand," Sam responded. "We turned him in to make this problem go away."

"And the problem has gone away. Aleman has been removed from the equation. Your families are no longer in danger."

"It's not that easy, sir," said Bill.

"No," General Franks replied, "it never is. The investigation is going to come out publically in less than a week, although I'm surprised it hasn't leaked already. But that's not the point. The point is that the severity of the fallout

361

it will do to our country needs to be minimized as much as humanly possible. My job, quite frankly, will be to spin this so the United States won't appear weak."

"What are you trying to say, sir?" Sam said matter-of-factly, and somewhat annoyed.

"Very well," General Franks said. "I need you to forget everything you know about General Robert Aleman."

"You want us to help you bury this investigation?" Bill exclaimed.

"I didn't say that but work it through with me. This isn't the time for our President to appear weak. The Cold War is nearly over and he needs to concentrate on that. I'm not asking you to turn a blind eye. Robert Aleman will pay for his crimes and, behind the scenes, my investigation will continue, but it will continue out of the public's eye."

"So you just want us to walk away from all this?" Sam tested.

"No." General Franks pulled out a folder from the bottom of the stack. "This dossier is all about your company, SANDBOX."

"What about it?" Sam replied defensively.

"Take it easy. I'm not threatening you or your company."

"Then why bring it up?"

"I bring it up for the following reasons. You both made a name for yourselves during your eight years in the Army. From completing Ranger school, HALO, SERE training and becoming Special Ops operators. You've seen, done it all and have earned that merit badge. Your company, SANDBOX, is up and coming but has already begun to earn the respect it deserves. Personally I think the services you offer are outstanding."

362

"Your point, sir."

"Thank you for keeping me on track, Mr. Paige. My point is simple. The United States Military wants to trade your silence on this matter for two things. The first is a check for five million dollars. The second should sweeten our deal even more. We're prepared to push more operators, who are exiting the military and looking for jobs, your way."

"This feels more like a bribe, sir."

"I would rather look at it as a situation that's not going away any time in the near future. I need to mitigate the fallout from this investigation, while at the same time bring the guilty to justice. It'll get done; it just needs to be handled under the table."

Sam stood up and Bill followed. "Will you give us a moment, sir?"

"Of course," General Franks replied.

Sam and Bill walked a few feet away and began a whispered conversation.

"Do you believe what he's telling us?" Sam asked.

"The crazy thing is that I actually do."

"Thoughts?"

Bill pondered for a moment. "This isn't our fight, not directly at least. We've done the right thing and we can hold our heads high because of it. We're neck deep in the realm of politics and I feel like I need to shower."

"Agreed. And as much as I don't want to admit it, what other choice do we have? Are we going to go to the press ourselves and put our entire lives under a microscope for something we haven't even been involved in? We can't afford to take on the United States Military."

"Not to mention we'd be looking over our backs for years to come. Our families deserve more than that. This isn't our fight."

"It sounds like we're in agreement then."

"It doesn't mean I'm happy with it," Bill stated.

"Neither am I."

Sam and Bill walked back.

"Do we have a deal?" General Franks asked.

"Yes sir, we do."

52
Friday January 27, 1989

Sam and Bill drove home from the airport and parked in Sam's driveway.

Julie and Kim, holding their baby daughters, walked out of the front door to meet them.

"Hi honey," Sam said as he greeted his wife and daughter.

"Hey babe," Bill said to Kim. He took his daughter from her arms and made faces at her. "How's my little girl doing today? Are you being a good girl? I know you are."

"We're so glad you're home," Kim responded. "What happened? Why did the Pentagon want with you?"

Sam and Bill shared a glance.

"You're not going to like our answer," Sam replied.

"Why not?" Julie asked.

"Because we can't talk about it," Bill responded.

"You can't tell your own wives what's going on, is that what I'm hearing?" Julie stated with a slight edge to her voice.

"I don't like it," Kim added. "What the hell are you hiding?"

"Everyone just stop," Sam commanded. "Jules. Kim. This is our job. This is how we do business. You need to understand that we can't tell you about everything. You know we used to be in Special Forces. Have we told you about what we did while we were part of that community? The answer is no. It's the same thing with most of the work we take on at SANDBOX." Sam paused for a few seconds and then continued. "The reality is that you don't have to like it but I assure you we're not hiding things, or what we do, from you on purpose. You know us better than that."

Julie wasn't finished. "So you rushing home, guns drawn and then whisking us away to the office 'for our safety' isn't something you can talk about?"

"No."

"I don't agree with that. We can't go through life thinking we're not going to be safe in our own homes Sam. That's insanity. What's worse is when my own husband won't tell me a Goddamn thing about it."

"I'm with my sister on this," Kim added. "You need to give us something. You scared the crap out of us barging in, guns out and bullet holes all over you."

"They weren't all over us Kim," Bill explained.

"That's not the point and you know it!" Kim shot back.

Sam put his hand up. "Alright."

Julie and Kim were puzzled. "What do you mean alright?"

"We'll try to explain some of this, but we before that can happen we need to head inside. I'm not going to continue this conversation outside in the driveway."

All of them walked inside and headed to the kitchen.

"We're listening," Kim said as she stood next to her sister.

Sam spoke up. "I know you're both on edge and don't have a great sense of safety at the moment. Without going into a tremendous amount of detail I'm going to try and alleviate that fear. We were shot at by a man we knew years ago. He used that relationship to catch us off guard. Before he escaped he threatened our families so Bill and I had no choice but to come protect the two of you and whisk you off to safety."

"But..."

"I'm not finished. Bill and I tracked down that man. We apprehended him and then turned him over to military. The meeting at the Pentagon was to assure us that he'll never see the light of day again. You're safe. We're all safe now."

Relief washed over Julie and Kim's face. Bill maintained his poker face knowing full well Sam had just told them a white lie to cover up the real truth.

"Thank you Sam," Julie said.

"Yes," added Kim, "that makes me feel a lot better."

"But," as Julie continued, "we still need to talk about those bullet holes."

"What about them?" Bill asked.

"That scared us," Kim said. "That scared us a lot."

"It comes with the territory," Sam tried to explain.

"No," Julie said as she pointed a finger in Sam's face. "You don't get to play super heroes anymore. You both have families to take care of."

Sam pulled Julie close. "Jules, sweetheart, you're right. SANDBOX is growing and we can pick and choose what jobs Bill and I work on. We enjoy what we do and there are certain risks that come with it, BUT," he emphasized, "that doesn't mean we have to take all of the risks now."

Julie squirmed in his arms. "You know that doesn't mean I have to like it."

Sam smiled. "I get it. You just want me safe. Trust me, I want the same thing. Bill and I don't take risks. We calculate everything and take the appropriate actions along the way. We know what we're doing."

"I just want you to come home to me," Julie said softly.

"And I want the same thing for you," Kim added as she hugged Bill.

"Everything's going to be all right," Bill said.

"It had better be," Kim replied as she gut punched him.

"Oof!"

Julie, Kim and Sam were all smiles as Bill overacted the punch and fell to the ground.

53
Friday January 27, 1989

Sam and Bill, after talking things out with their wives, headed back to SANDBOX and made a bee-line to their office.

"You think we're in the clear?" Bill asked as he sat down on his side of the desk.

Sam took his seat opposite his friend and let out a big sigh. "I don't know. We just made a deal with the same government we used to work for just to keep our mouths shut."

Bill nodded. "It does feel a bit slimy but unfortunately I did see Generals Franks' point."

"Me too. It doesn't mean I like how it makes me feel."

"I hear you there brother. The only good news out of all this, aside from General Aleman rotting in a hole somewhere, is that it looks like our company is going to grow even larger now."

Sam smiled. "I had no idea our reputation was that prolific."

"We need to seriously look at expanding. We have a solid track record and we could easily provide our services all over the country."

"That same idea has been on my mind as well. The Bay Area was a great place to start but now we can develop even more."

Bill stood up. "We need to powwow on this at some point. However, for the moment I'm going to take this check down to Roberta so she can deposit it."

"Good idea. We wouldn't want Uncle Sam to put a hold on that check."

"Exactly," Bill replied with a grin.

Bill left their office and headed down to Roberta's desk. "Hey Roberta."

She had the phone up to her ear. "Would you mind holding for a moment? Thank you." She looked up at her boss. "Bill. How are you?"

"Good good."

"Anything to report back on from your Pentagon trip?"

"Funny you should ask," he said as he handed over the check. "Please deposit this in our operating accounts."

She took the check and whistled. "Five million. Business must be good."

Bill smiled. "It's not bad, that's for sure. With that said, we're going to start receiving dossiers from the military on specific soldiers. Let me know when that pipeline is up and running."

"Absolutely."

"Thanks Roberta," Bill said as he left her desk and headed back upstairs.

She took her caller off hold. "Thank you for holding."

"Do you believe they suspect anything?" the man on the other end asked.

"No. Nothing. I've been very careful," Roberta replied.

"Good. We'll limit our contact to quarterly updates. In the meantime I need you to continue to send us reports on SANDBOX contracts. We're still finalizing how we want to use the company, but as soon as we do we'll let you know what we require of you."

"I understand."

"You're still with us, right Roberta? They haven't caused you to falter?"

"No, of course not. I know they're responsible for the death of my son, and I want to make them pay."

"Excellent. We're happy to hear that."

* * *

Bill walked back into his office and sat back down.

"How'd it go with Roberta?" Sam asked.

"Easy as always. I have to say she's the best hire we ever made."

"No argument there. She runs this place like a well-oiled machine. It takes a lot of the day-to-day pressure of us."

"No shit. Hard to complain to that. But speaking of complaining..."

Sam looked up from what he was working on. "What?"

"I'm trying not to over think this, but what do we do now?"

"In what aspect?"

Bill sat up straight. "Can and should we trust General Franks?"

"Maybe, maybe not. At this point it seems he has as much to lose as we do. And, not that he knows, but we made a copy of everything that was in Aleman's briefcase just in case. The bottom line is that he wants this to go away as much as we do."

"So you think it's over then?"

"What, the fact that Aleman said he worked for other people? No, I don't think this is over. I think we might have poked the hornet's nest without realizing how big it really was before we did it."

Bill nodded. "Yeah, I'm right there with you. We'll be watching our backs for a while."

Sam smiled. "What else is new?"

Bill chuckled. "Oh well. Business as usual. And, speaking of, we have a business to build so stop distracting me you bastard."

"Oh, it's like that is it?" Sam joked back.

"You know what this banter reminds me of?"

"Our good old days with Thomas?"

"You read my mind yet again," Bill replied. "We haven't talked to him in a long time. Let's call and see what he's up to in that remote place he calls home up there in the mountains."

Visit my website at

http://www.dwneuman.com

If you enjoyed this novel please consider
taking a moment and writing a quick review
about it (on Amazon). It helps me out
more than you know and fuels my
motivation!
Of course, word of mouth
works wonders too! ;)

Thank you!

And you can look forward to book seven,
Shadows of the Serpent,
in the future.

www.ingramcontent.com/pod-product-compliance
Lightning Source LLC
Chambersburg PA
CBHW072340020726
47506CB00004B/945